THE
TROLLS WILL FEAST!

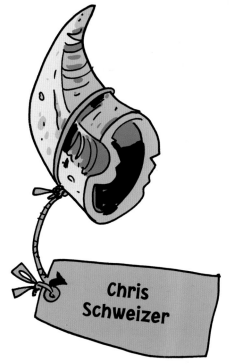

Chris
Schweizer

AMULET BOOKS
NEW YORK

[redacted]

Library of Congress Control Number: 2015944618

Hardcover ISBN: 978-1-4197-1882-3
Paperback ISBN: 978-1-4197-1883-0

Book design by Pamela Notarantonio
Color assistance by Liz Schweizer

Printed and bound in China
10 9 8 7 6 5 4 3 2 1

Amulet Books are available at special discounts when purchased in quantity for premiums and promotions as well as fundraising or educational use. Special editions can also be created to specification. For details, contact specialsales@abramsbooks.com or the address below.

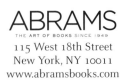

ABRAMS
THE ART OF BOOKS SINCE 1949
115 West 18th Street
New York, NY 10011
www.abramsbooks.com

TO MY NIECE, ADDIE

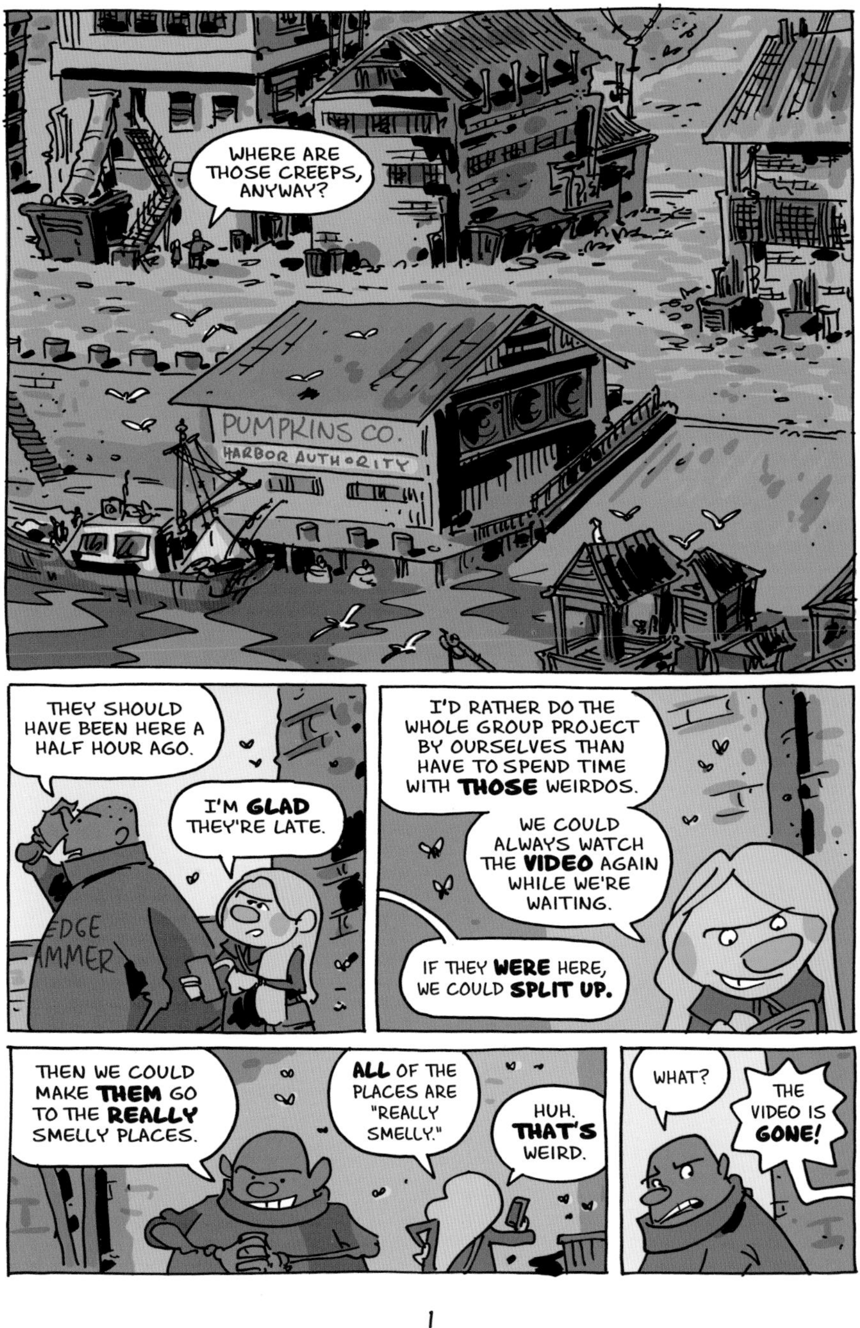

WHERE ARE THOSE CREEPS, ANYWAY?
PUMPKINS CO.
HARBOR AUTHORITY
THEY SHOULD HAVE BEEN HERE A HALF HOUR AGO.
I'M **GLAD** THEY'RE LATE.
I'D RATHER DO THE WHOLE GROUP PROJECT BY OURSELVES THAN HAVE TO SPEND TIME WITH **THOSE** WEIRDOS.
WE COULD ALWAYS WATCH THE **VIDEO** AGAIN WHILE WE'RE WAITING.
IF THEY **WERE** HERE, WE COULD **SPLIT UP.**
THEN WE COULD MAKE **THEM** GO TO THE **REALLY** SMELLY PLACES.
ALL OF THE PLACES ARE "REALLY SMELLY."
HUH. **THAT'S** WEIRD.
WHAT?
THE VIDEO IS **GONE!**

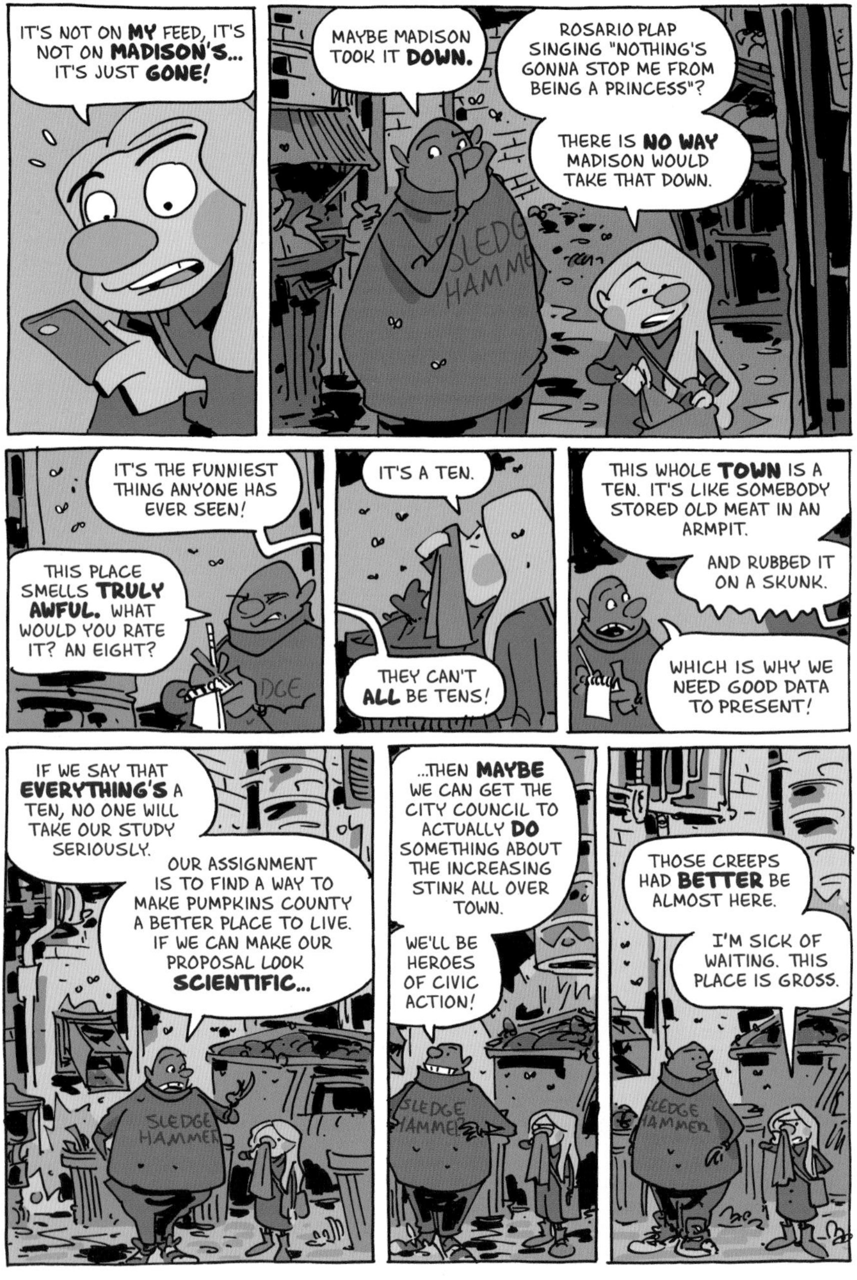
IT'S NOT ON MY FEED, IT'S NOT ON MADISON'S... IT'S JUST GONE!
MAYBE MADISON TOOK IT DOWN.
ROSARIO PLAP SINGING "NOTHING'S GONNA STOP ME FROM BEING A PRINCESS"?
THERE IS NO WAY MADISON WOULD TAKE THAT DOWN.
IT'S THE FUNNIEST THING ANYONE HAS EVER SEEN!
THIS PLACE SMELLS TRULY AWFUL. WHAT WOULD YOU RATE IT? AN EIGHT?
IT'S A TEN.
THEY CAN'T ALL BE TENS!
THIS WHOLE TOWN IS A TEN. IT'S LIKE SOMEBODY STORED OLD MEAT IN AN ARMPIT.
AND RUBBED IT ON A SKUNK.
WHICH IS WHY WE NEED GOOD DATA TO PRESENT!
IF WE SAY THAT EVERYTHING'S A TEN, NO ONE WILL TAKE OUR STUDY SERIOUSLY.
OUR ASSIGNMENT IS TO FIND A WAY TO MAKE PUMPKINS COUNTY A BETTER PLACE TO LIVE. IF WE CAN MAKE OUR PROPOSAL LOOK SCIENTIFIC...
...THEN MAYBE WE CAN GET THE CITY COUNCIL TO ACTUALLY DO SOMETHING ABOUT THE INCREASING STINK ALL OVER TOWN.
WE'LL BE HEROES OF CIVIC ACTION!
THOSE CREEPS HAD BETTER BE ALMOST HERE.
I'M SICK OF WAITING. THIS PLACE IS GROSS.

STILL... I THINK WE'VE WAITED HERE LONG ENOUGH.

I'M WITH YOU THERE.

SLEDGE HAMMER

GRAB MY BODY SPRAY, WILL YOU?

NO PROBLEM.

YOINK

ERNEST!

AAAUGH!

NO NO NOOOU

CHOMP

W-W-

CHOMP CHOMP HMM

GULP!

PTEWH

THUNK!

WHUAAGH! WAUUAAAAAGH!

5

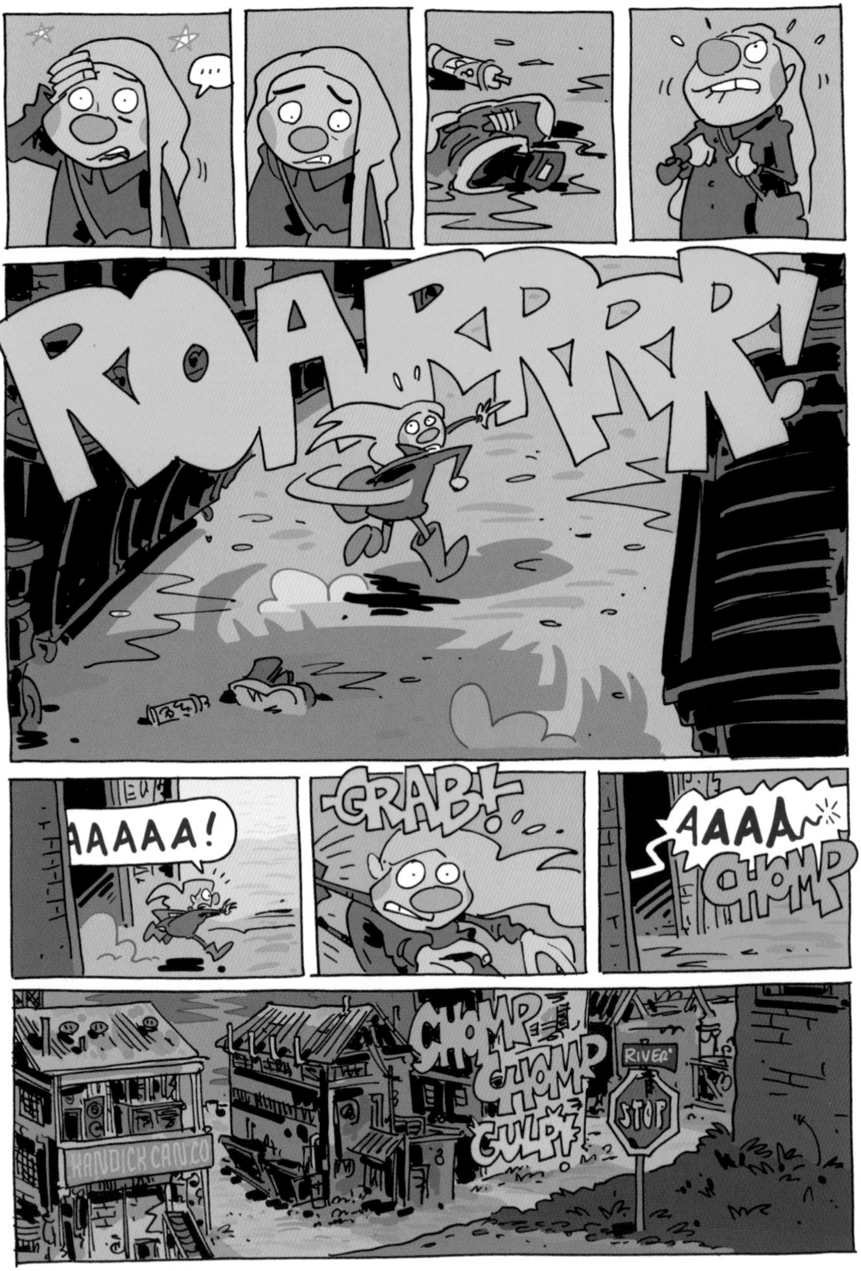
...
ROARRRR!
AAAAA!
GRAB!
AAAA
CHOMP
CHOMP
CHOMP
GULP!
RIVER
STOP
KANDICK CAN CO

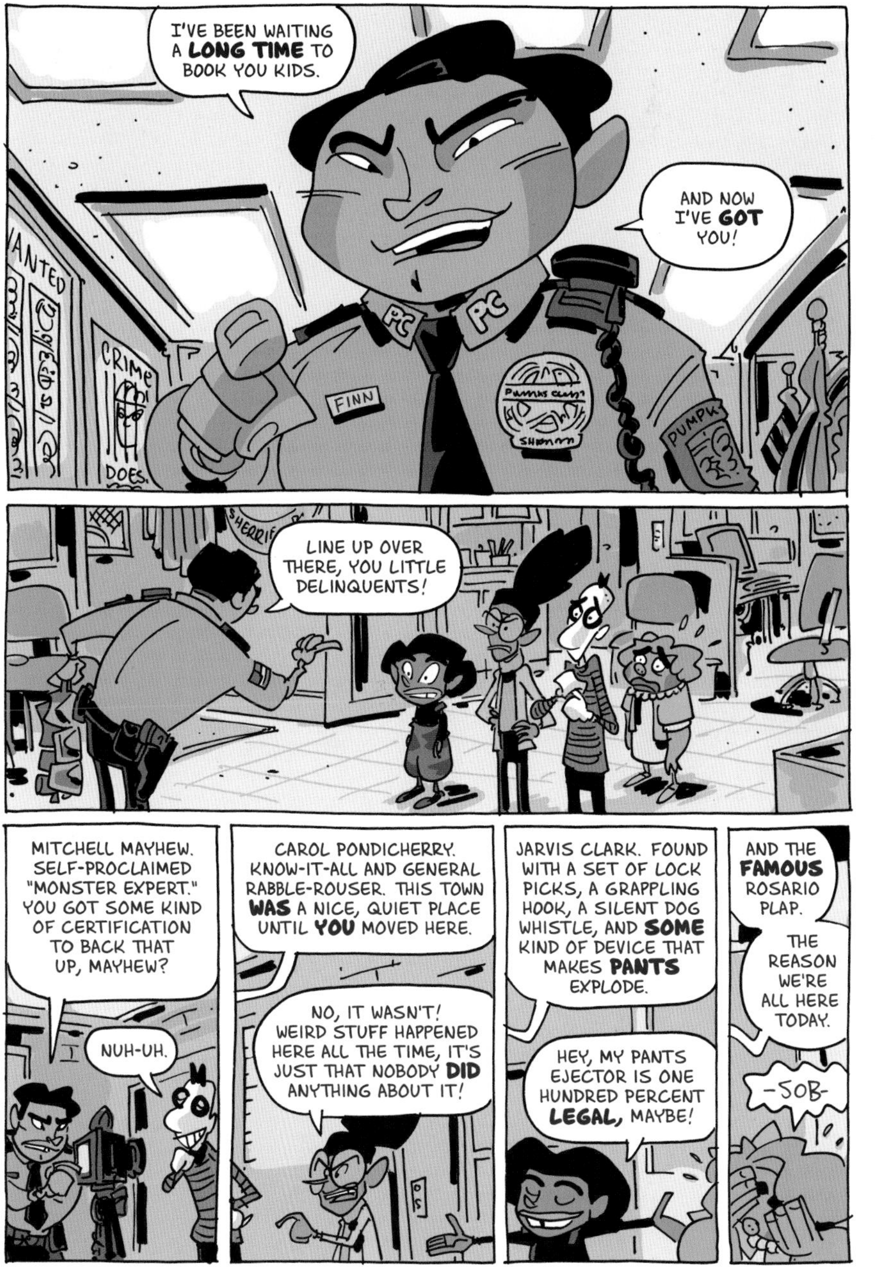
I'VE BEEN WAITING A **LONG TIME** TO BOOK YOU KIDS.
AND NOW I'VE **GOT** YOU!
WANTED
CRIME DOES.
FINN
PC
PC
LINE UP OVER THERE, YOU LITTLE DELINQUENTS!
MITCHELL MAYHEW. SELF-PROCLAIMED "MONSTER EXPERT." YOU GOT SOME KIND OF CERTIFICATION TO BACK THAT UP, MAYHEW?
NUH-UH.
CAROL PONDICHERRY. KNOW-IT-ALL AND GENERAL RABBLE-ROUSER. THIS TOWN **WAS** A NICE, QUIET PLACE UNTIL **YOU** MOVED HERE.
NO, IT WASN'T! WEIRD STUFF HAPPENED HERE ALL THE TIME, IT'S JUST THAT NOBODY **DID** ANYTHING ABOUT IT!
JARVIS CLARK. FOUND WITH A SET OF LOCK PICKS, A GRAPPLING HOOK, A SILENT DOG WHISTLE, AND **SOME** KIND OF DEVICE THAT MAKES **PANTS** EXPLODE.
HEY, MY PANTS EJECTOR IS ONE HUNDRED PERCENT **LEGAL,** MAYBE!
AND THE **FAMOUS** ROSARIO PLAP.
THE REASON WE'RE ALL HERE TODAY.
-SOB-

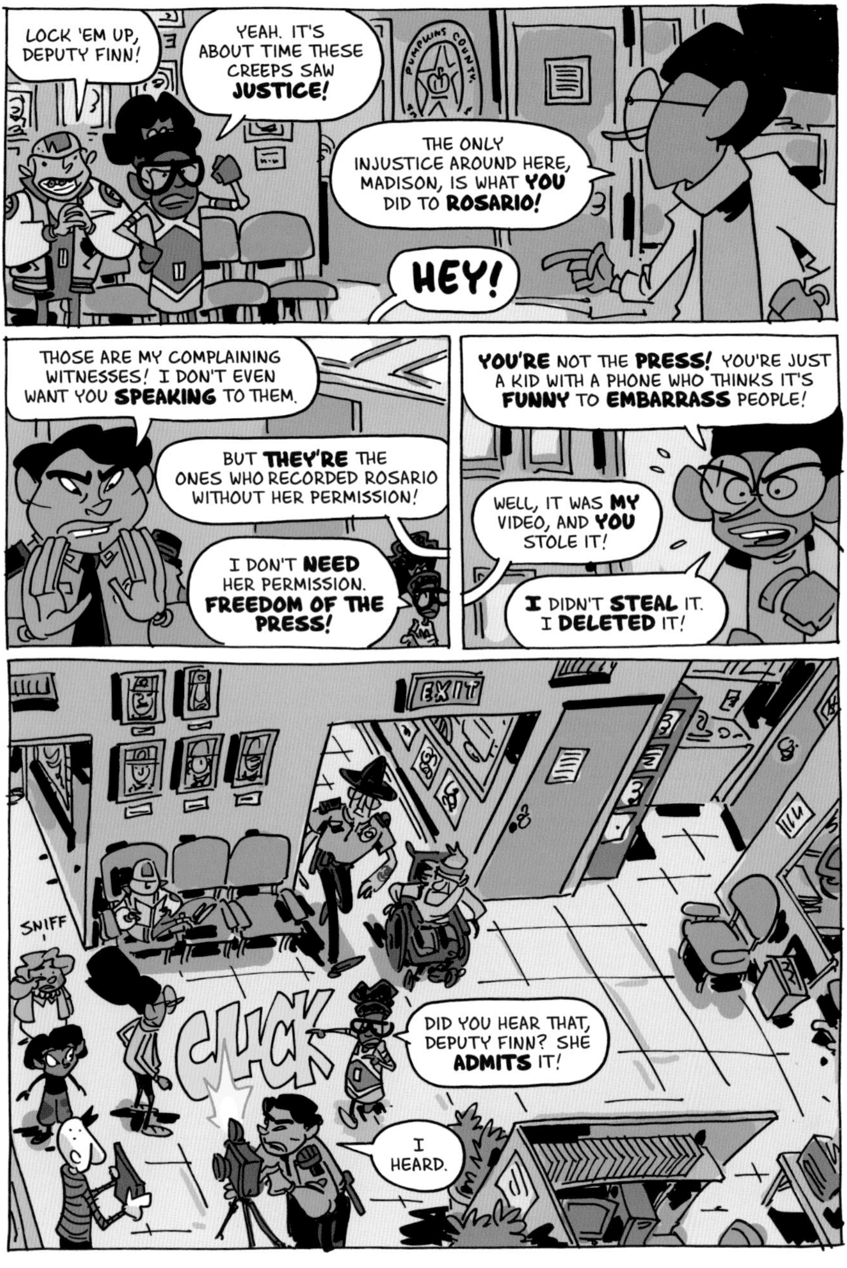
LOCK 'EM UP, DEPUTY FINN!
YEAH. IT'S ABOUT TIME THESE CREEPS SAW **JUSTICE!**
PUMPKINS COUNTY
THE ONLY INJUSTICE AROUND HERE, MADISON, IS WHAT **YOU** DID TO **ROSARIO!**
HEY!
THOSE ARE MY COMPLAINING WITNESSES! I DON'T EVEN WANT YOU **SPEAKING** TO THEM.
BUT **THEY'RE** THE ONES WHO RECORDED ROSARIO WITHOUT HER PERMISSION!
I DON'T **NEED** HER PERMISSION. **FREEDOM OF THE PRESS!**
YOU'RE NOT THE **PRESS!** YOU'RE JUST A KID WITH A PHONE WHO THINKS IT'S **FUNNY** TO **EMBARRASS** PEOPLE!
WELL, IT WAS **MY** VIDEO, AND **YOU** STOLE IT!
I DIDN'T **STEAL** IT. I **DELETED** IT!
EXIT
SNIFF
CLICK
DID YOU HEAR THAT, DEPUTY FINN? SHE **ADMITS** IT!
I HEARD.

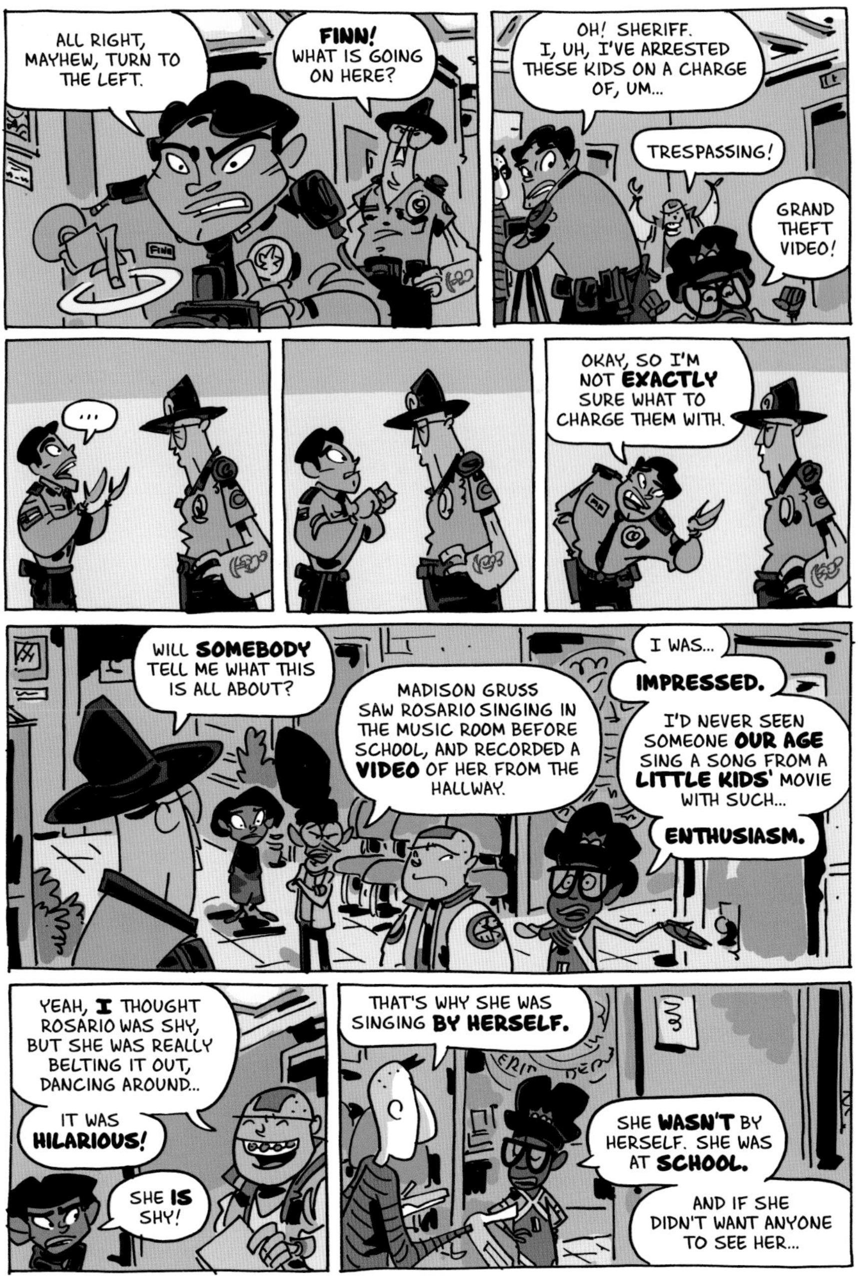
ALL RIGHT, MAYHEW, TURN TO THE LEFT.
FINN! WHAT IS GOING ON HERE?
OH! SHERIFF. I, UH, I'VE ARRESTED THESE KIDS ON A CHARGE OF, UM...
TRESPASSING!
GRAND THEFT VIDEO!
...
OKAY, SO I'M NOT EXACTLY SURE WHAT TO CHARGE THEM WITH.
WILL SOMEBODY TELL ME WHAT THIS IS ALL ABOUT?
MADISON GRUSS SAW ROSARIO SINGING IN THE MUSIC ROOM BEFORE SCHOOL, AND RECORDED A VIDEO OF HER FROM THE HALLWAY.
I WAS...
IMPRESSED.
I'D NEVER SEEN SOMEONE OUR AGE SING A SONG FROM A LITTLE KIDS' MOVIE WITH SUCH...
ENTHUSIASM.
YEAH, I THOUGHT ROSARIO WAS SHY, BUT SHE WAS REALLY BELTING IT OUT, DANCING AROUND...
IT WAS HILARIOUS!
SHE IS SHY!
THAT'S WHY SHE WAS SINGING BY HERSELF.
SHE WASN'T BY HERSELF. SHE WAS AT SCHOOL.
AND IF SHE DIDN'T WANT ANYONE TO SEE HER...

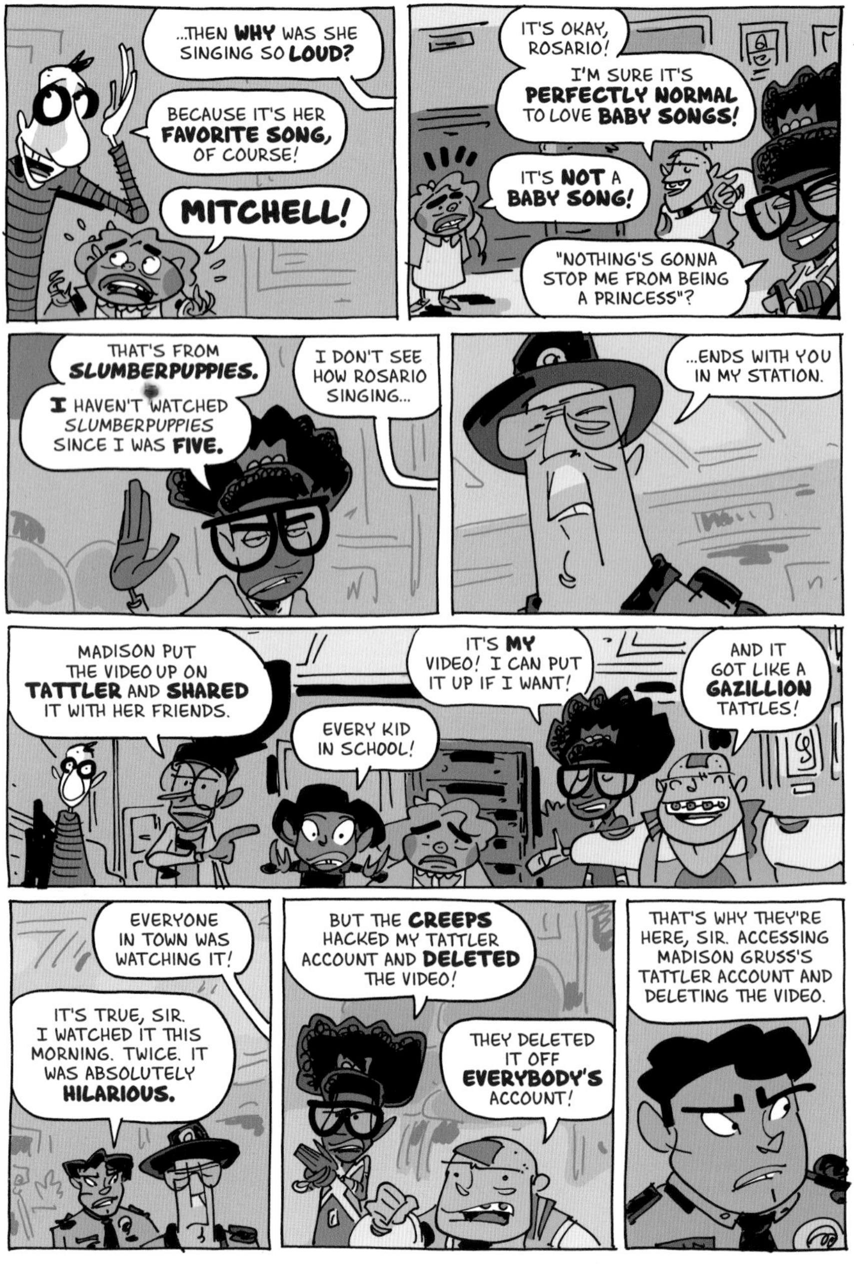
...THEN **WHY** WAS SHE SINGING SO **LOUD?**
BECAUSE IT'S HER **FAVORITE SONG,** OF COURSE!
MITCHELL!
IT'S OKAY, ROSARIO!
I'M SURE IT'S **PERFECTLY NORMAL** TO LOVE **BABY SONGS!**
IT'S **NOT** A **BABY SONG!**
"NOTHING'S GONNA STOP ME FROM BEING A PRINCESS"?
THAT'S FROM **SLUMBERPUPPIES.**
I HAVEN'T WATCHED *SLUMBERPUPPIES* SINCE I WAS **FIVE.**
I DON'T SEE HOW ROSARIO SINGING...
...ENDS WITH YOU IN MY STATION.
MADISON PUT THE VIDEO UP ON **TATTLER** AND **SHARED** IT WITH HER FRIENDS.
EVERY KID IN SCHOOL!
IT'S **MY** VIDEO! I CAN PUT IT UP IF I WANT!
AND IT GOT LIKE A **GAZILLION** TATTLES!
EVERYONE IN TOWN WAS WATCHING IT!
IT'S TRUE, SIR. I WATCHED IT THIS MORNING. TWICE. IT WAS ABSOLUTELY **HILARIOUS.**
BUT THE **CREEPS** HACKED MY TATTLER ACCOUNT AND **DELETED** THE VIDEO!
THEY DELETED IT OFF **EVERYBODY'S** ACCOUNT!
THAT'S WHY THEY'RE HERE, SIR. ACCESSING MADISON GRUSS'S TATTLER ACCOUNT AND DELETING THE VIDEO.

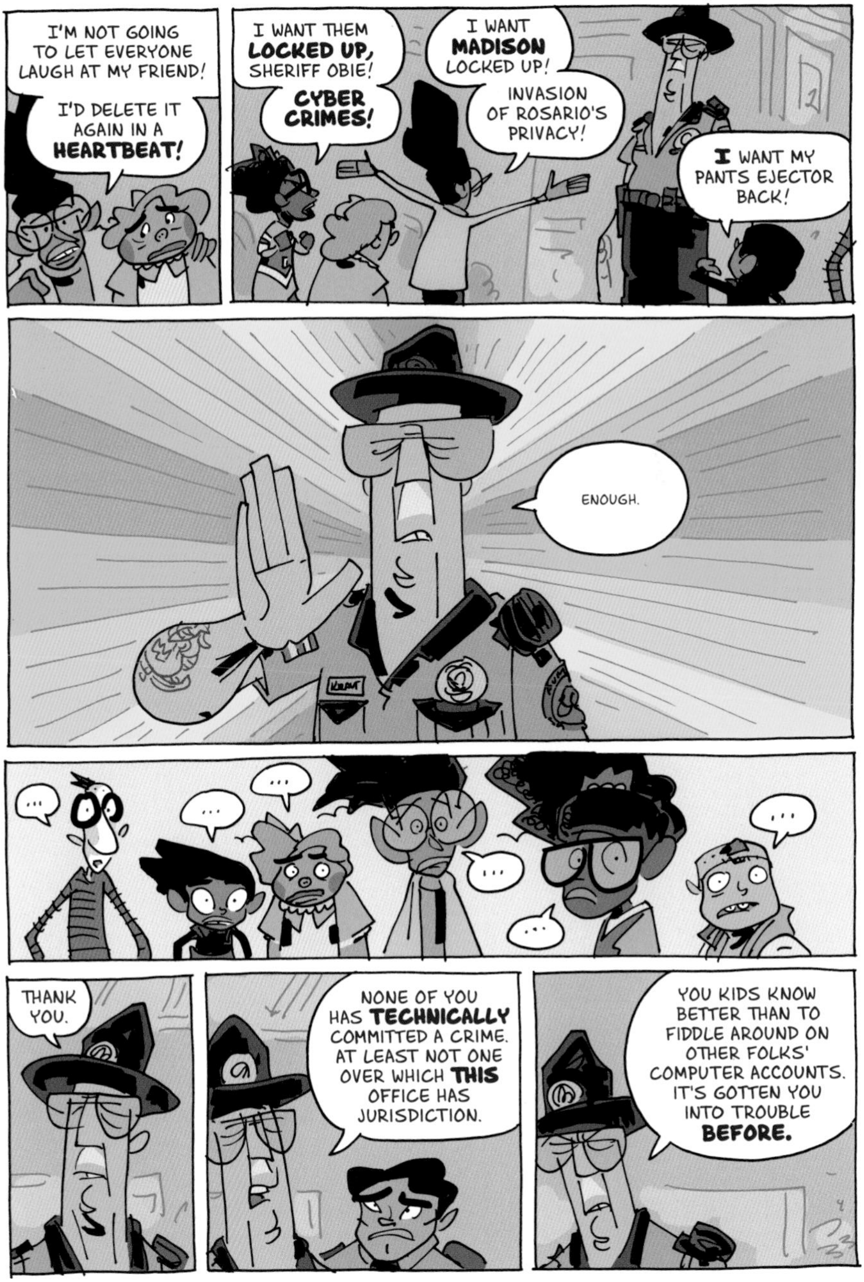

I'M NOT GOING TO LET EVERYONE LAUGH AT MY FRIEND!
I'D DELETE IT AGAIN IN A **HEARTBEAT!**
I WANT THEM **LOCKED UP,** SHERIFF OBIE!
CYBER CRIMES!
I WANT **MADISON** LOCKED UP!
INVASION OF ROSARIO'S PRIVACY!
I WANT MY PANTS EJECTOR BACK!
ENOUGH.
...
...
...
...
...
...
...
THANK YOU.
NONE OF YOU HAS **TECHNICALLY** COMMITTED A CRIME. AT LEAST NOT ONE OVER WHICH **THIS** OFFICE HAS JURISDICTION.
YOU KIDS KNOW BETTER THAN TO FIDDLE AROUND ON OTHER FOLKS' COMPUTER ACCOUNTS. IT'S GOTTEN YOU INTO TROUBLE **BEFORE.**

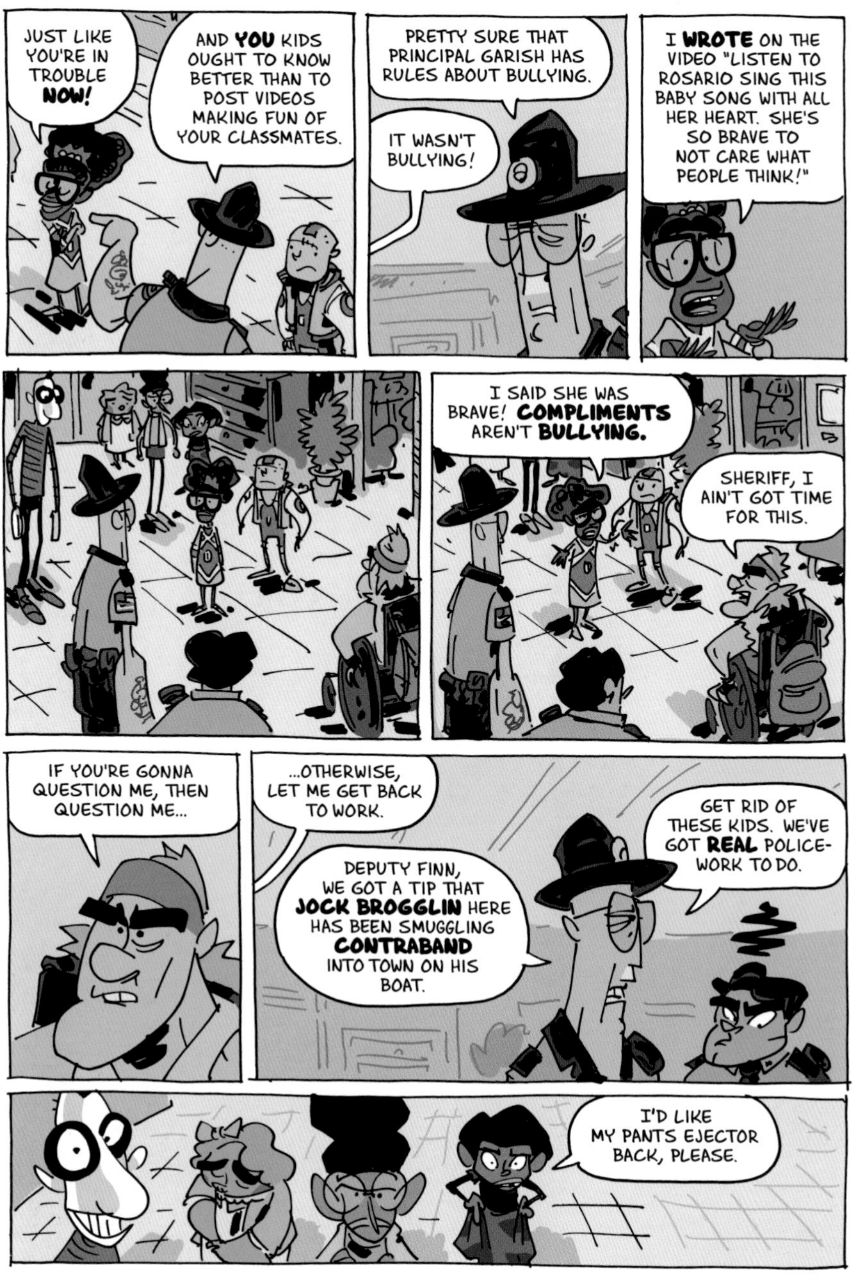
JUST LIKE YOU'RE IN TROUBLE **NOW!**
AND **YOU** KIDS OUGHT TO KNOW BETTER THAN TO POST VIDEOS MAKING FUN OF YOUR CLASSMATES.
PRETTY SURE THAT PRINCIPAL GARISH HAS RULES ABOUT BULLYING.
IT WASN'T BULLYING!
I **WROTE** ON THE VIDEO "LISTEN TO ROSARIO SING THIS BABY SONG WITH ALL HER HEART. SHE'S SO BRAVE TO NOT CARE WHAT PEOPLE THINK!"
I SAID SHE WAS BRAVE! **COMPLIMENTS** AREN'T **BULLYING.**
SHERIFF, I AIN'T GOT TIME FOR THIS.
IF YOU'RE GONNA QUESTION ME, THEN QUESTION ME...
...OTHERWISE, LET ME GET BACK TO WORK.
DEPUTY FINN, WE GOT A TIP THAT **JOCK BROGGLIN** HERE HAS BEEN SMUGGLING **CONTRABAND** INTO TOWN ON HIS BOAT.
GET RID OF THESE KIDS. WE'VE GOT **REAL** POLICE-WORK TO DO.
I'D LIKE MY PANTS EJECTOR BACK, PLEASE.

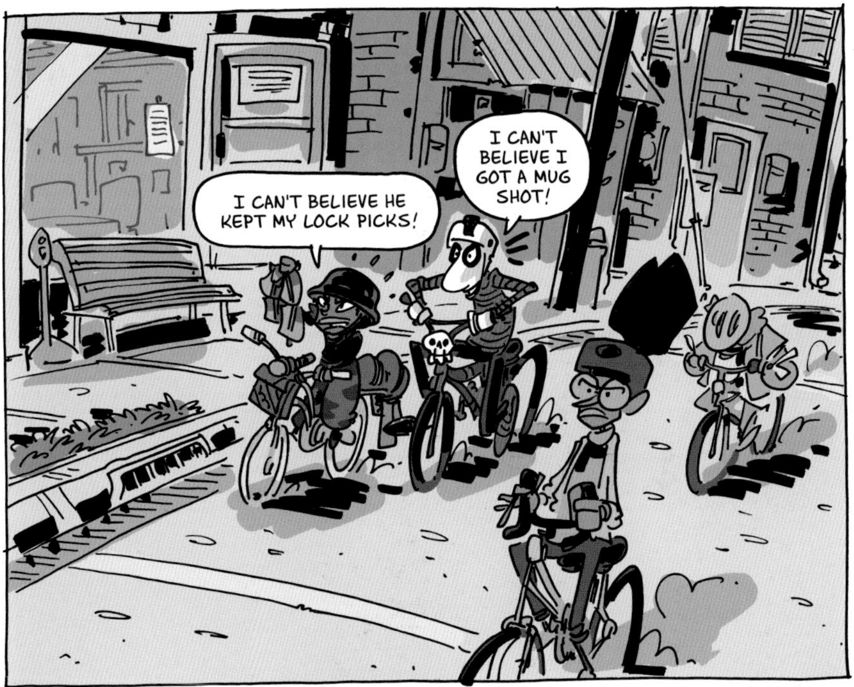
I CAN'T BELIEVE HE KEPT MY LOCK PICKS!
I CAN'T BELIEVE I GOT A MUG SHOT!

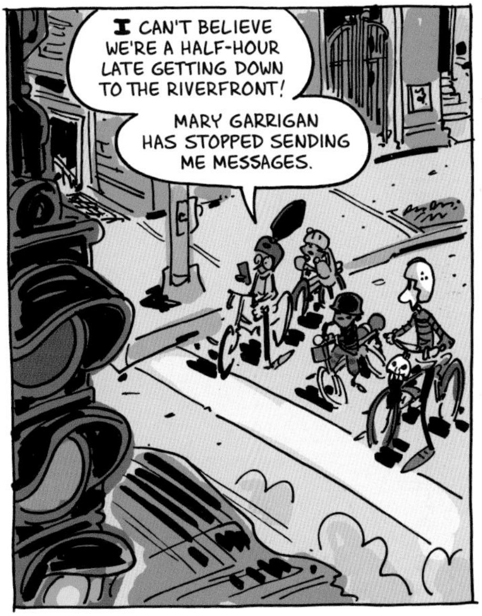
I CAN'T BELIEVE WE'RE A HALF-HOUR LATE GETTING DOWN TO THE RIVERFRONT!
MARY GARRIGAN HAS STOPPED SENDING ME MESSAGES.

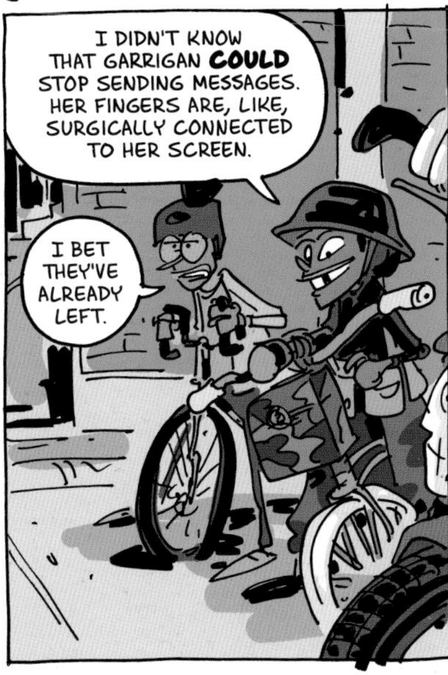
I DIDN'T KNOW THAT GARRIGAN COULD STOP SENDING MESSAGES. HER FINGERS ARE, LIKE, SURGICALLY CONNECTED TO HER SCREEN.
I BET THEY'VE ALREADY LEFT.

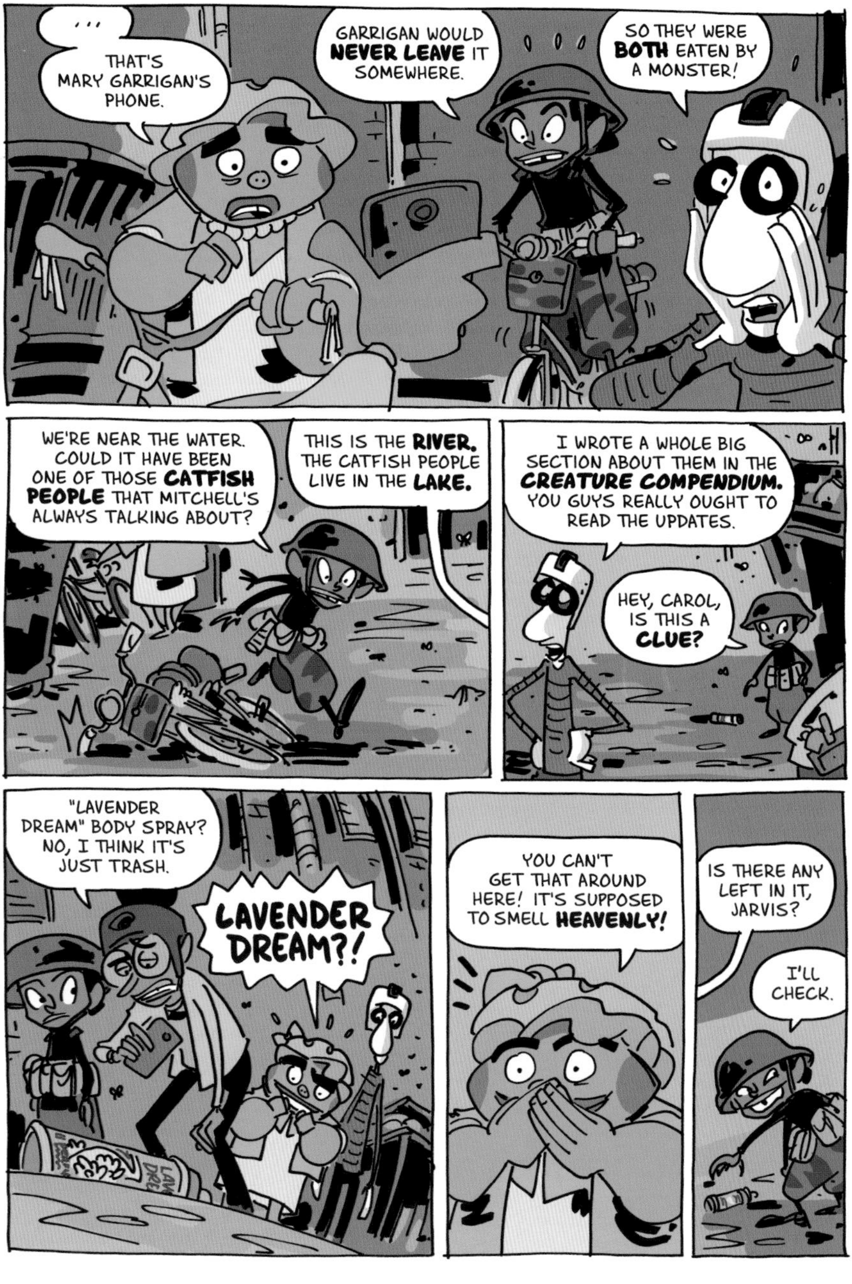
...
THAT'S MARY GARRIGAN'S PHONE.
GARRIGAN WOULD **NEVER LEAVE** IT SOMEWHERE.
SO THEY WERE **BOTH** EATEN BY A MONSTER!
WE'RE NEAR THE WATER. COULD IT HAVE BEEN ONE OF THOSE **CATFISH PEOPLE** THAT MITCHELL'S ALWAYS TALKING ABOUT?
THIS IS THE **RIVER.** THE CATFISH PEOPLE LIVE IN THE **LAKE.**
I WROTE A WHOLE BIG SECTION ABOUT THEM IN THE ***CREATURE COMPENDIUM.*** YOU GUYS REALLY OUGHT TO READ THE UPDATES.
HEY, CAROL, IS THIS A **CLUE?**
"LAVENDER DREAM" BODY SPRAY? NO, I THINK IT'S JUST TRASH.
LAVENDER DREAM?!
YOU CAN'T GET THAT AROUND HERE! IT'S SUPPOSED TO SMELL **HEAVENLY!**
IS THERE ANY LEFT IN IT, JARVIS?
I'LL CHECK.

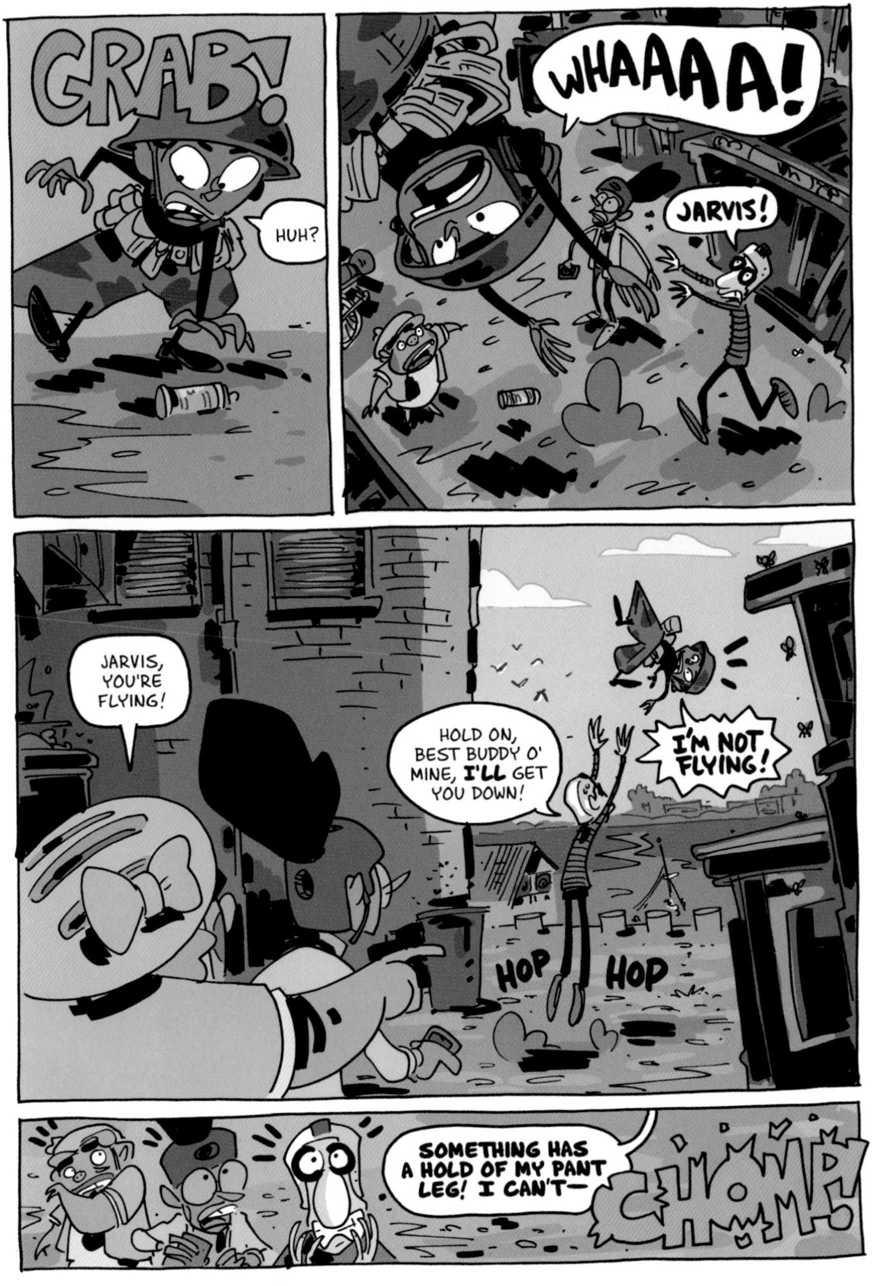
GRAB!
HUH?
WHAAAA!
JARVIS!
JARVIS, YOU'RE FLYING!
HOLD ON, BEST BUDDY O' MINE, **I'LL** GET YOU DOWN!
I'M NOT FLYING!
HOP
HOP
SOMETHING HAS A HOLD OF MY PANT LEG! I CAN'T—
CHOMP!

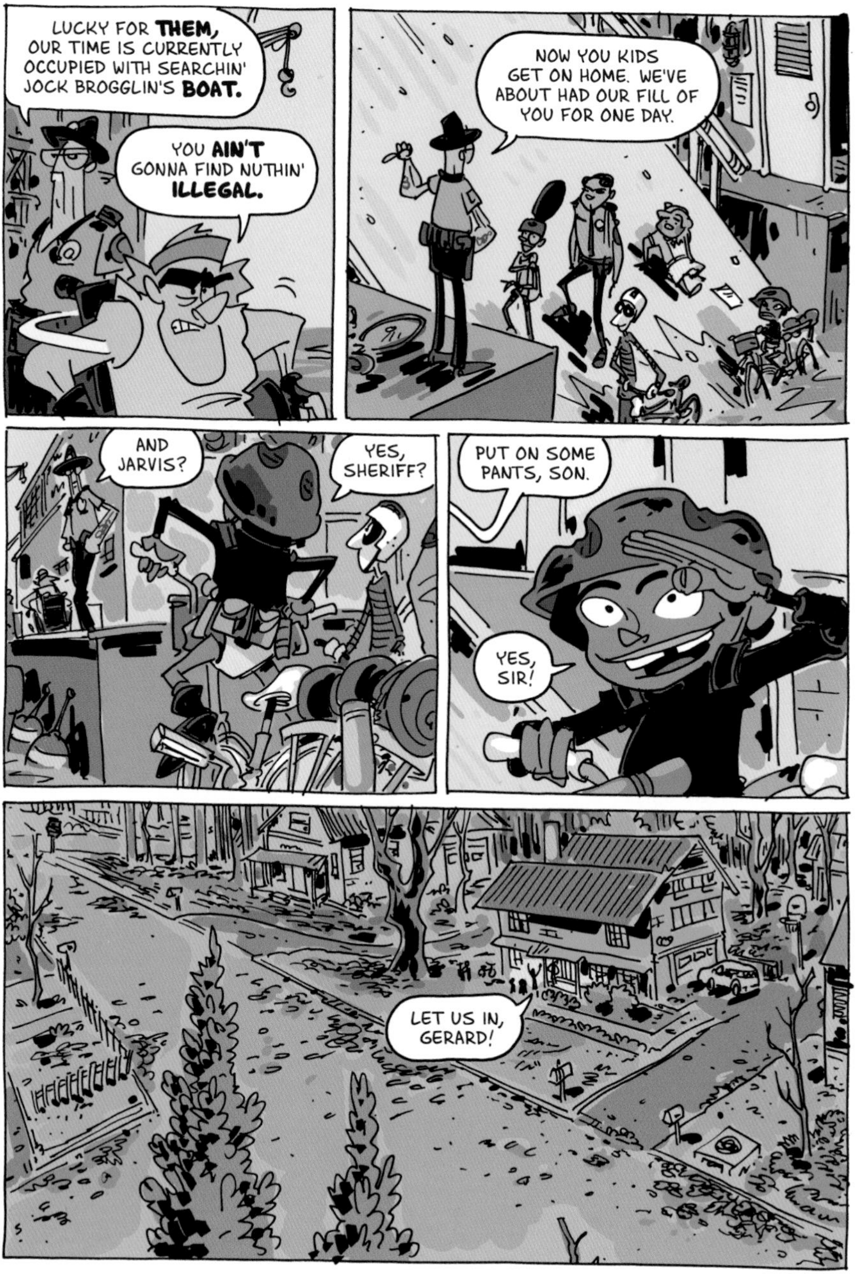
LUCKY FOR THEM, OUR TIME IS CURRENTLY OCCUPIED WITH SEARCHIN' JOCK BROGGLIN'S BOAT.
YOU AIN'T GONNA FIND NUTHIN' ILLEGAL.
NOW YOU KIDS GET ON HOME. WE'VE ABOUT HAD OUR FILL OF YOU FOR ONE DAY.
AND JARVIS?
YES, SHERIFF?
PUT ON SOME PANTS, SON.
YES, SIR!
LET US IN, GERARD!

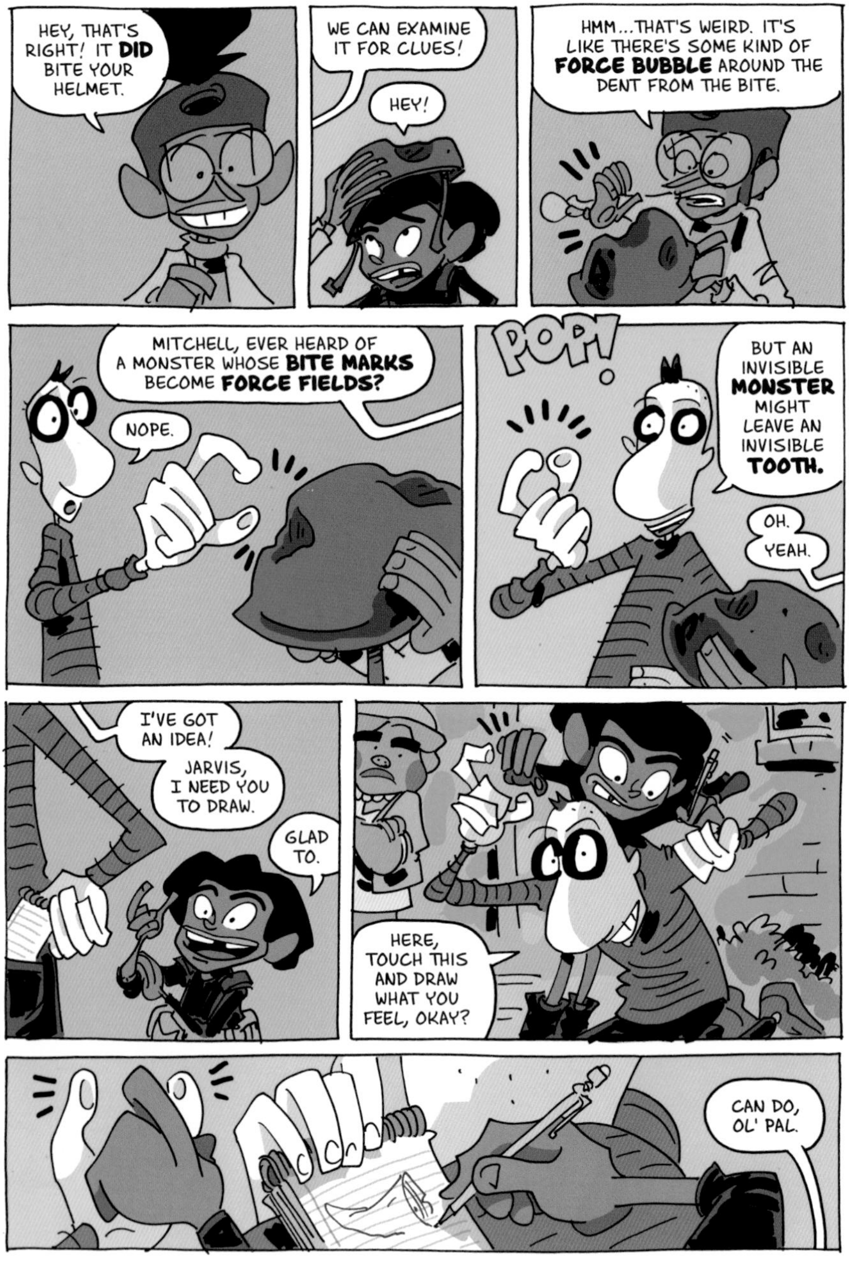
HEY, THAT'S RIGHT! IT **DID** BITE YOUR HELMET.
WE CAN EXAMINE IT FOR CLUES!
HEY!
HMM...THAT'S WEIRD. IT'S LIKE THERE'S SOME KIND OF **FORCE BUBBLE** AROUND THE DENT FROM THE BITE.
MITCHELL, EVER HEARD OF A MONSTER WHOSE **BITE MARKS** BECOME **FORCE FIELDS?**
NOPE.
POP!
BUT AN INVISIBLE **MONSTER** MIGHT LEAVE AN INVISIBLE **TOOTH.**
OH.
YEAH.
I'VE GOT AN IDEA!
JARVIS, I NEED YOU TO DRAW.
GLAD TO.
HERE, TOUCH THIS AND DRAW WHAT YOU FEEL, OKAY?
CAN DO, OL' PAL.

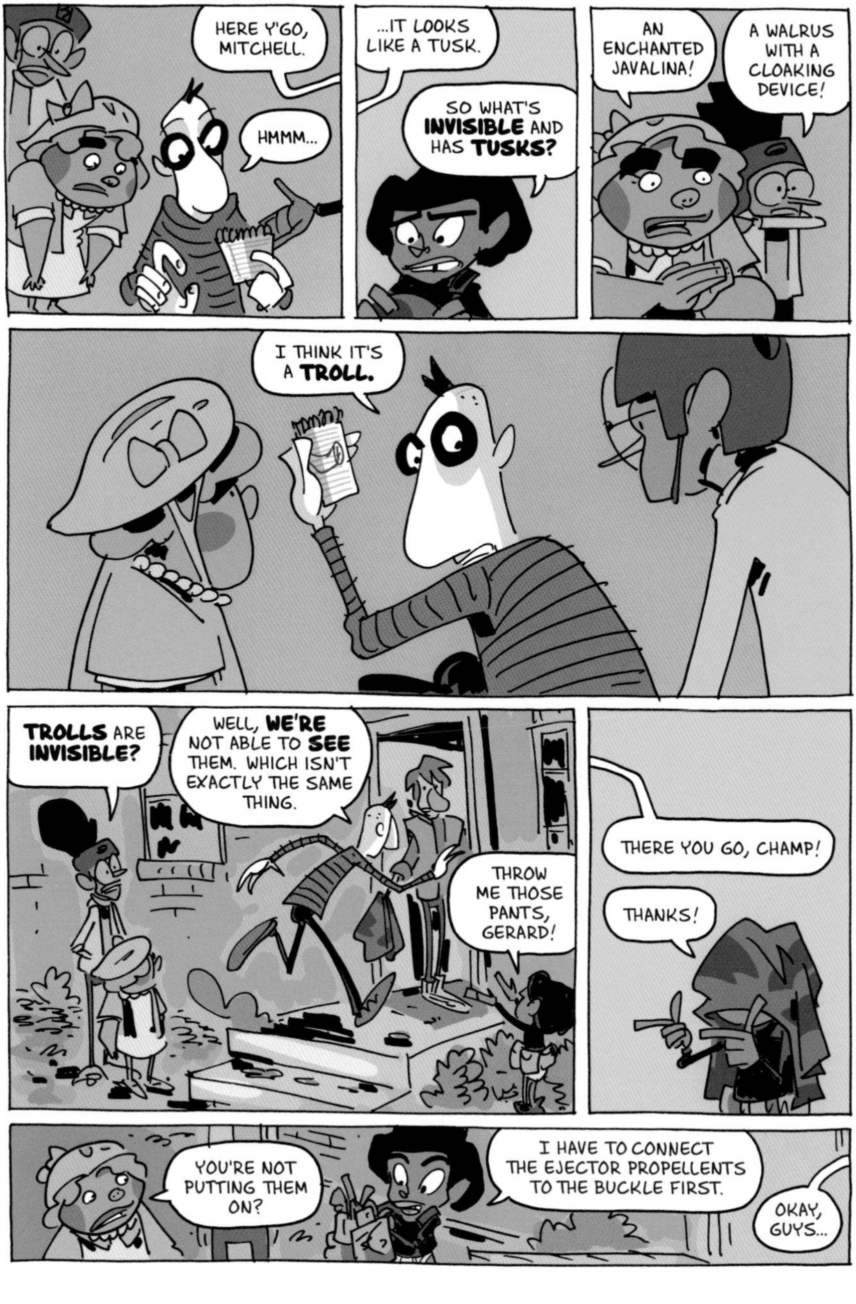
HERE Y'GO, MITCHELL.
HMMM...
...IT LOOKS LIKE A TUSK.
SO WHAT'S INVISIBLE AND HAS TUSKS?
AN ENCHANTED JAVALINA!
A WALRUS WITH A CLOAKING DEVICE!
I THINK IT'S A TROLL.
TROLLS ARE INVISIBLE?
WELL, WE'RE NOT ABLE TO SEE THEM. WHICH ISN'T EXACTLY THE SAME THING.
THROW ME THOSE PANTS, GERARD!
THERE YOU GO, CHAMP!
THANKS!
YOU'RE NOT PUTTING THEM ON?
I HAVE TO CONNECT THE EJECTOR PROPELLENTS TO THE BUCKLE FIRST.
OKAY, GUYS...

...WHAT KIND OF TROUBLE ARE YOU GETTING UP TO?

SOMETHING ATE OUR CLASSMATES. MITCHELL THINKS IT MIGHT BE A **TROLL**.

AW, COME ON, GUYS. EVERY TIME YOU SHOUT "MONSTER" THE WHOLE TOWN GETS MAD AT YOU. JUST **BE COOL.**

YOU GUYS MIGHT BE A LITTLE WEIRD AND STUFF, BUT YOU'RE ALL RIGHT.

JUST TONE DOWN THE MONSTER STUFF. IT BUMS ME OUT THAT EVERYONE THINKS OF YOU GUYS AS, WELL...

...YOU KNOW...

REAL NICE, GERARD.

CREEPS.

EVERYONE TREATS **US** LIKE DIRT, AND **WE'RE** THE ONES WHO NEED TO CHANGE?

I'M NOT SAYING THAT YOU **DESERVE** TO BE PICKED ON. I'M JUST SAYING THAT YOU MAKE YOURSELVES REALLY EASY TARGETS.

YOU CAN **LIKE** STUFF THAT'S UNUSUAL...

I MEAN, **I'M** BONKERS FOR FARM-CRAFTED ARTISANAL CHEESES...

...BUT, YOU KNOW, PLAY IT CLOSE TO THE VEST.

SO PRETEND THAT WE DON'T CARE ABOUT THE STUFF WE CARE ABOUT?

EXACTLY!

PASSION IS A LUXURY AFFORDED LITTLE KIDS AND GROWN-UPS.

THE WATERS OF ADOLESCENT SOCIAL STANDING ARE CHOPPY, MY LITTLE FRIENDS, AND IT HELPS TO HAVE...

UM...

I DON'T KNOW, A BOAT OR SOMETHING?

I KIND OF LOST THE METAPHOR, BUT IF PEOPLE THINK THAT **YOU'RE** MORE OR LESS LIKE **THEM**, THEN THEY'LL **LIKE** YOU MORE.

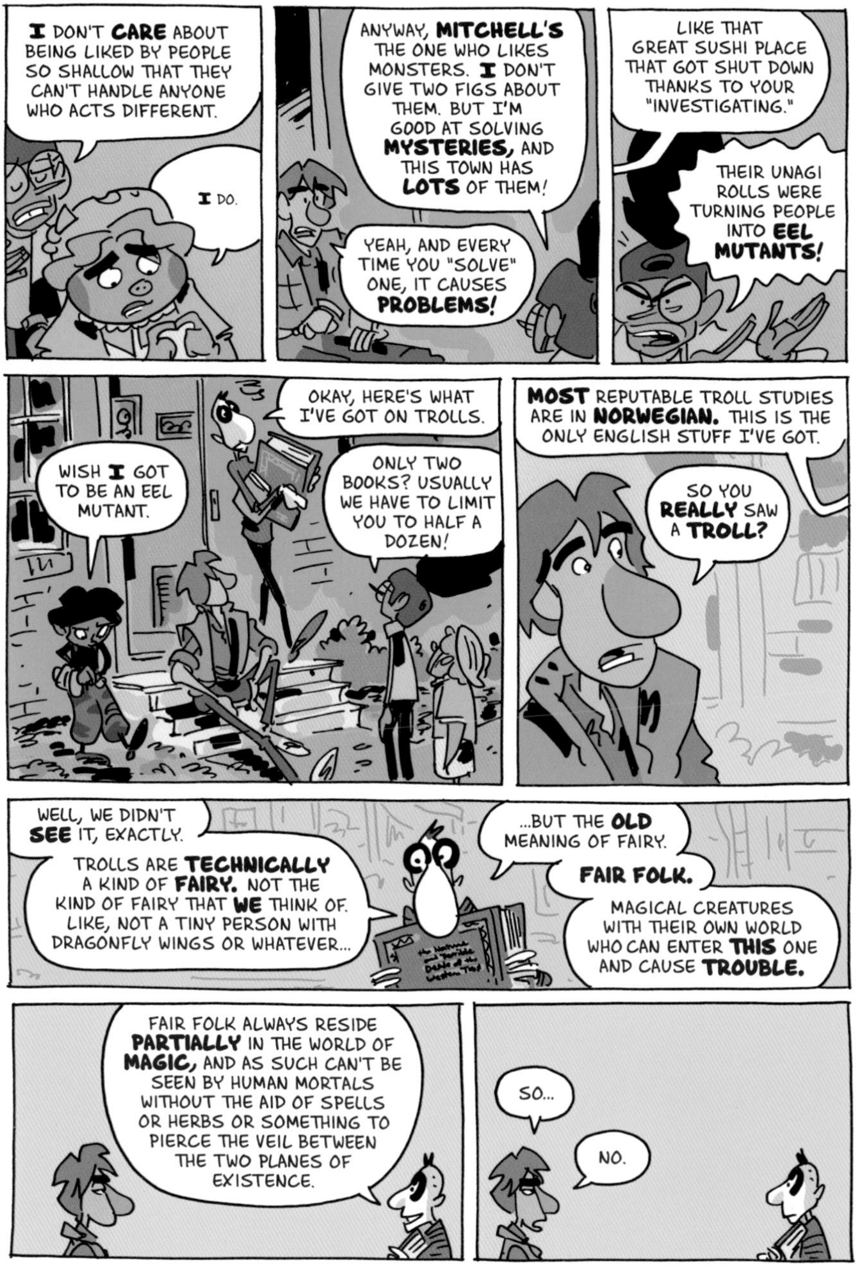
I DON'T CARE ABOUT BEING LIKED BY PEOPLE SO SHALLOW THAT THEY CAN'T HANDLE ANYONE WHO ACTS DIFFERENT.
I DO.
ANYWAY, MITCHELL'S THE ONE WHO LIKES MONSTERS. I DON'T GIVE TWO FIGS ABOUT THEM. BUT I'M GOOD AT SOLVING MYSTERIES, AND THIS TOWN HAS LOTS OF THEM!
YEAH, AND EVERY TIME YOU "SOLVE" ONE, IT CAUSES PROBLEMS!
LIKE THAT GREAT SUSHI PLACE THAT GOT SHUT DOWN THANKS TO YOUR "INVESTIGATING."
THEIR UNAGI ROLLS WERE TURNING PEOPLE INTO EEL MUTANTS!
WISH I GOT TO BE AN EEL MUTANT.
OKAY, HERE'S WHAT I'VE GOT ON TROLLS.
ONLY TWO BOOKS? USUALLY WE HAVE TO LIMIT YOU TO HALF A DOZEN!
MOST REPUTABLE TROLL STUDIES ARE IN NORWEGIAN. THIS IS THE ONLY ENGLISH STUFF I'VE GOT.
SO YOU REALLY SAW A TROLL?
WELL, WE DIDN'T SEE IT, EXACTLY.
TROLLS ARE TECHNICALLY A KIND OF FAIRY. NOT THE KIND OF FAIRY THAT WE THINK OF. LIKE, NOT A TINY PERSON WITH DRAGONFLY WINGS OR WHATEVER...
...BUT THE OLD MEANING OF FAIRY.
FAIR FOLK.
MAGICAL CREATURES WITH THEIR OWN WORLD WHO CAN ENTER THIS ONE AND CAUSE TROUBLE.
FAIR FOLK ALWAYS RESIDE PARTIALLY IN THE WORLD OF MAGIC, AND AS SUCH CAN'T BE SEEN BY HUMAN MORTALS WITHOUT THE AID OF SPELLS OR HERBS OR SOMETHING TO PIERCE THE VEIL BETWEEN THE TWO PLANES OF EXISTENCE.
SO...
NO.

-SIGH-

YOU KIDS DO YOUR THING, I GUESS.

FAIRIES, MITCHELL? **FAIRIES?**

I'D **LOVE** TO SEE A REAL FAIRY!

WELL, **THESE** FAIRIES ARE GIANT, MEAN, AND STINKY.

RESEARCH TIME!

THUD

LET'S READ THROUGH TOGETHER, SHALL WE?

SO WE'RE PROBABLY NOT LOOKING AT **ONE** TROLL, BUT A **LOT** OF THEM.

THEY LIVE IN TRIBES OR CLANS. THEY EVEN **HIBERNATE** COMMUNALLY.

Slumb'r lengthy is the beast's rospite
With men their gullets swell'd to stem their water
Wherefore they gorge not outside single night
One way o'erhead their hungr for to slake

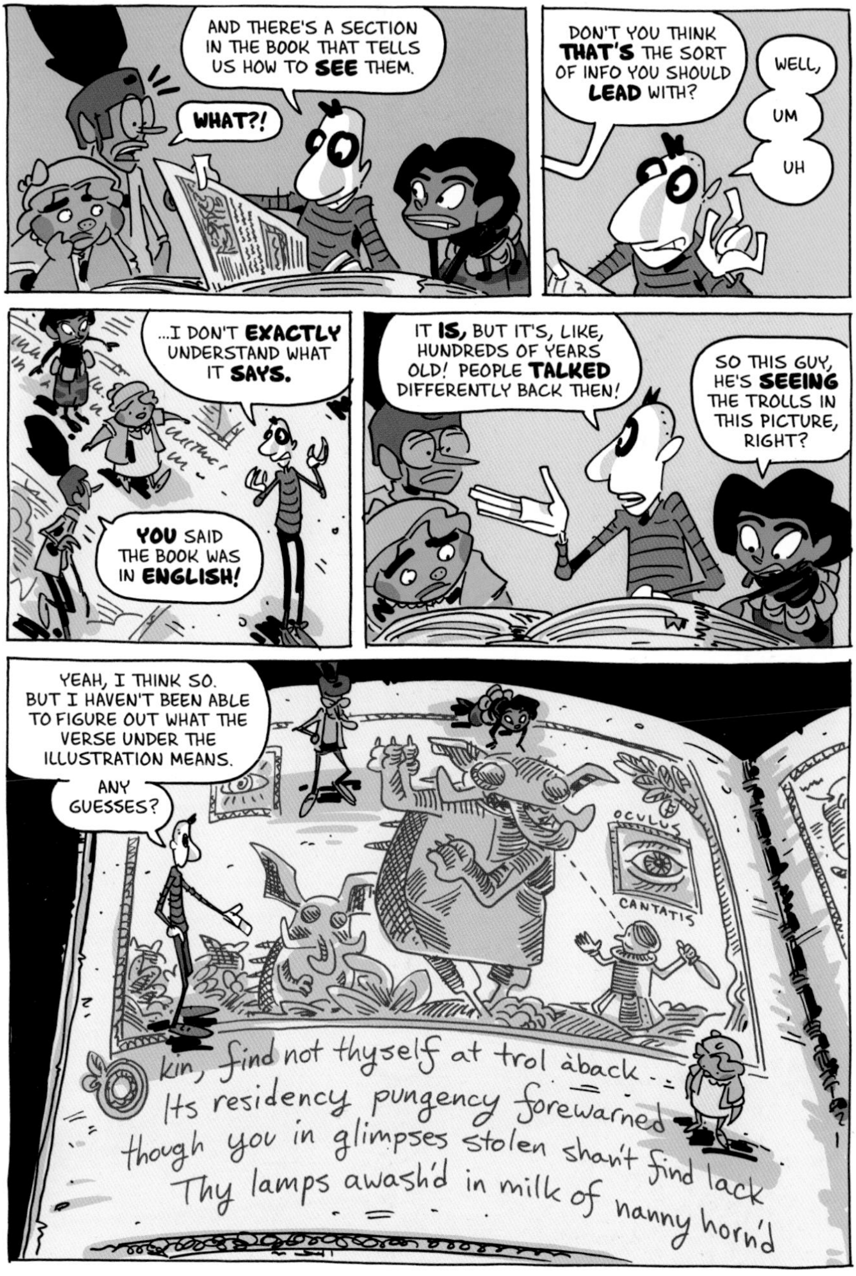
AND THERE'S A SECTION IN THE BOOK THAT TELLS US HOW TO **SEE** THEM.
WHAT?!
DON'T YOU THINK **THAT'S** THE SORT OF INFO YOU SHOULD **LEAD** WITH?
WELL,
UM
UH
...I DON'T **EXACTLY** UNDERSTAND WHAT IT **SAYS.**
YOU SAID THE BOOK WAS IN **ENGLISH!**
IT **IS,** BUT IT'S, LIKE, HUNDREDS OF YEARS OLD! PEOPLE **TALKED** DIFFERENTLY BACK THEN!
SO THIS GUY, HE'S **SEEING** THE TROLLS IN THIS PICTURE, RIGHT?
YEAH, I THINK SO. BUT I HAVEN'T BEEN ABLE TO FIGURE OUT WHAT THE VERSE UNDER THE ILLUSTRATION MEANS.
ANY GUESSES?
OCULUS
CANTATIS
kin, find not thyself at trol àback
Its residency pungency forewarned
though you in glimpses stolen shan't find lack
Thy lamps awash'd in milk of nanny horn'd

NOPE. NO GUESSES.

WHAT DOES THIS PART ABOUT **LAMPS** MEAN?

"THY LAMPS AWASH'D IN MILK OF NANNY HORN'D."

MAYBE IF WE PUT A SPECIAL KIND OF MILK ON AN OLD LAMP, LIKE AN OIL LAMP, MAYBE THE LIGHT SHINING OUT WOULD SHOW THE TROLLS?

OR MAYBE YOU'RE SUPPOSED TO PUT THE MILK **IN** THE LAMP, INSTEAD OF **OIL**.

THERE'S AN OLD OIL LAMP IN OUR **SHED!**

EASY, GUYS...

LIKE YOU SAID, A "SPECIAL KIND" OF MILK. A "NANNY" MIGHT MEAN, LIKE, A NURSEMAID, BUT **I** DON'T **KNOW** ANY NURSEMAIDS.

MUCH LESS ANY THAT HAVE HORNS.

WHAT HAS HORNS? A SATYR?

I THINK SATYRS ARE MALE. YOU CAN'T MILK MALES.

I'M NOT MILKING ANYTHING.

I THINK IT'S A DEAD END CLUE, GUYS. IT WAS WRITTEN HUNDREDS OF YEARS AGO. FOR ALL WE KNOW, A "NANNY HORN'D" COULD BE A TYPE OF MILK BOTTLE, OR A TOWN, OR WHO KNOWS WHAT. WE GOT NUTHIN'.

COME ON, MITCHELL. IF I KNOW YOU, THEN YOU'VE **PORED** OVER THIS BOOK. YOU **MUST** HAVE FOUND SOME OTHER CLUES OR **SOMETHING** THAT CAN HELP!

I'VE DONE MY BEST, CAROL, BUT I DON'T UNDERSTAND MUCH OF THE WRITING, AND MOST OF THE ILLUSTRATIONS ARE EITHER PICTURES OF TROLLS SLEEPING OR DIAGRAMS OF THEIR DIGESTIVE SYSTEMS.

EWW!

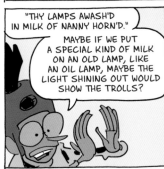

SO WE COULDN'T FIGURE OUT THE BIT ABOUT HOW TO **SEE** THEM...

...IS THERE ANYTHING IN THE BOOK ABOUT HOW TO **STOP** THEM?

MITCHELL...

OKAY, MAYBE THERE'S **SOMETHING.**

BUT I THINK IT MIGHT BE ABOUT HOW TO **KILL** TROLLS. **I** DON'T WANT TO KILL **ANYTHING.**

FOR ALL WE KNOW, THEY'RE GENTLE AT HEART AND JUST WANT TO BE LEFT ALONE.

THEY ATE MARY AND ERNEST.

THAT DOESN'T SAY "GENTLE" TO **ME.**

GOOD POINT.

OKAY, HERE IN THE BACK. I COULDN'T FIGURE THIS SECTION OUT, EITHER.

YEP. THAT TROLL LOOKS DEADER THAN A DOORNAIL.

THIS VERSE DOESN'T MAKE ANY MORE SENSE THAN THE **OTHER** ONE.

HERE!

If seek ye monsters' end as end betide
A trill from passions fountainhead declare
Its heart untanned, a pole against its hide
For strain believed is more than it can bear

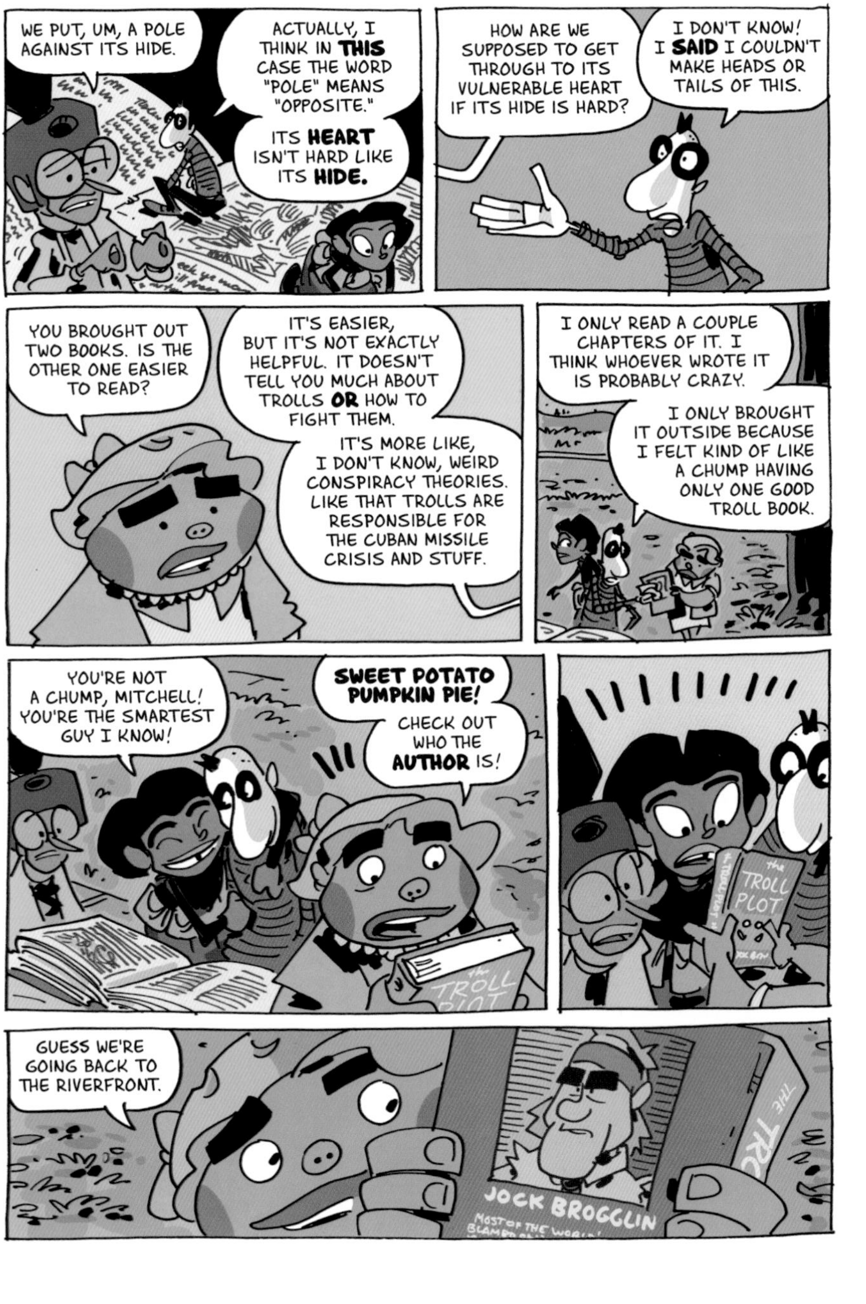
WE PUT, UM, A POLE AGAINST ITS HIDE.
ACTUALLY, I THINK IN **THIS** CASE THE WORD "POLE" MEANS "OPPOSITE."
ITS **HEART** ISN'T HARD LIKE ITS **HIDE.**
HOW ARE WE SUPPOSED TO GET THROUGH TO ITS VULNERABLE HEART IF ITS HIDE IS HARD?
I DON'T KNOW! I **SAID** I COULDN'T MAKE HEADS OR TAILS OF THIS.
YOU BROUGHT OUT TWO BOOKS. IS THE OTHER ONE EASIER TO READ?
IT'S EASIER, BUT IT'S NOT EXACTLY HELPFUL. IT DOESN'T TELL YOU MUCH ABOUT TROLLS **OR** HOW TO FIGHT THEM.
IT'S MORE LIKE, I DON'T KNOW, WEIRD CONSPIRACY THEORIES. LIKE THAT TROLLS ARE RESPONSIBLE FOR THE CUBAN MISSILE CRISIS AND STUFF.
I ONLY READ A COUPLE CHAPTERS OF IT. I THINK WHOEVER WROTE IT IS PROBABLY CRAZY.
I ONLY BROUGHT IT OUTSIDE BECAUSE I FELT KIND OF LIKE A CHUMP HAVING ONLY ONE GOOD TROLL BOOK.
YOU'RE NOT A CHUMP, MITCHELL! YOU'RE THE SMARTEST GUY I KNOW!
SWEET POTATO PUMPKIN PIE!
CHECK OUT WHO THE **AUTHOR** IS!
THE TROLL PLOT
GUESS WE'RE GOING BACK TO THE RIVERFRONT.
JOCK BROGGLIN

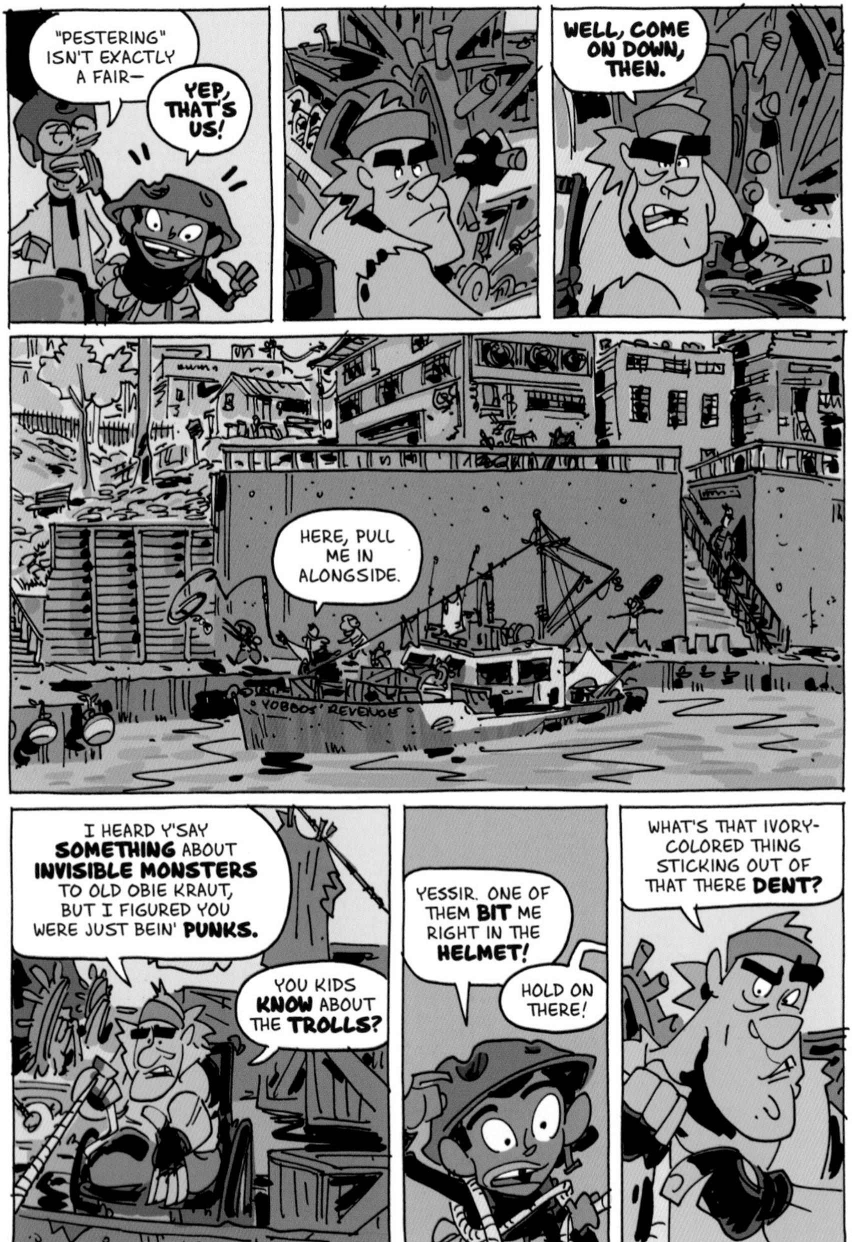
"PESTERING" ISN'T EXACTLY A FAIR—
YEP, THAT'S US!
WELL, COME ON DOWN, THEN.
HERE, PULL ME IN ALONGSIDE.
YOBBOS' REVENGE
I HEARD Y'SAY SOMETHING ABOUT INVISIBLE MONSTERS TO OLD OBIE KRAUT, BUT I FIGURED YOU WERE JUST BEIN' PUNKS.
YOU KIDS KNOW ABOUT THE TROLLS?
YESSIR. ONE OF THEM BIT ME RIGHT IN THE HELMET!
HOLD ON THERE!
WHAT'S THAT IVORY-COLORED THING STICKING OUT OF THAT THERE DENT?

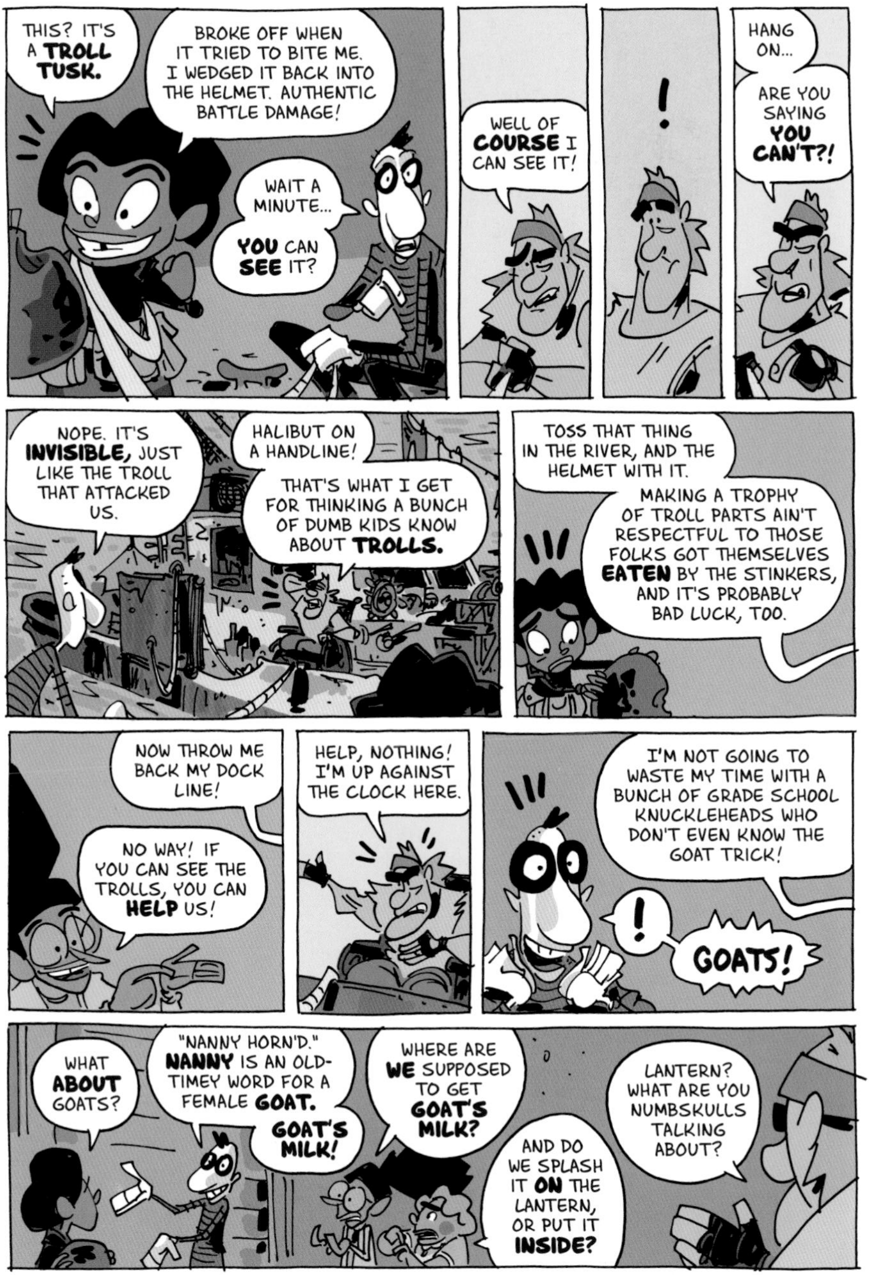
THIS? IT'S A **TROLL TUSK.**
BROKE OFF WHEN IT TRIED TO BITE ME. I WEDGED IT BACK INTO THE HELMET. AUTHENTIC BATTLE DAMAGE!
WAIT A MINUTE...
YOU CAN **SEE** IT?
WELL OF **COURSE** I CAN SEE IT!
!
HANG ON...
ARE YOU SAYING **YOU CAN'T?!**
NOPE. IT'S **INVISIBLE,** JUST LIKE THE TROLL THAT ATTACKED US.
HALIBUT ON A HANDLINE!
THAT'S WHAT I GET FOR THINKING A BUNCH OF DUMB KIDS KNOW ABOUT **TROLLS.**
TOSS THAT THING IN THE RIVER, AND THE HELMET WITH IT.
MAKING A TROPHY OF TROLL PARTS AIN'T RESPECTFUL TO THOSE FOLKS GOT THEMSELVES **EATEN** BY THE STINKERS, AND IT'S PROBABLY BAD LUCK, TOO.
NOW THROW ME BACK MY DOCK LINE!
NO WAY! IF YOU CAN SEE THE TROLLS, YOU CAN **HELP** US!
HELP, NOTHING! I'M UP AGAINST THE CLOCK HERE.
I'M NOT GOING TO WASTE MY TIME WITH A BUNCH OF GRADE SCHOOL KNUCKLEHEADS WHO DON'T EVEN KNOW THE GOAT TRICK!
!
GOATS!
WHAT **ABOUT** GOATS?
"NANNY HORN'D." **NANNY** IS AN OLD-TIMEY WORD FOR A FEMALE **GOAT.**
GOAT'S MILK!
WHERE ARE **WE** SUPPOSED TO GET **GOAT'S MILK?**
AND DO WE SPLASH IT **ON** THE LANTERN, OR PUT IT **INSIDE?**
LANTERN? WHAT ARE YOU NUMBSKULLS TALKING ABOUT?

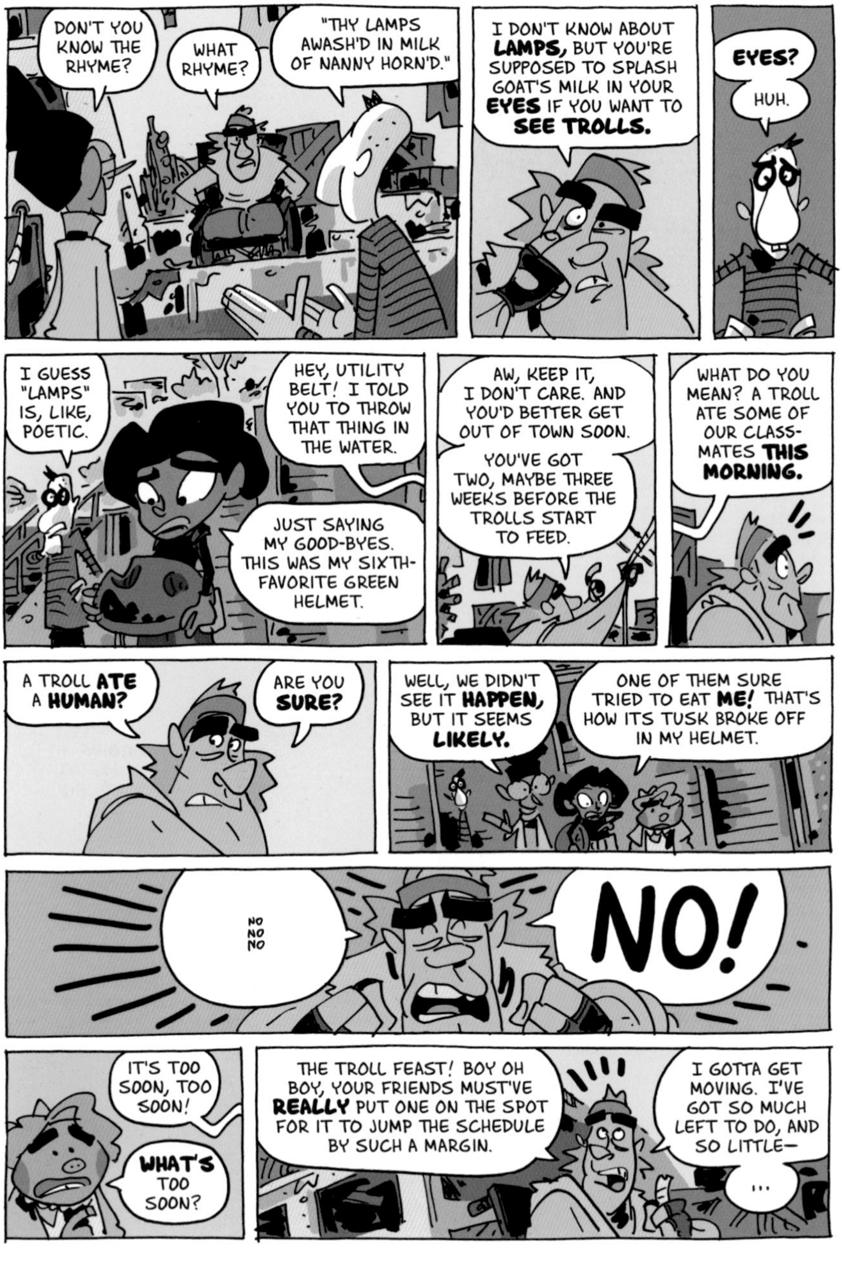
DON'T YOU KNOW THE RHYME?
WHAT RHYME?
"THY LAMPS AWASH'D IN MILK OF NANNY HORN'D."
I DON'T KNOW ABOUT LAMPS, BUT YOU'RE SUPPOSED TO SPLASH GOAT'S MILK IN YOUR EYES IF YOU WANT TO SEE TROLLS.
EYES?
HUH.
I GUESS "LAMPS" IS, LIKE, POETIC.
HEY, UTILITY BELT! I TOLD YOU TO THROW THAT THING IN THE WATER.
JUST SAYING MY GOOD-BYES. THIS WAS MY SIXTH-FAVORITE GREEN HELMET.
AW, KEEP IT, I DON'T CARE. AND YOU'D BETTER GET OUT OF TOWN SOON.
YOU'VE GOT TWO, MAYBE THREE WEEKS BEFORE THE TROLLS START TO FEED.
WHAT DO YOU MEAN? A TROLL ATE SOME OF OUR CLASSMATES THIS MORNING.
A TROLL ATE A HUMAN?
ARE YOU SURE?
WELL, WE DIDN'T SEE IT HAPPEN, BUT IT SEEMS LIKELY.
ONE OF THEM SURE TRIED TO EAT ME! THAT'S HOW ITS TUSK BROKE OFF IN MY HELMET.
NO NO NO
NO!
IT'S TOO SOON, TOO SOON!
WHAT'S TOO SOON?
THE TROLL FEAST! BOY OH BOY, YOUR FRIENDS MUST'VE REALLY PUT ONE ON THE SPOT FOR IT TO JUMP THE SCHEDULE BY SUCH A MARGIN.
I GOTTA GET MOVING. I'VE GOT SO MUCH LEFT TO DO, AND SO LITTLE—
...

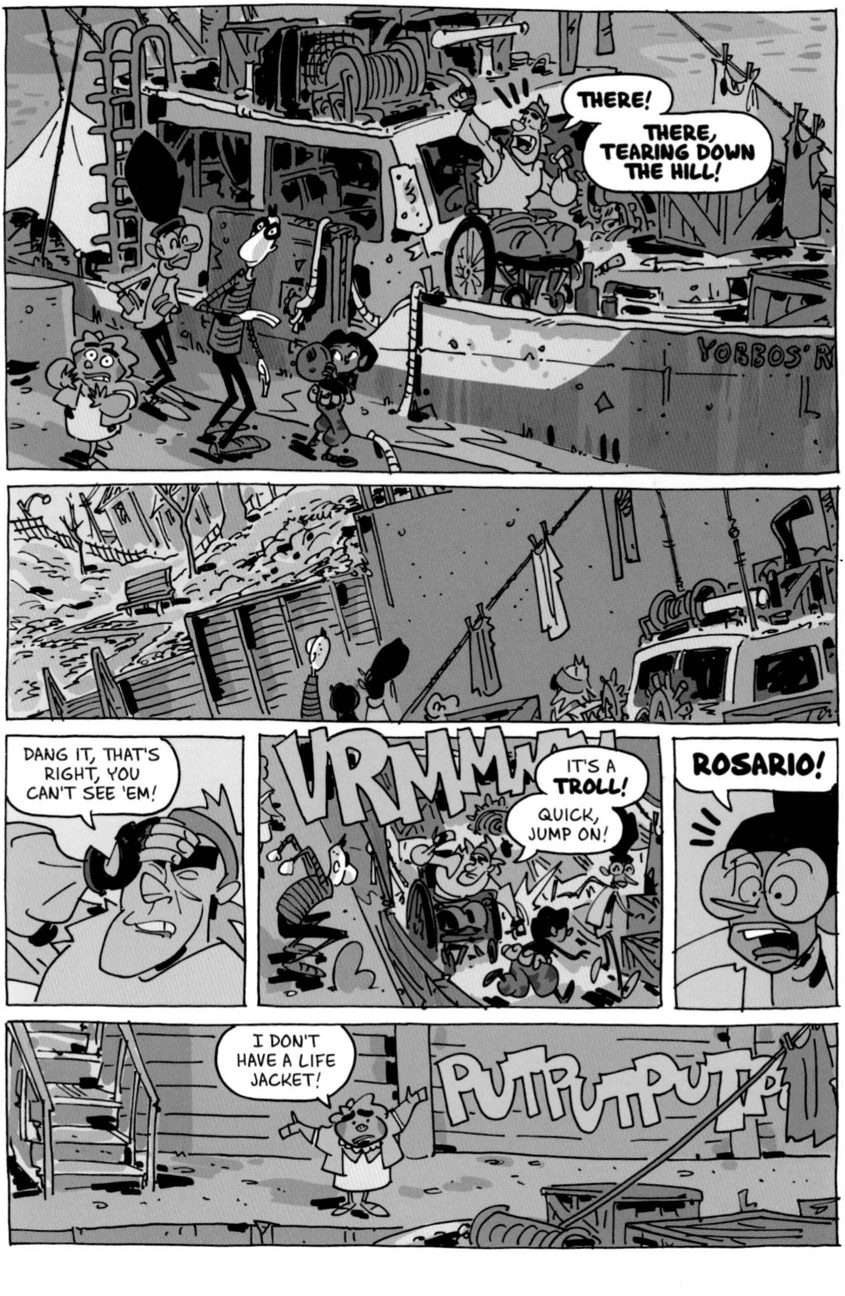
THERE!
THERE, TEARING DOWN THE HILL!
YOBBOS' R
DANG IT, THAT'S RIGHT, YOU CAN'T SEE 'EM!
VRMMM
IT'S A TROLL!
QUICK, JUMP ON!
ROSARIO!
I DON'T HAVE A LIFE JACKET!
PUTPUTPUTP

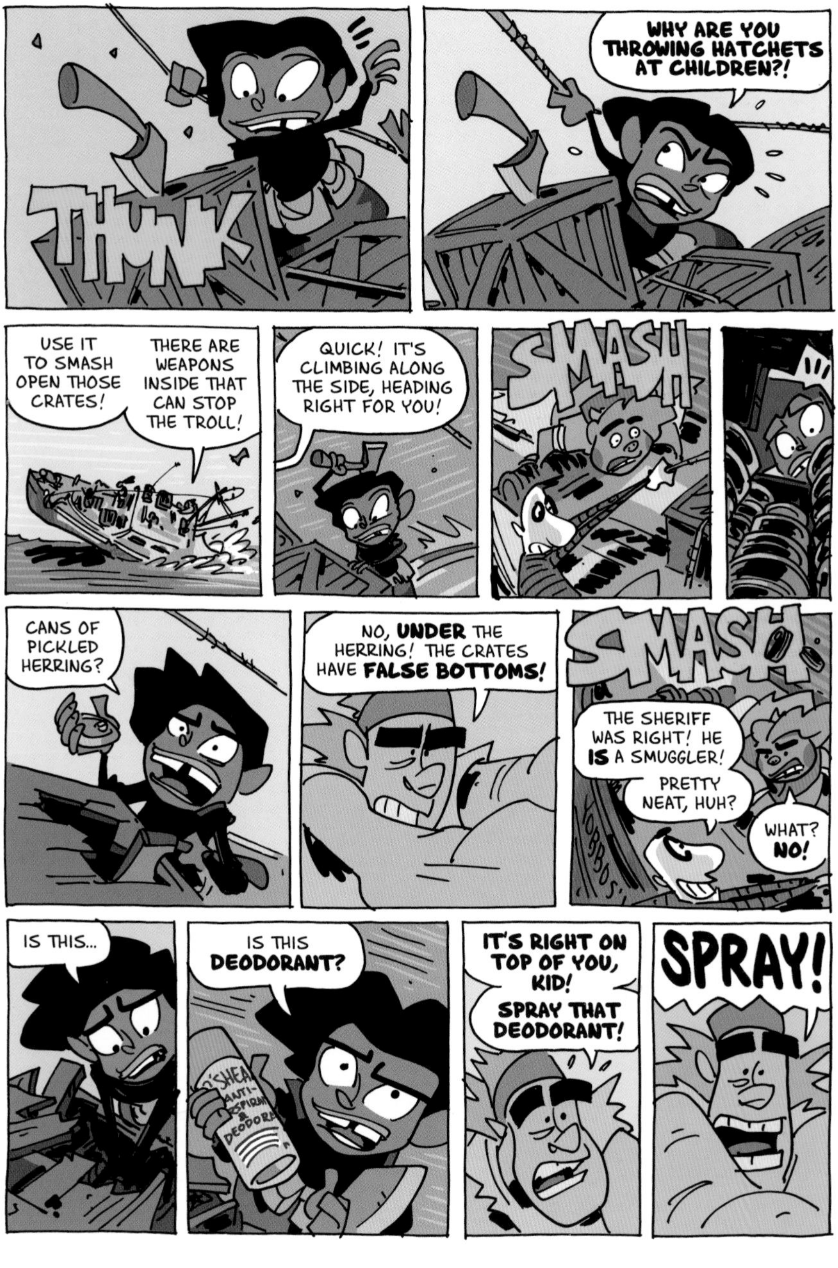
THUNK
WHY ARE YOU THROWING HATCHETS AT CHILDREN?!
USE IT TO SMASH OPEN THOSE CRATES!
THERE ARE WEAPONS INSIDE THAT CAN STOP THE TROLL!
QUICK! IT'S CLIMBING ALONG THE SIDE, HEADING RIGHT FOR YOU!
SMASH
CANS OF PICKLED HERRING?
NO, UNDER THE HERRING! THE CRATES HAVE FALSE BOTTOMS!
SMASH
THE SHERIFF WAS RIGHT! HE IS A SMUGGLER!
PRETTY NEAT, HUH?
WHAT? NO!
IS THIS...
IS THIS DEODORANT?
IT'S RIGHT ON TOP OF YOU, KID!
SPRAY THAT DEODORANT!
SPRAY!

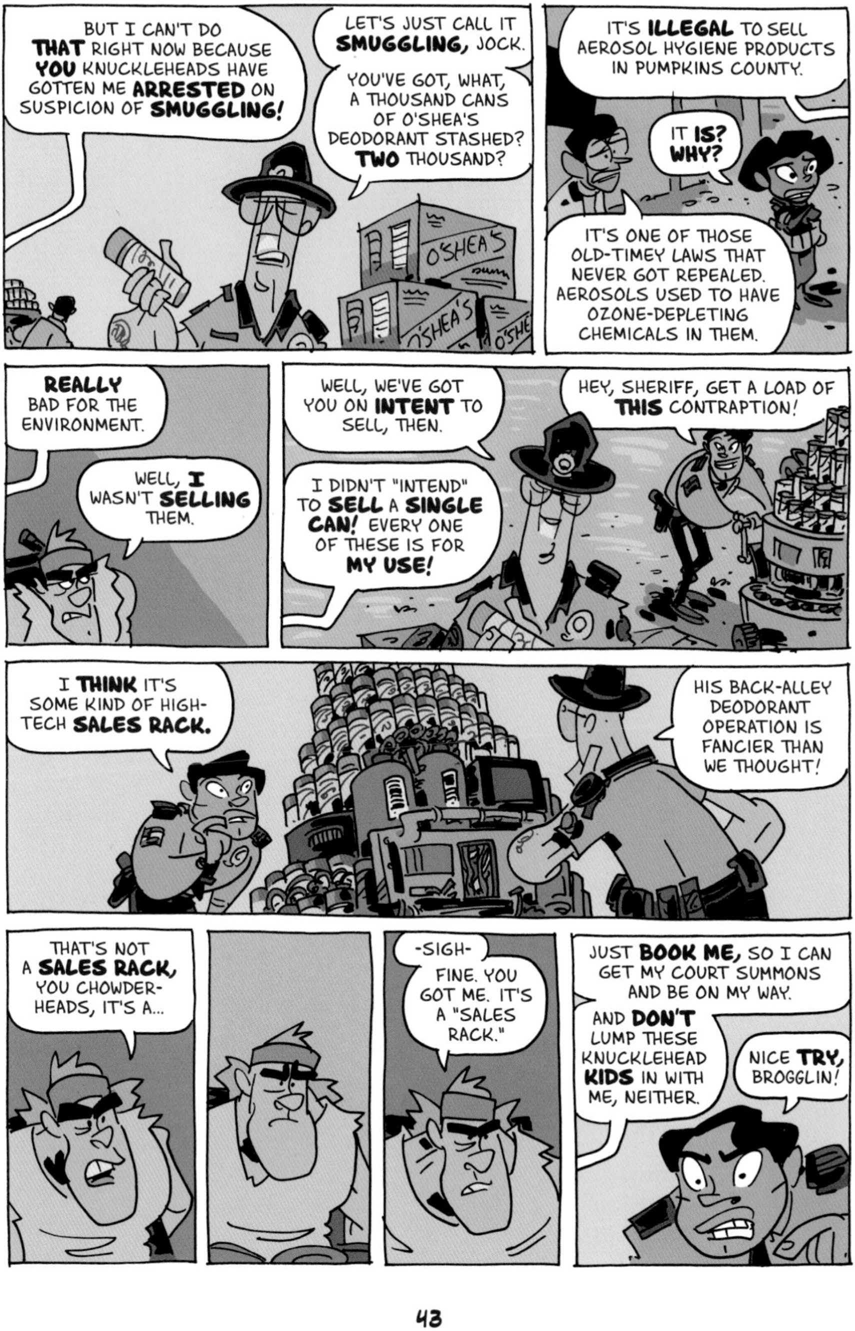
BUT I CAN'T DO THAT RIGHT NOW BECAUSE YOU KNUCKLEHEADS HAVE GOTTEN ME ARRESTED ON SUSPICION OF SMUGGLING!
LET'S JUST CALL IT SMUGGLING, JOCK.
YOU'VE GOT, WHAT, A THOUSAND CANS OF O'SHEA'S DEODORANT STASHED? TWO THOUSAND?
O'SHEA'S
IT'S ILLEGAL TO SELL AEROSOL HYGIENE PRODUCTS IN PUMPKINS COUNTY.
IT IS? WHY?
IT'S ONE OF THOSE OLD-TIMEY LAWS THAT NEVER GOT REPEALED. AEROSOLS USED TO HAVE OZONE-DEPLETING CHEMICALS IN THEM.
REALLY BAD FOR THE ENVIRONMENT.
WELL, I WASN'T SELLING THEM.
WELL, WE'VE GOT YOU ON INTENT TO SELL, THEN.
I DIDN'T "INTEND" TO SELL A SINGLE CAN! EVERY ONE OF THESE IS FOR MY USE!
HEY, SHERIFF, GET A LOAD OF THIS CONTRAPTION!
I THINK IT'S SOME KIND OF HIGH-TECH SALES RACK.
HIS BACK-ALLEY DEODORANT OPERATION IS FANCIER THAN WE THOUGHT!
THAT'S NOT A SALES RACK, YOU CHOWDER-HEADS, IT'S A...
-SIGH-
FINE. YOU GOT ME. IT'S A "SALES RACK."
JUST BOOK ME, SO I CAN GET MY COURT SUMMONS AND BE ON MY WAY.
AND DON'T LUMP THESE KNUCKLEHEAD KIDS IN WITH ME, NEITHER.
NICE TRY, BROGGLIN!

THESE CREEPS ARE A **CONSTANT** IRRITATION TO THE CITIZENS OF PUMPKINS COUNTY.

NOW THEY'VE BEEN CAUGHT HELPING **YOU** WITH YOUR **MUSK-RUNNING** OUTFIT—

FINN, WE'VE GOT A **LOT** OF EVIDENCE **AND** A SUSPECT TO BRING DOWN TO THE STATION...

...AND WE'VE ONLY GOT **ONE** VEHICLE NOW.

...!

FINE. FINE, WE CAUGHT OUR SMUGGLER. **THAT'S** ENOUGH.

BUT OUR **JOB** IS TO **PROTECT** AND **SERVE** THIS COMMUNITY, AND WE'RE DOING **NEITHER** BY LETTING **THESE** TROUBLEMAKERS RUN **WILD**.

PSST!

LISTEN UP, YOU GOOBERS!

YOU'VE ONLY GOT A **FEW HOURS** BEFORE THE TROLLS **EAT** HALF THE PEOPLE IN THIS TOWN, SO GET YOURSELVES **VERY FAR AWAY**.

THE **CYCLE** HAS **BEGUN**!

ALL RIGHT, CRAZY PANTS, TIME TO GO.

AND KIDS?

I'VE SEEN YOU THREE TIMES TOO MANY TODAY.

SCRAM.

JEEZ!

45

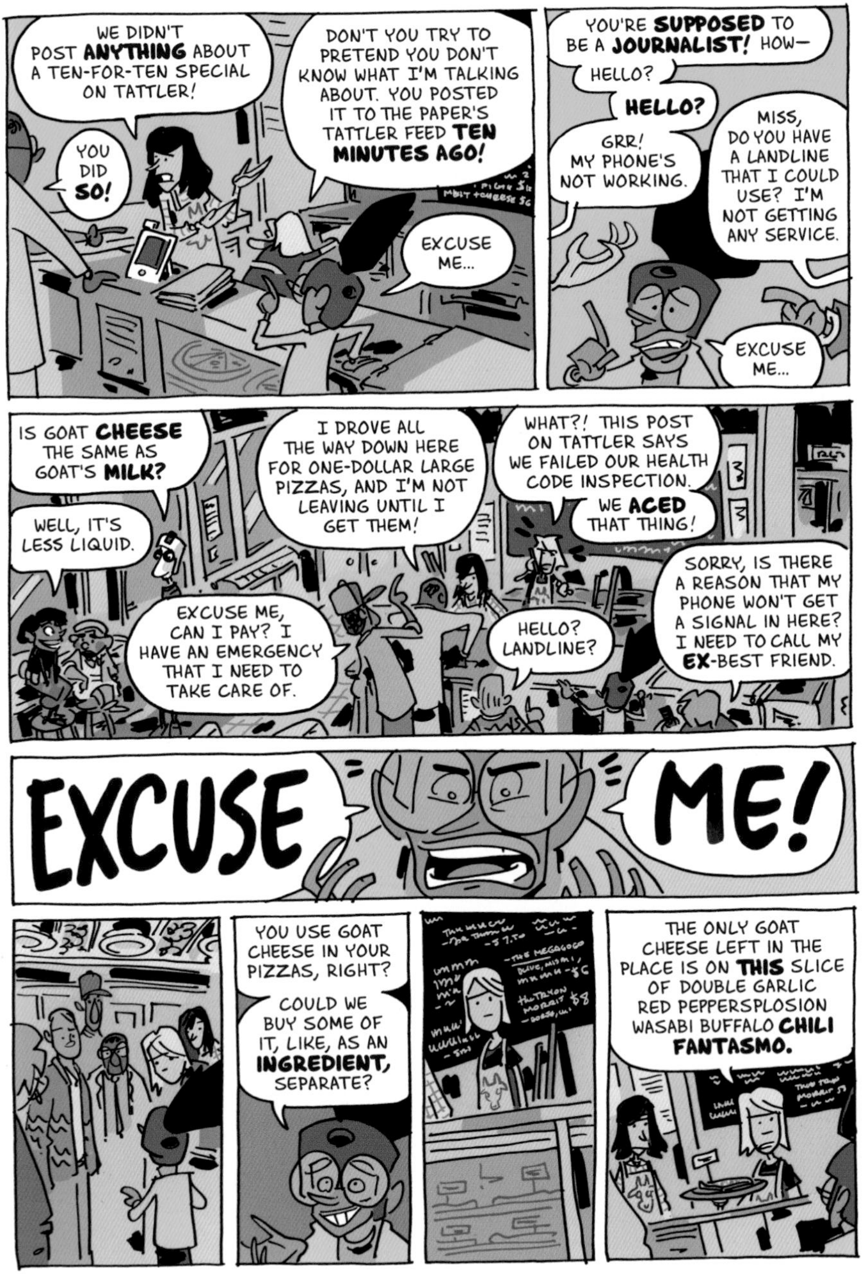
WE DIDN'T POST **ANYTHING** ABOUT A TEN-FOR-TEN SPECIAL ON TATTLER!
YOU DID **SO!**
DON'T YOU TRY TO PRETEND YOU DON'T KNOW WHAT I'M TALKING ABOUT. YOU POSTED IT TO THE PAPER'S TATTLER FEED **TEN MINUTES AGO!**
EXCUSE ME...
YOU'RE **SUPPOSED** TO BE A **JOURNALIST!** HOW—
HELLO?
HELLO?
GRR! MY PHONE'S NOT WORKING.
MISS, DO YOU HAVE A LANDLINE THAT I COULD USE? I'M NOT GETTING ANY SERVICE.
EXCUSE ME...
IS GOAT **CHEESE** THE SAME AS GOAT'S **MILK?**
WELL, IT'S LESS LIQUID.
I DROVE ALL THE WAY DOWN HERE FOR ONE-DOLLAR LARGE PIZZAS, AND I'M NOT LEAVING UNTIL I GET THEM!
WHAT?! THIS POST ON TATTLER SAYS WE FAILED OUR HEALTH CODE INSPECTION.
WE **ACED** THAT THING!
EXCUSE ME, CAN I PAY? I HAVE AN EMERGENCY THAT I NEED TO TAKE CARE OF.
HELLO? LANDLINE?
SORRY, IS THERE A REASON THAT MY PHONE WON'T GET A SIGNAL IN HERE? I NEED TO CALL MY **EX**-BEST FRIEND.
EXCUSE
ME!
YOU USE GOAT CHEESE IN YOUR PIZZAS, RIGHT?
COULD WE BUY SOME OF IT, LIKE, AS AN **INGREDIENT,** SEPARATE?
THE ONLY GOAT CHEESE LEFT IN THE PLACE IS ON **THIS** SLICE OF DOUBLE GARLIC RED PEPPERSPLOSION WASABI BUFFALO **CHILI FANTASMO.**

WHAAA

AEIIEE

I'M BLIND! **BLIND!**

CAROL, THIS WAS A **TERRIBLE** IDEA!

IT WAS

AAA

THE BEST I COULD COME UP WITH, OKA**AA**

AUGGH

VENABLE'S PIZZA

WAAGHH

VENABLE'S PIZZA

UNGH

COUGH COUGH

RRR!

WOOF!

VENABLE'S PIZZA

OKAY. RUBBING PIZZA IN OUR EYES **WAS** A BAD IDEA.

BUT WE CAN SEE **TROLLS** NOW, RIGHT?

I DON'T KNOW. **I** DON'T SEE ANY.

AT LEAST ALL THOSE CRAZY SPICES KEPT US FROM SMELLING THIS ALLEY.

TEMPORARILY, AT LEAST.

YOU'RE RIGHT, IT **IS** WORSE HERE THAN IT WAS AT THE RIVERFRONT.

WHAT DO YOU THINK IS CAUSING IT? THOSE GREASE-TRAPS, OR THE DUMPSTERS?

I DON'T THINK WHAT **WE'RE** SMELLING IS **EITHER** OF THOSE THINGS.

47

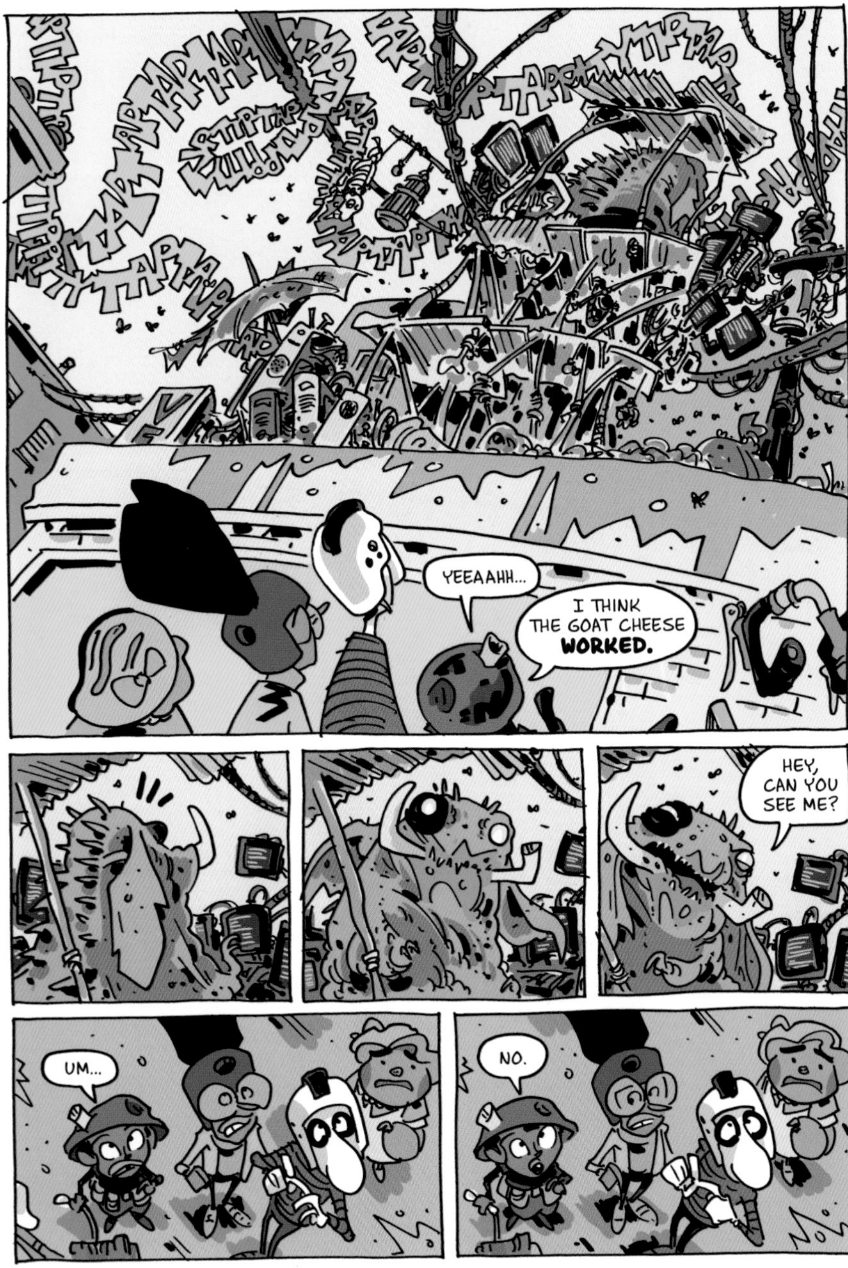
YEEAAHH...
I THINK THE GOAT CHEESE **WORKED.**
HEY, CAN YOU SEE ME?
UM...
NO.

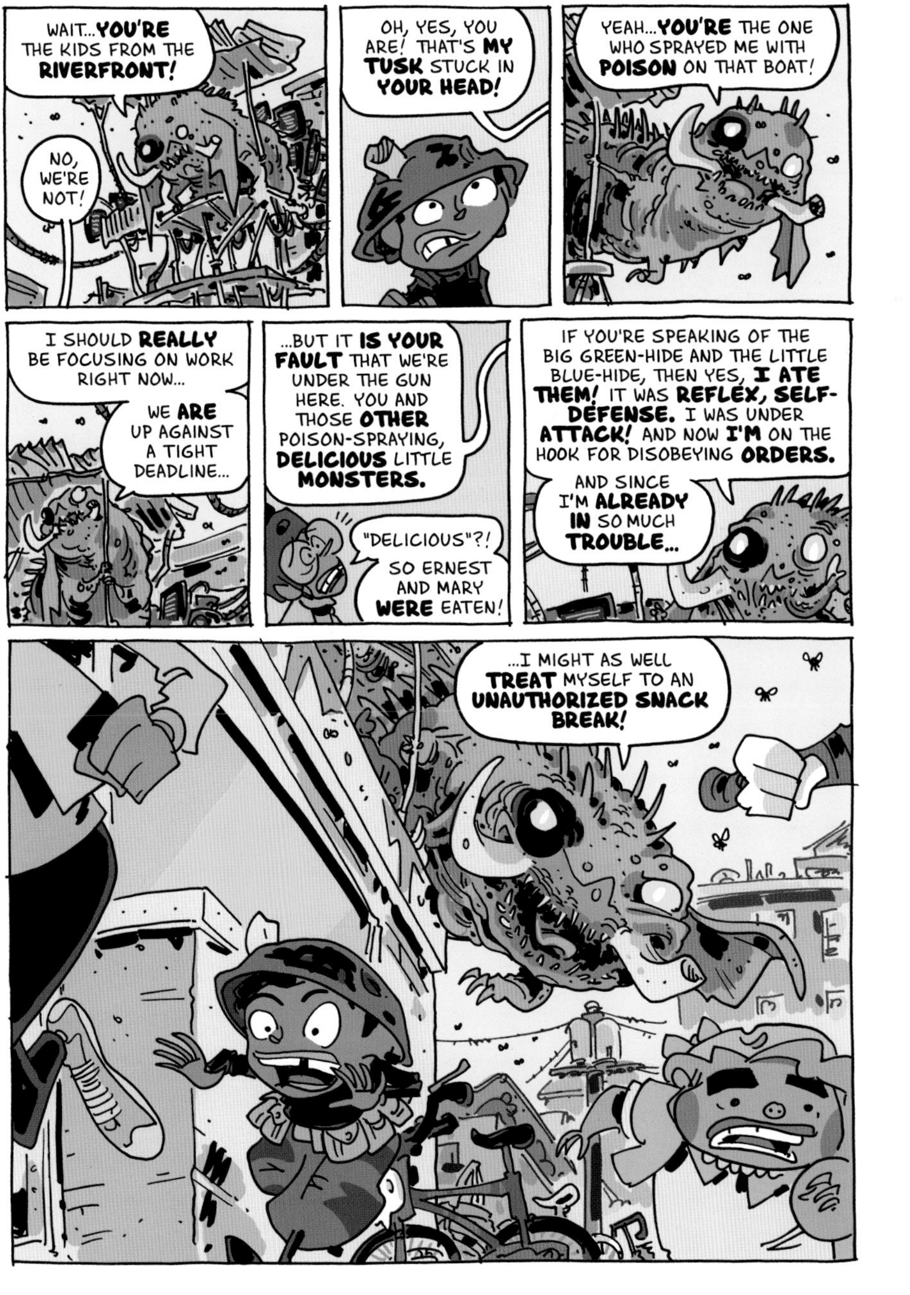
WAIT...YOU'RE THE KIDS FROM THE RIVERFRONT!
NO, WE'RE NOT!
OH, YES, YOU ARE! THAT'S MY TUSK STUCK IN YOUR HEAD!
YEAH...YOU'RE THE ONE WHO SPRAYED ME WITH POISON ON THAT BOAT!
I SHOULD REALLY BE FOCUSING ON WORK RIGHT NOW...
WE ARE UP AGAINST A TIGHT DEADLINE...
...BUT IT IS YOUR FAULT THAT WE'RE UNDER THE GUN HERE. YOU AND THOSE OTHER POISON-SPRAYING, DELICIOUS LITTLE MONSTERS.
"DELICIOUS"?!
SO ERNEST AND MARY WERE EATEN!
IF YOU'RE SPEAKING OF THE BIG GREEN-HIDE AND THE LITTLE BLUE-HIDE, THEN YES, I ATE THEM! IT WAS REFLEX, SELF-DEFENSE. I WAS UNDER ATTACK! AND NOW I'M ON THE HOOK FOR DISOBEYING ORDERS.
AND SINCE I'M ALREADY IN SO MUCH TROUBLE...
...I MIGHT AS WELL TREAT MYSELF TO AN UNAUTHORIZED SNACK BREAK!

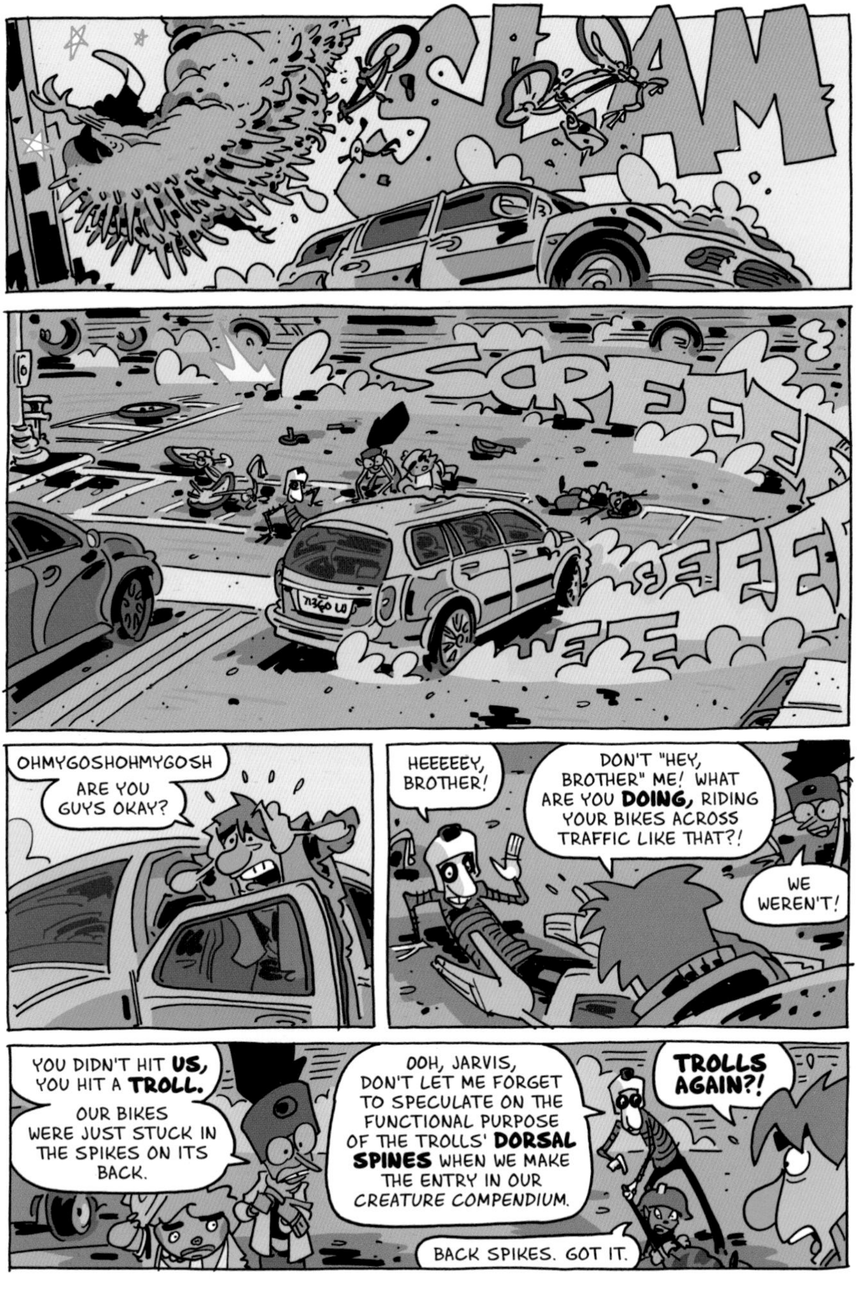
SLAM
SCREEEEEEEE
OHMYGOSHOHMYGOSH ARE YOU GUYS OKAY?
HEEEEEY, BROTHER!
DON'T "HEY, BROTHER" ME! WHAT ARE YOU **DOING,** RIDING YOUR BIKES ACROSS TRAFFIC LIKE THAT?!
WE WEREN'T!
YOU DIDN'T HIT **US,** YOU HIT A **TROLL.**
OUR BIKES WERE JUST STUCK IN THE SPIKES ON ITS BACK.
OOH, JARVIS, DON'T LET ME FORGET TO SPECULATE ON THE FUNCTIONAL PURPOSE OF THE TROLLS' **DORSAL SPINES** WHEN WE MAKE THE ENTRY IN OUR CREATURE COMPENDIUM.
TROLLS AGAIN?!
BACK SPIKES. GOT IT.

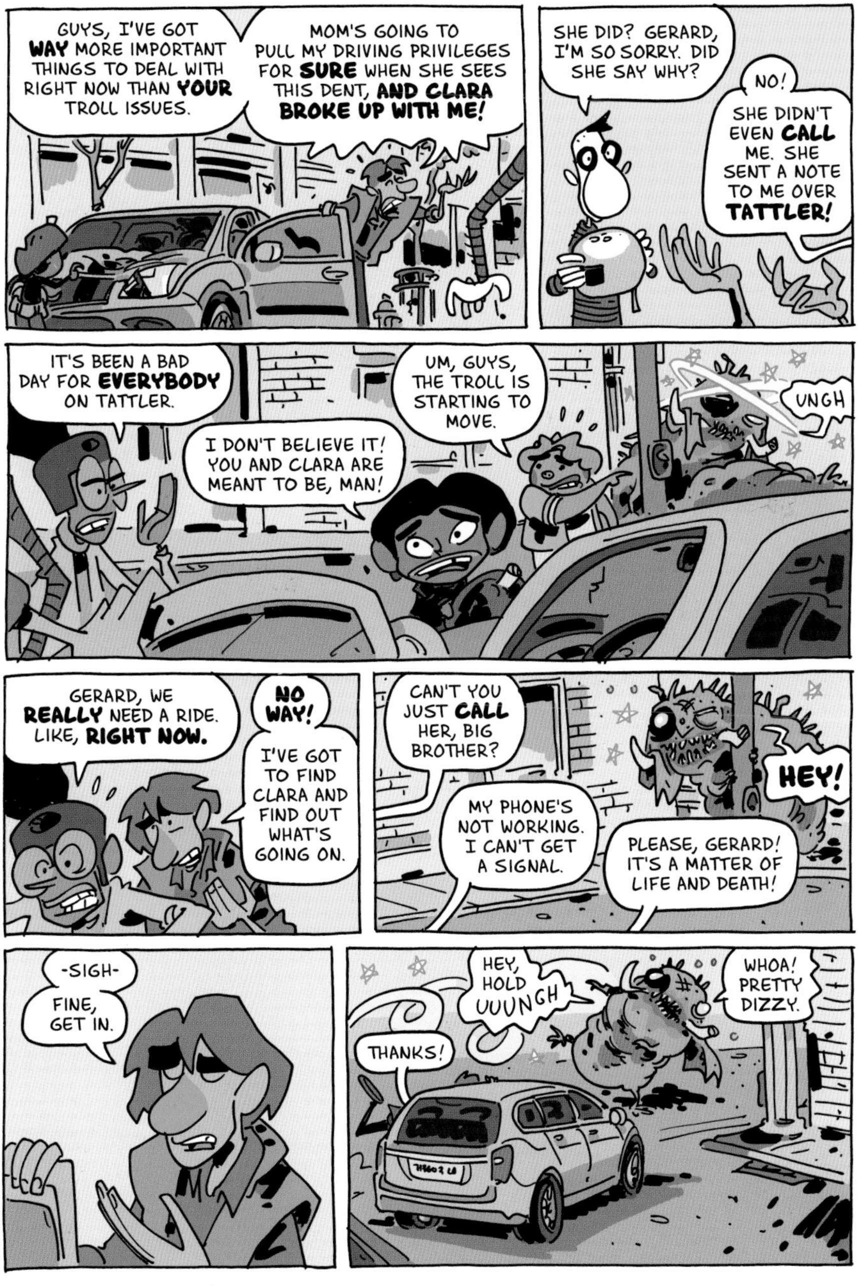
GUYS, I'VE GOT **WAY** MORE IMPORTANT THINGS TO DEAL WITH RIGHT NOW THAN **YOUR** TROLL ISSUES.
MOM'S GOING TO PULL MY DRIVING PRIVILEGES FOR **SURE** WHEN SHE SEES THIS DENT, **AND CLARA BROKE UP WITH ME!**
SHE DID? GERARD, I'M SO SORRY. DID SHE SAY WHY?
NO!
SHE DIDN'T EVEN **CALL** ME. SHE SENT A NOTE TO ME OVER **TATTLER!**
IT'S BEEN A BAD DAY FOR **EVERYBODY** ON TATTLER.
I DON'T BELIEVE IT! YOU AND CLARA ARE MEANT TO BE, MAN!
UM, GUYS, THE TROLL IS STARTING TO MOVE.
UNGH
GERARD, WE **REALLY** NEED A RIDE. LIKE, **RIGHT NOW.**
NO WAY!
I'VE GOT TO FIND CLARA AND FIND OUT WHAT'S GOING ON.
CAN'T YOU JUST **CALL** HER, BIG BROTHER?
MY PHONE'S NOT WORKING. I CAN'T GET A SIGNAL.
HEY!
PLEASE, GERARD! IT'S A MATTER OF LIFE AND DEATH!
-SIGH-
FINE, GET IN.
HEY, HOLD UUUNGH
THANKS!
WHOA! PRETTY DIZZY.

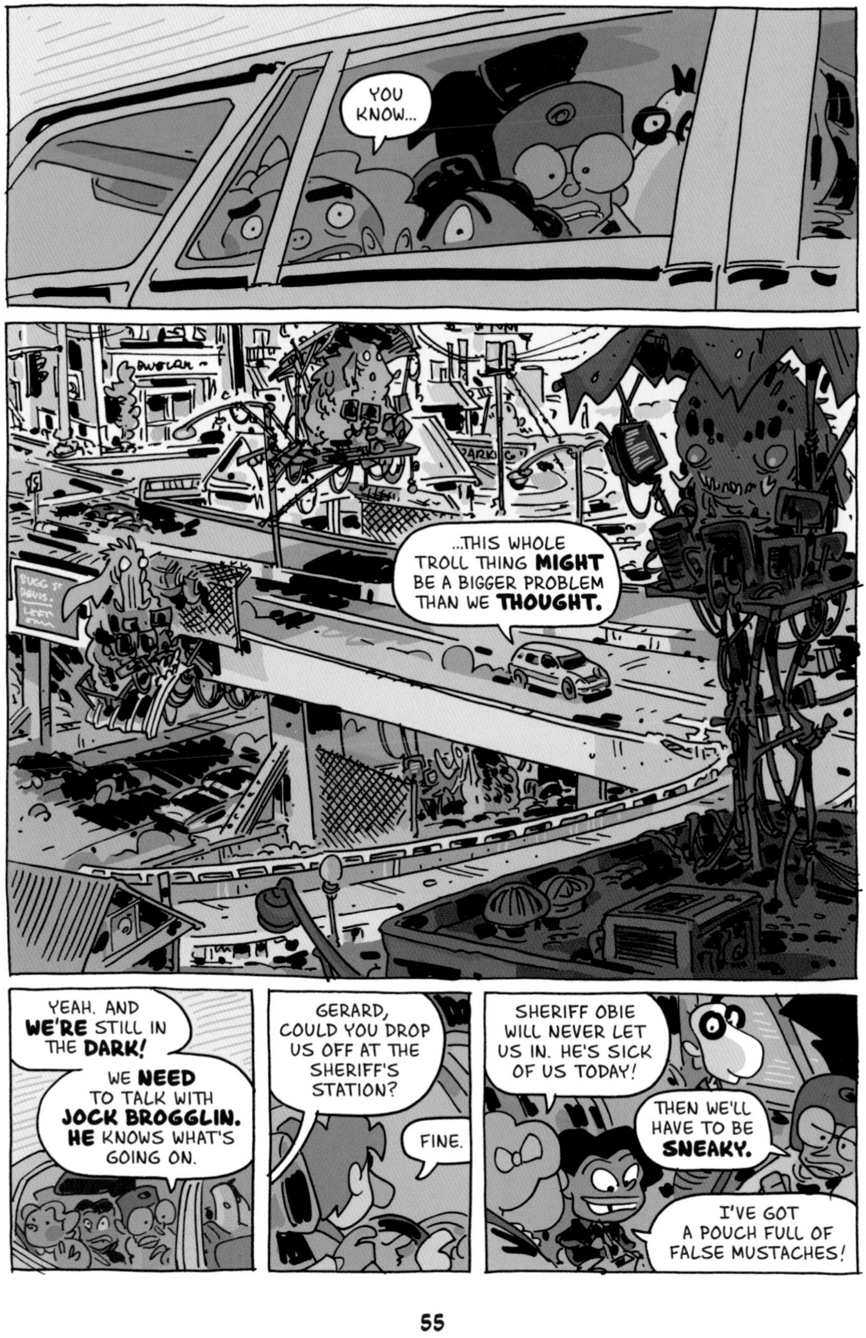
YOU KNOW...
...THIS WHOLE TROLL THING **MIGHT** BE A BIGGER PROBLEM THAN WE **THOUGHT.**
YEAH. AND **WE'RE** STILL IN THE **DARK!**
WE **NEED** TO TALK WITH **JOCK BROGGLIN. HE** KNOWS WHAT'S GOING ON.
GERARD, COULD YOU DROP US OFF AT THE SHERIFF'S STATION?
FINE.
SHERIFF OBIE WILL NEVER LET US IN. HE'S SICK OF US TODAY!
THEN WE'LL HAVE TO BE **SNEAKY.**
I'VE GOT A POUCH FULL OF FALSE MUSTACHES!

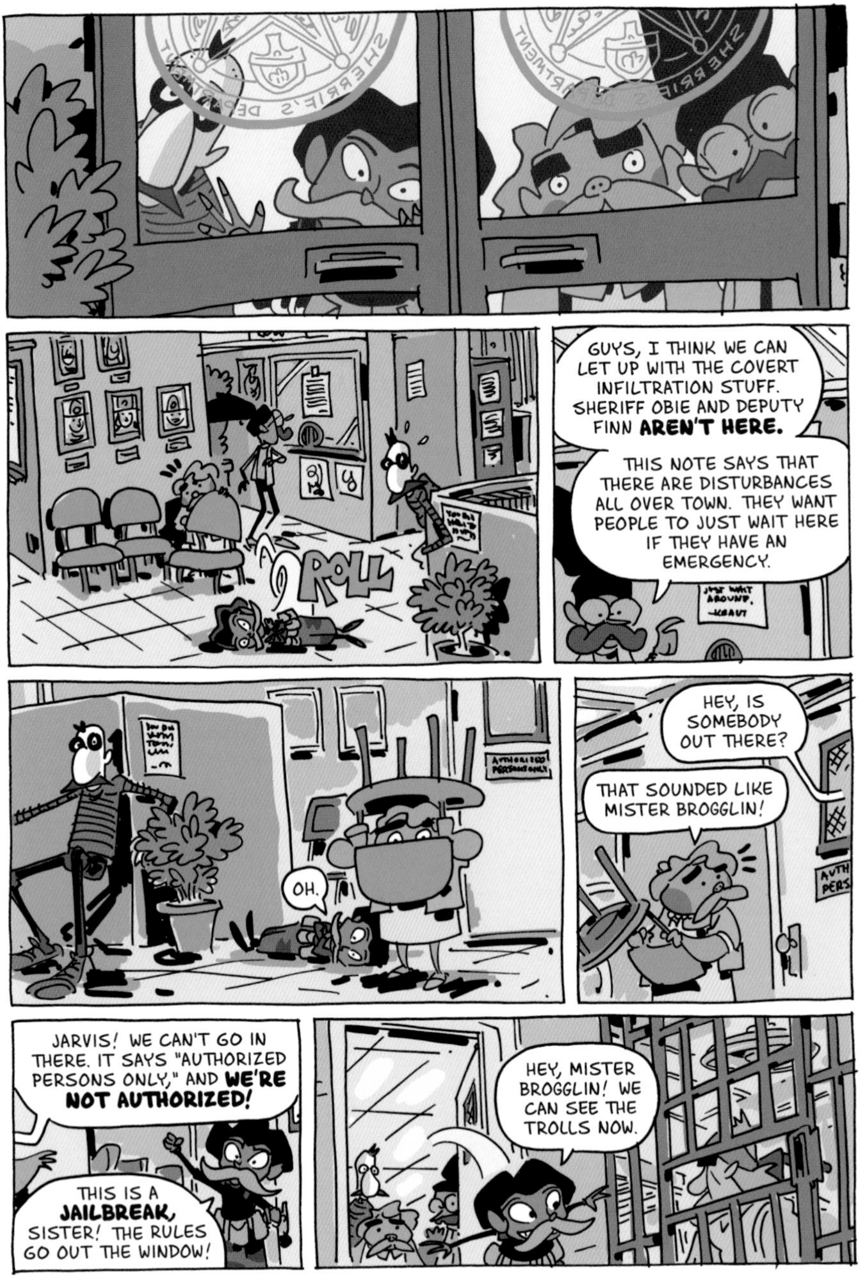
ROLL
GUYS, I THINK WE CAN LET UP WITH THE COVERT INFILTRATION STUFF. SHERIFF OBIE AND DEPUTY FINN **AREN'T HERE.**
THIS NOTE SAYS THAT THERE ARE DISTURBANCES ALL OVER TOWN. THEY WANT PEOPLE TO JUST WAIT HERE IF THEY HAVE AN EMERGENCY.
OH.
HEY, IS SOMEBODY OUT THERE?
THAT SOUNDED LIKE MISTER BROGGLIN!
JARVIS! WE CAN'T GO IN THERE. IT SAYS "AUTHORIZED PERSONS ONLY," AND **WE'RE NOT AUTHORIZED!**
THIS IS A **JAILBREAK,** SISTER! THE RULES GO OUT THE WINDOW!
HEY, MISTER BROGGLIN! WE CAN SEE THE TROLLS NOW.

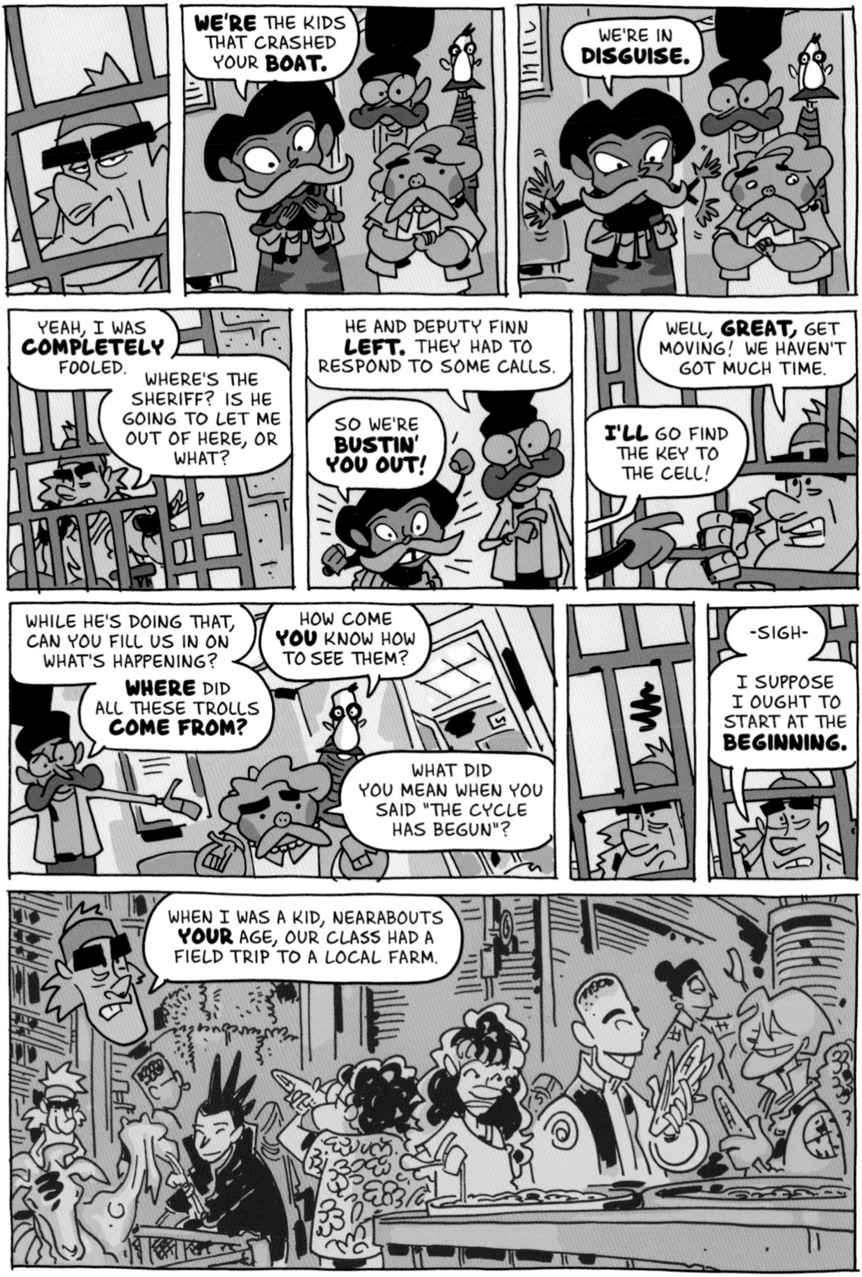
WE'RE THE KIDS THAT CRASHED YOUR BOAT.
WE'RE IN DISGUISE.
YEAH, I WAS COMPLETELY FOOLED.
WHERE'S THE SHERIFF? IS HE GOING TO LET ME OUT OF HERE, OR WHAT?
HE AND DEPUTY FINN LEFT. THEY HAD TO RESPOND TO SOME CALLS.
SO WE'RE BUSTIN' YOU OUT!
WELL, GREAT, GET MOVING! WE HAVEN'T GOT MUCH TIME.
I'LL GO FIND THE KEY TO THE CELL!
WHILE HE'S DOING THAT, CAN YOU FILL US IN ON WHAT'S HAPPENING?
WHERE DID ALL THESE TROLLS COME FROM?
HOW COME YOU KNOW HOW TO SEE THEM?
WHAT DID YOU MEAN WHEN YOU SAID "THE CYCLE HAS BEGUN"?
-SIGH-
I SUPPOSE I OUGHT TO START AT THE BEGINNING.
WHEN I WAS A KID, NEARABOUTS YOUR AGE, OUR CLASS HAD A FIELD TRIP TO A LOCAL FARM.

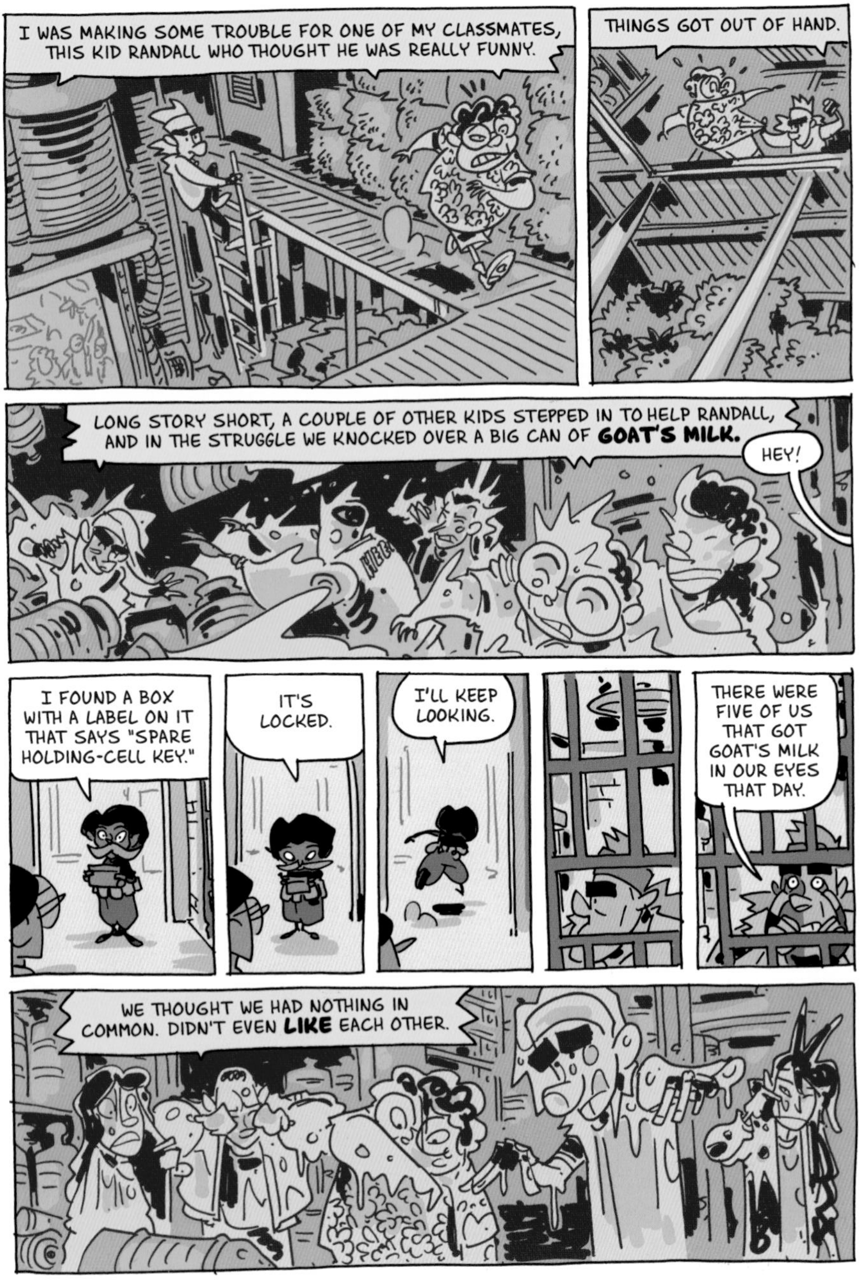
I WAS MAKING SOME TROUBLE FOR ONE OF MY CLASSMATES, THIS KID RANDALL WHO THOUGHT HE WAS REALLY FUNNY.
THINGS GOT OUT OF HAND.
LONG STORY SHORT, A COUPLE OF OTHER KIDS STEPPED IN TO HELP RANDALL, AND IN THE STRUGGLE WE KNOCKED OVER A BIG CAN OF GOAT'S MILK.
HEY!
I FOUND A BOX WITH A LABEL ON IT THAT SAYS "SPARE HOLDING-CELL KEY."
IT'S LOCKED.
I'LL KEEP LOOKING.
THERE WERE FIVE OF US THAT GOT GOAT'S MILK IN OUR EYES THAT DAY.
WE THOUGHT WE HAD NOTHING IN COMMON. DIDN'T EVEN LIKE EACH OTHER.

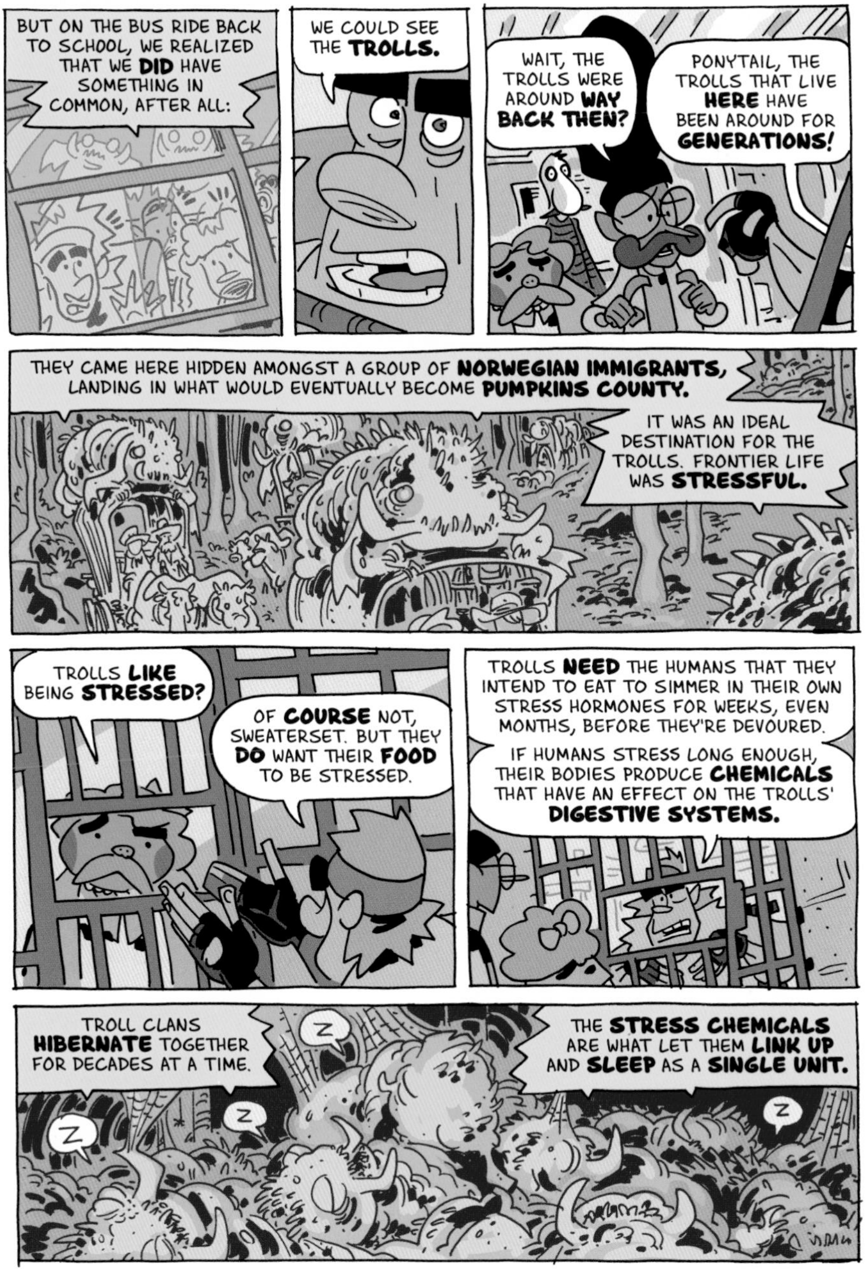

BUT ON THE BUS RIDE BACK TO SCHOOL, WE REALIZED THAT WE **DID** HAVE SOMETHING IN COMMON, AFTER ALL:
WE COULD SEE THE **TROLLS.**
WAIT, THE TROLLS WERE AROUND **WAY BACK THEN?**
PONYTAIL, THE TROLLS THAT LIVE **HERE** HAVE BEEN AROUND FOR **GENERATIONS!**
THEY CAME HERE HIDDEN AMONGST A GROUP OF **NORWEGIAN IMMIGRANTS,** LANDING IN WHAT WOULD EVENTUALLY BECOME **PUMPKINS COUNTY.**
IT WAS AN IDEAL DESTINATION FOR THE TROLLS. FRONTIER LIFE WAS **STRESSFUL.**
TROLLS **LIKE** BEING **STRESSED?**
OF **COURSE** NOT, SWEATERSET. BUT THEY **DO** WANT THEIR **FOOD** TO BE STRESSED.
TROLLS **NEED** THE HUMANS THAT THEY INTEND TO EAT TO SIMMER IN THEIR OWN STRESS HORMONES FOR WEEKS, EVEN MONTHS, BEFORE THEY'RE DEVOURED.
IF HUMANS STRESS LONG ENOUGH, THEIR BODIES PRODUCE **CHEMICALS** THAT HAVE AN EFFECT ON THE TROLLS' **DIGESTIVE SYSTEMS.**
TROLL CLANS **HIBERNATE** TOGETHER FOR DECADES AT A TIME.
Z
THE **STRESS CHEMICALS** ARE WHAT LET THEM **LINK UP** AND **SLEEP** AS A **SINGLE UNIT.**
Z
Z
Z

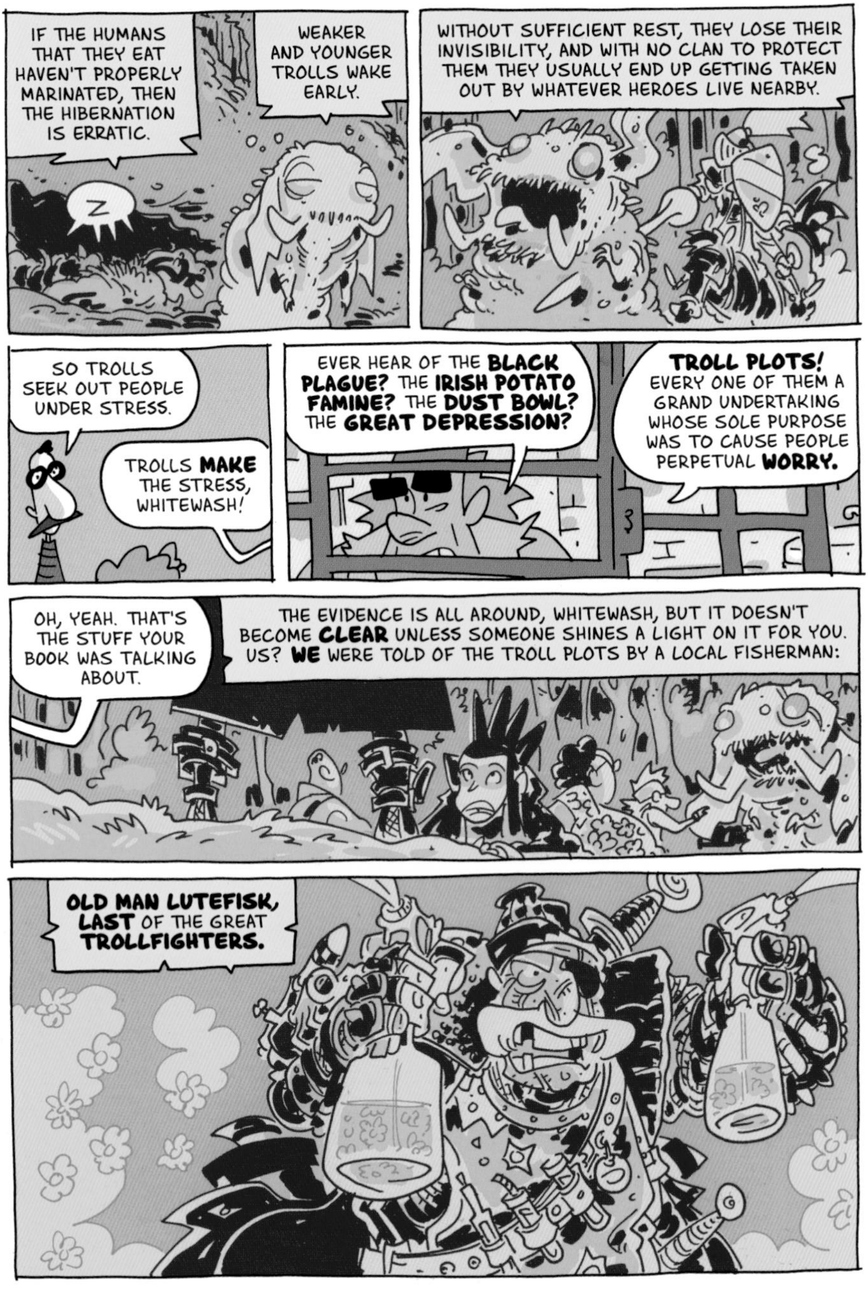
IF THE HUMANS THAT THEY EAT HAVEN'T PROPERLY MARINATED, THEN THE HIBERNATION IS ERRATIC.
WEAKER AND YOUNGER TROLLS WAKE EARLY.
Z
WITHOUT SUFFICIENT REST, THEY LOSE THEIR INVISIBILITY, AND WITH NO CLAN TO PROTECT THEM THEY USUALLY END UP GETTING TAKEN OUT BY WHATEVER HEROES LIVE NEARBY.
SO TROLLS SEEK OUT PEOPLE UNDER STRESS.
TROLLS **MAKE** THE STRESS, WHITEWASH!
EVER HEAR OF THE **BLACK PLAGUE?** THE **IRISH POTATO FAMINE?** THE **DUST BOWL?** THE **GREAT DEPRESSION?**
TROLL PLOTS! EVERY ONE OF THEM A GRAND UNDERTAKING WHOSE SOLE PURPOSE WAS TO CAUSE PEOPLE PERPETUAL **WORRY.**
OH, YEAH. THAT'S THE STUFF YOUR BOOK WAS TALKING ABOUT.
THE EVIDENCE IS ALL AROUND, WHITEWASH, BUT IT DOESN'T BECOME **CLEAR** UNLESS SOMEONE SHINES A LIGHT ON IT FOR YOU. US? **WE** WERE TOLD OF THE TROLL PLOTS BY A LOCAL FISHERMAN:
OLD MAN LUTEFISK, LAST OF THE GREAT **TROLLFIGHTERS.**

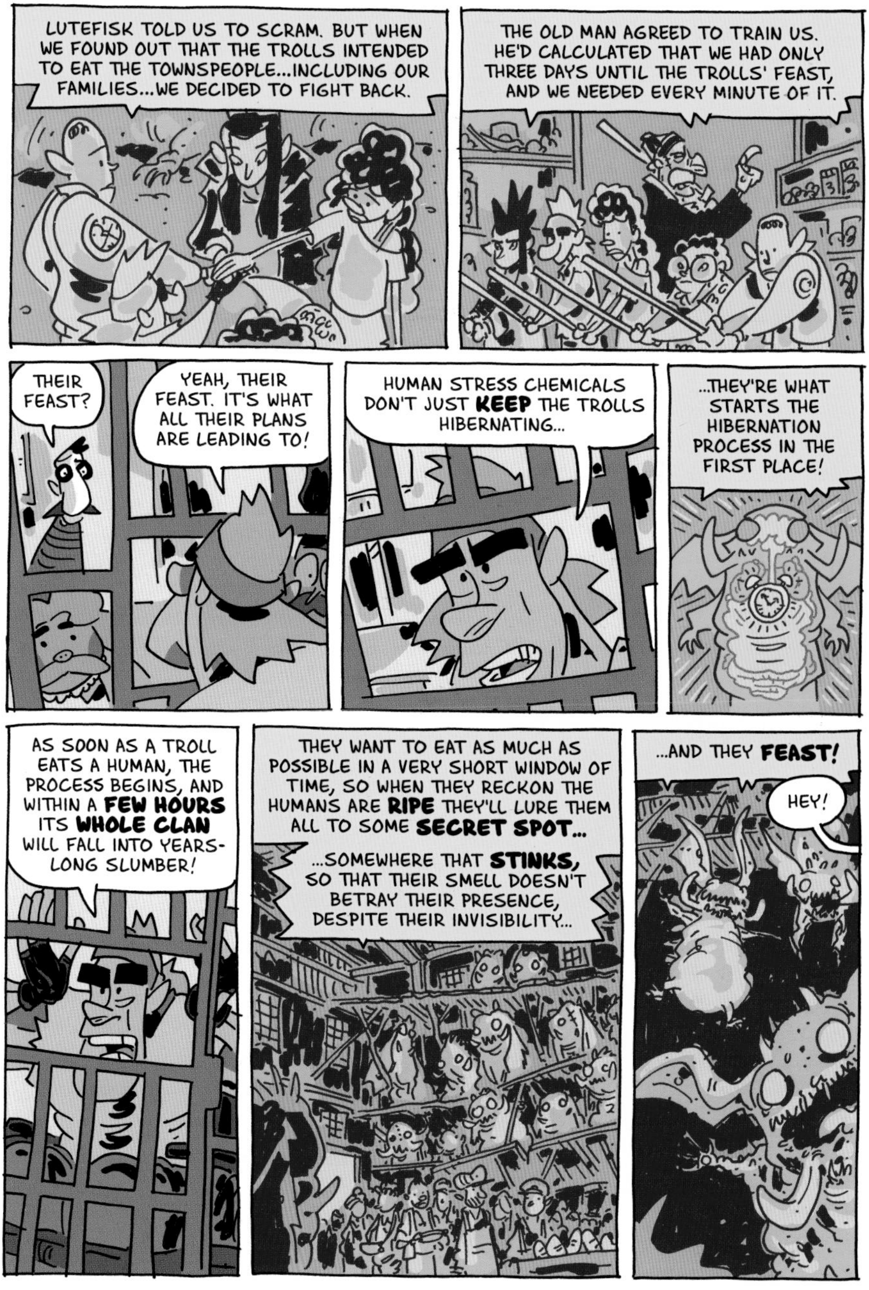

LUTEFISK TOLD US TO SCRAM. BUT WHEN WE FOUND OUT THAT THE TROLLS INTENDED TO EAT THE TOWNSPEOPLE...INCLUDING OUR FAMILIES...WE DECIDED TO FIGHT BACK.
THE OLD MAN AGREED TO TRAIN US. HE'D CALCULATED THAT WE HAD ONLY THREE DAYS UNTIL THE TROLLS' FEAST, AND WE NEEDED EVERY MINUTE OF IT.
THEIR FEAST?
YEAH, THEIR FEAST. IT'S WHAT ALL THEIR PLANS ARE LEADING TO!
HUMAN STRESS CHEMICALS DON'T JUST **KEEP** THE TROLLS HIBERNATING...
...THEY'RE WHAT STARTS THE HIBERNATION PROCESS IN THE FIRST PLACE!
AS SOON AS A TROLL EATS A HUMAN, THE PROCESS BEGINS, AND WITHIN A **FEW HOURS** ITS **WHOLE CLAN** WILL FALL INTO YEARS-LONG SLUMBER!
THEY WANT TO EAT AS MUCH AS POSSIBLE IN A VERY SHORT WINDOW OF TIME, SO WHEN THEY RECKON THE HUMANS ARE **RIPE** THEY'LL LURE THEM ALL TO SOME **SECRET SPOT...**
...SOMEWHERE THAT **STINKS,** SO THAT THEIR SMELL DOESN'T BETRAY THEIR PRESENCE, DESPITE THEIR INVISIBILITY...
...AND THEY **FEAST!**
HEY!

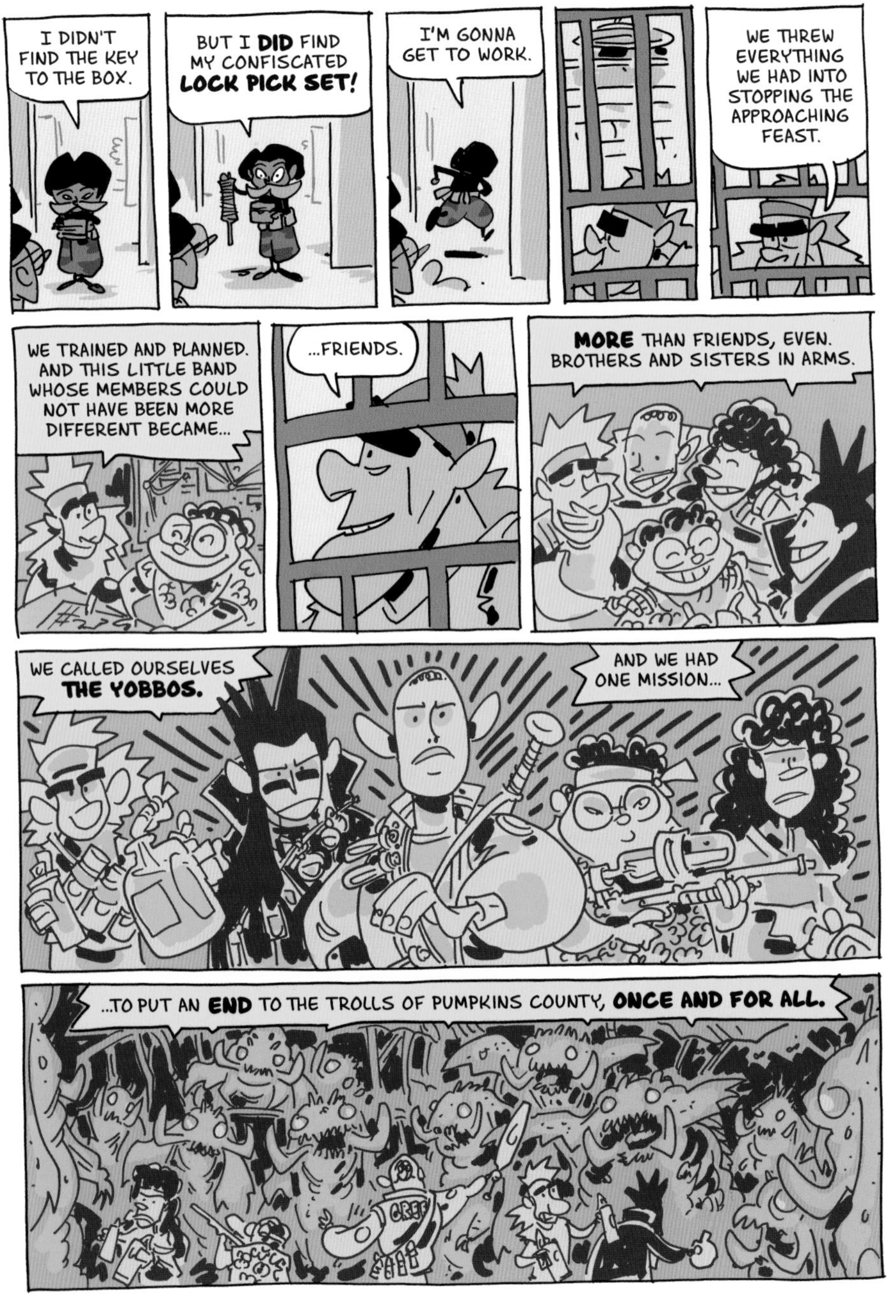
I DIDN'T FIND THE KEY TO THE BOX.
BUT I **DID** FIND MY CONFISCATED **LOCK PICK SET!**
I'M GONNA GET TO WORK.
WE THREW EVERYTHING WE HAD INTO STOPPING THE APPROACHING FEAST.
WE TRAINED AND PLANNED. AND THIS LITTLE BAND WHOSE MEMBERS COULD NOT HAVE BEEN MORE DIFFERENT BECAME...
...FRIENDS.
MORE THAN FRIENDS, EVEN. BROTHERS AND SISTERS IN ARMS.
WE CALLED OURSELVES **THE YOBBOS.**
AND WE HAD ONE MISSION...
...TO PUT AN **END** TO THE TROLLS OF PUMPKINS COUNTY, **ONCE AND FOR ALL.**

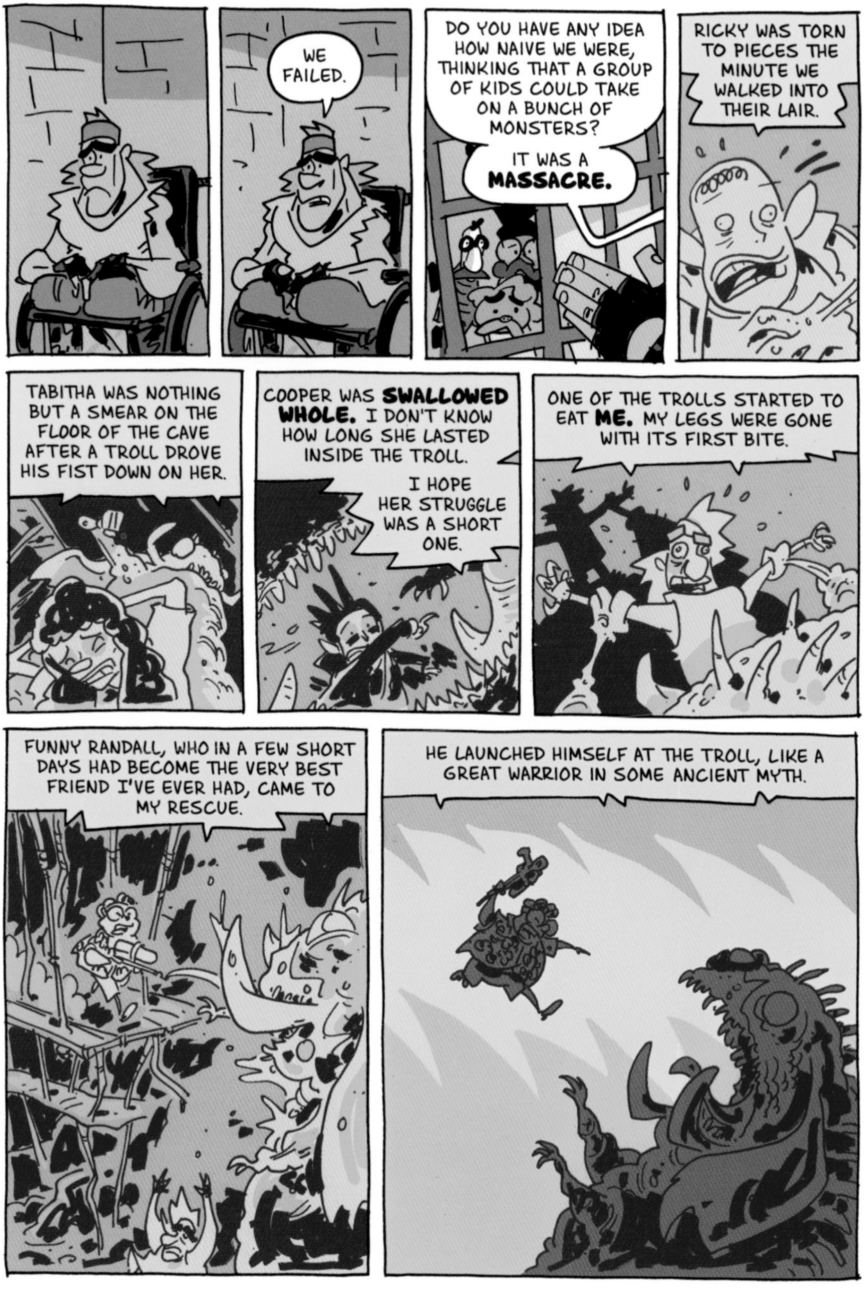
WE FAILED.
DO YOU HAVE ANY IDEA HOW NAIVE WE WERE, THINKING THAT A GROUP OF KIDS COULD TAKE ON A BUNCH OF MONSTERS?
IT WAS A MASSACRE.
RICKY WAS TORN TO PIECES THE MINUTE WE WALKED INTO THEIR LAIR.
TABITHA WAS NOTHING BUT A SMEAR ON THE FLOOR OF THE CAVE AFTER A TROLL DROVE HIS FIST DOWN ON HER.
COOPER WAS SWALLOWED WHOLE. I DON'T KNOW HOW LONG SHE LASTED INSIDE THE TROLL.
I HOPE HER STRUGGLE WAS A SHORT ONE.
ONE OF THE TROLLS STARTED TO EAT ME. MY LEGS WERE GONE WITH ITS FIRST BITE.
FUNNY RANDALL, WHO IN A FEW SHORT DAYS HAD BECOME THE VERY BEST FRIEND I'VE EVER HAD, CAME TO MY RESCUE.
HE LAUNCHED HIMSELF AT THE TROLL, LIKE A GREAT WARRIOR IN SOME ANCIENT MYTH.

BUT RANDALL **WASN'T** A GREAT WARRIOR. HE WAS JUST A BRAVE KID WITH A HEART TOO BIG TO REALIZE THAT A JERK LIKE **ME** WASN'T WORTH SAVING.

WE COULDN'T STOP THEM. THE TROLLS WENT ON TO FEAST AS PLANNED.

MY **PARENTS** WERE AMONG THE ONES DEVOURED TO FUEL THE TROLLS' LONG RESPITE.

LUTEFISK TOOK ME IN, AND **TRAINED** ME IN THE DYING ART OF **TROLLFIGHTING.**

THE OLD MAN FIGURED I'D HAVE TO FACE THEM EVENTUALLY. ONE **DID** EAT MY LEGS, AFTER ALL.

ONCE A TROLL HAS SUPPED ON YOUR FLESH, IT'S **BOUND TO YOU FOREVER,** AND WILL ALWAYS SNIFF YOU OUT AND **FIND** YOU AFTER IT AWAKENS FROM ITS HIBERNATION.

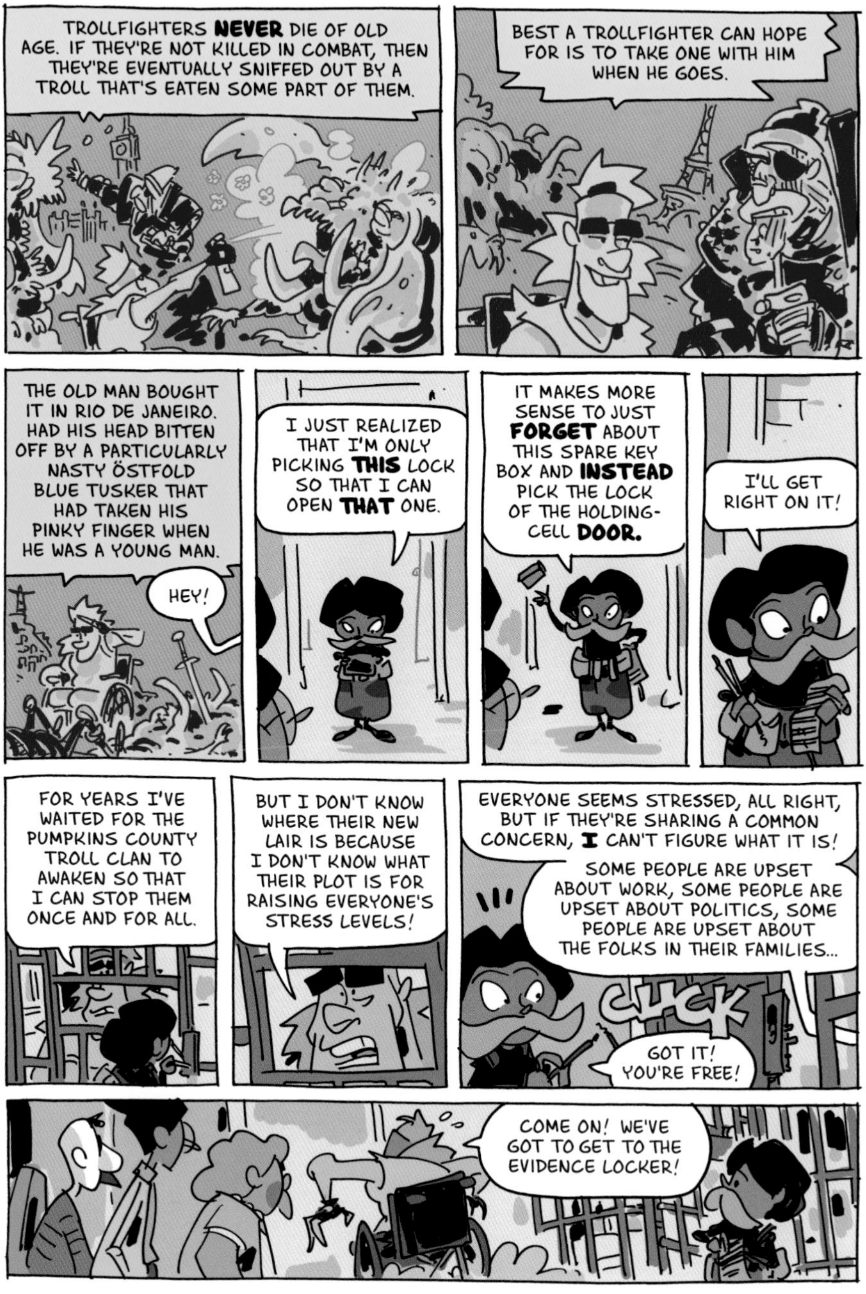

TROLLFIGHTERS **NEVER** DIE OF OLD AGE. IF THEY'RE NOT KILLED IN COMBAT, THEN THEY'RE EVENTUALLY SNIFFED OUT BY A TROLL THAT'S EATEN SOME PART OF THEM.
BEST A TROLLFIGHTER CAN HOPE FOR IS TO TAKE ONE WITH HIM WHEN HE GOES.
THE OLD MAN BOUGHT IT IN RIO DE JANEIRO. HAD HIS HEAD BITTEN OFF BY A PARTICULARLY NASTY ÖSTFOLD BLUE TUSKER THAT HAD TAKEN HIS PINKY FINGER WHEN HE WAS A YOUNG MAN.
HEY!
I JUST REALIZED THAT I'M ONLY PICKING **THIS** LOCK SO THAT I CAN OPEN **THAT** ONE.
IT MAKES MORE SENSE TO JUST **FORGET** ABOUT THIS SPARE KEY BOX AND **INSTEAD** PICK THE LOCK OF THE HOLDING-CELL **DOOR.**
I'LL GET RIGHT ON IT!
FOR YEARS I'VE WAITED FOR THE PUMPKINS COUNTY TROLL CLAN TO AWAKEN SO THAT I CAN STOP THEM ONCE AND FOR ALL.
BUT I DON'T KNOW WHERE THEIR NEW LAIR IS BECAUSE I DON'T KNOW WHAT THEIR PLOT IS FOR RAISING EVERYONE'S STRESS LEVELS!
EVERYONE SEEMS STRESSED, ALL RIGHT, BUT IF THEY'RE SHARING A COMMON CONCERN, **I** CAN'T FIGURE WHAT IT IS!
SOME PEOPLE ARE UPSET ABOUT WORK, SOME PEOPLE ARE UPSET ABOUT POLITICS, SOME PEOPLE ARE UPSET ABOUT THE FOLKS IN THEIR FAMILIES...
CLICK
GOT IT! YOU'RE FREE!
COME ON! WE'VE GOT TO GET TO THE EVIDENCE LOCKER!

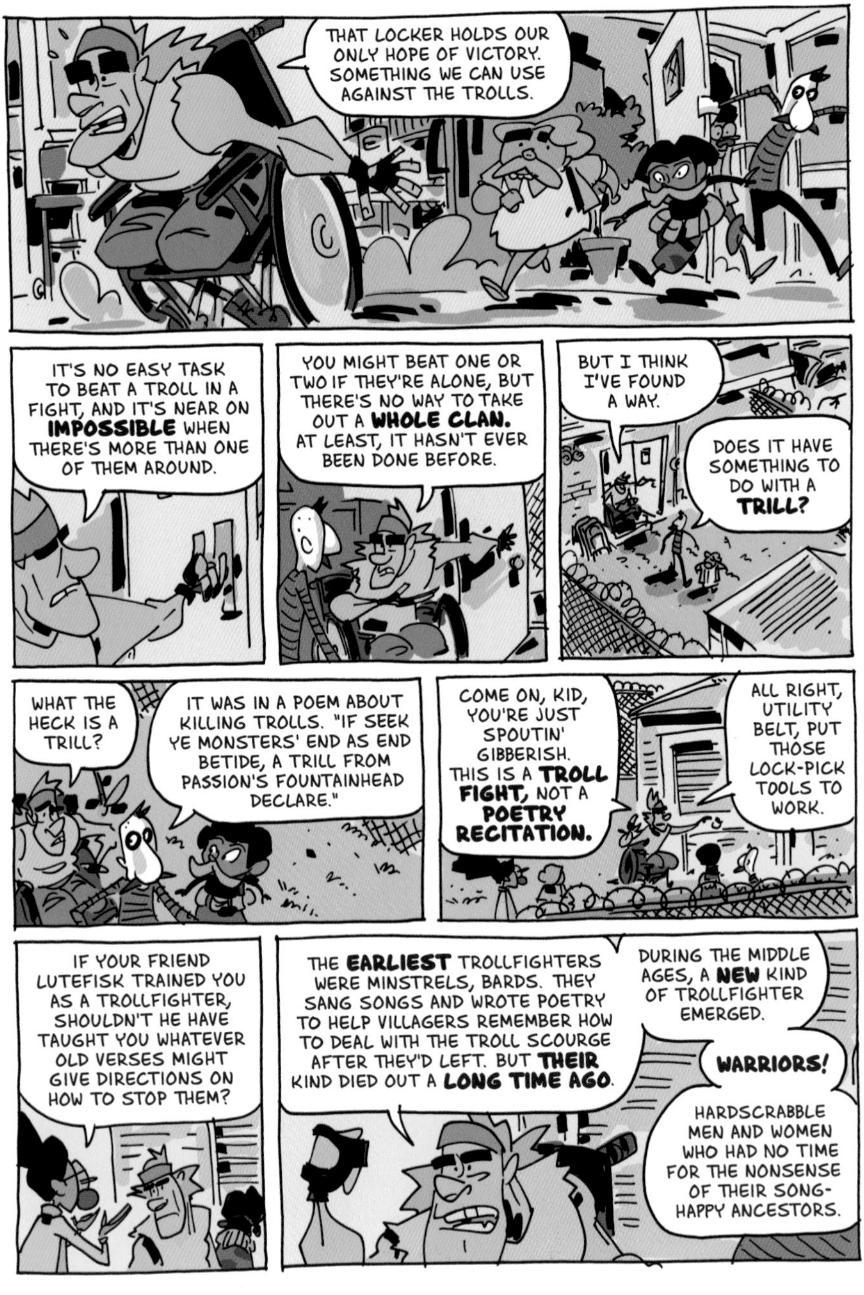
THAT LOCKER HOLDS OUR ONLY HOPE OF VICTORY. SOMETHING WE CAN USE AGAINST THE TROLLS.
IT'S NO EASY TASK TO BEAT A TROLL IN A FIGHT, AND IT'S NEAR ON IMPOSSIBLE WHEN THERE'S MORE THAN ONE OF THEM AROUND.
YOU MIGHT BEAT ONE OR TWO IF THEY'RE ALONE, BUT THERE'S NO WAY TO TAKE OUT A WHOLE CLAN. AT LEAST, IT HASN'T EVER BEEN DONE BEFORE.
BUT I THINK I'VE FOUND A WAY.
DOES IT HAVE SOMETHING TO DO WITH A TRILL?
WHAT THE HECK IS A TRILL?
IT WAS IN A POEM ABOUT KILLING TROLLS. "IF SEEK YE MONSTERS' END AS END BETIDE, A TRILL FROM PASSION'S FOUNTAINHEAD DECLARE."
COME ON, KID, YOU'RE JUST SPOUTIN' GIBBERISH. THIS IS A TROLL FIGHT, NOT A POETRY RECITATION.
ALL RIGHT, UTILITY BELT, PUT THOSE LOCK-PICK TOOLS TO WORK.
IF YOUR FRIEND LUTEFISK TRAINED YOU AS A TROLLFIGHTER, SHOULDN'T HE HAVE TAUGHT YOU WHATEVER OLD VERSES MIGHT GIVE DIRECTIONS ON HOW TO STOP THEM?
THE EARLIEST TROLLFIGHTERS WERE MINSTRELS, BARDS. THEY SANG SONGS AND WROTE POETRY TO HELP VILLAGERS REMEMBER HOW TO DEAL WITH THE TROLL SCOURGE AFTER THEY'D LEFT. BUT THEIR KIND DIED OUT A LONG TIME AGO.
DURING THE MIDDLE AGES, A NEW KIND OF TROLLFIGHTER EMERGED.
WARRIORS!
HARDSCRABBLE MEN AND WOMEN WHO HAD NO TIME FOR THE NONSENSE OF THEIR SONG-HAPPY ANCESTORS.

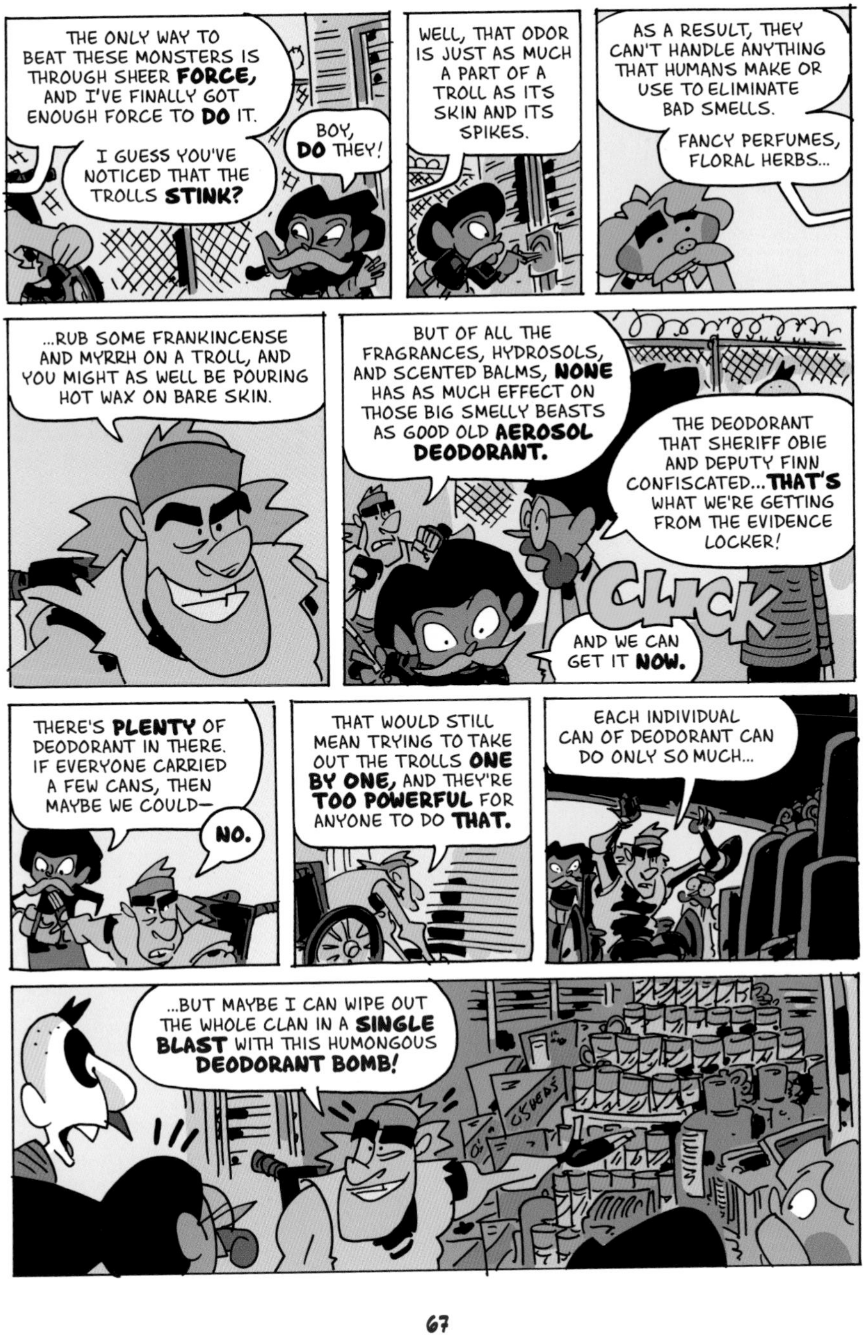
THE ONLY WAY TO BEAT THESE MONSTERS IS THROUGH SHEER FORCE, AND I'VE FINALLY GOT ENOUGH FORCE TO DO IT.
I GUESS YOU'VE NOTICED THAT THE TROLLS STINK?
BOY, DO THEY!
WELL, THAT ODOR IS JUST AS MUCH A PART OF A TROLL AS ITS SKIN AND ITS SPIKES.
AS A RESULT, THEY CAN'T HANDLE ANYTHING THAT HUMANS MAKE OR USE TO ELIMINATE BAD SMELLS.
FANCY PERFUMES, FLORAL HERBS...
...RUB SOME FRANKINCENSE AND MYRRH ON A TROLL, AND YOU MIGHT AS WELL BE POURING HOT WAX ON BARE SKIN.
BUT OF ALL THE FRAGRANCES, HYDROSOLS, AND SCENTED BALMS, NONE HAS AS MUCH EFFECT ON THOSE BIG SMELLY BEASTS AS GOOD OLD AEROSOL DEODORANT.
THE DEODORANT THAT SHERIFF OBIE AND DEPUTY FINN CONFISCATED...THAT'S WHAT WE'RE GETTING FROM THE EVIDENCE LOCKER!
CLICK
AND WE CAN GET IT NOW.
THERE'S PLENTY OF DEODORANT IN THERE. IF EVERYONE CARRIED A FEW CANS, THEN MAYBE WE COULD—
NO.
THAT WOULD STILL MEAN TRYING TO TAKE OUT THE TROLLS ONE BY ONE, AND THEY'RE TOO POWERFUL FOR ANYONE TO DO THAT.
EACH INDIVIDUAL CAN OF DEODORANT CAN DO ONLY SO MUCH...
...BUT MAYBE I CAN WIPE OUT THE WHOLE CLAN IN A SINGLE BLAST WITH THIS HUMONGOUS DEODORANT BOMB!

ISN'T A BOMB...
DANGEROUS?
RIDICULOUSLY DANGEROUS. THE DEODORANT PART MAY NOT HURT US, BUT THE BOMB PART COULD BLOW US TO PIECES!
THE ONLY TROUBLE IS THAT I DON'T HAVE THE SLIGHTEST IDEA WHERE TO SET IT OFF.
THE TROLLS WILL HERD THE VICTIMS TO THEIR LAIR, BUT I DON'T KNOW WHERE THEIR LAIR IS.
IF I COULD JUST FIGURE OUT WHAT THEIR PLOT IS, HOW THEY'RE MANAGING TO STRESS EVERYONE OUT, THAT MIGHT BE ENOUGH OF A CLUE, BUT I'M STUMPED.
NO GUESSES AT ALL?
NOPE. USUALLY I CAN INVESTIGATE A CLAN'S OPERATIONS BEFORE THEY STRIKE, BUT THE PUMPKINS COUNTY CLAN IS A SPECIAL CIRCUMSTANCE.
THIS IS WHERE THE TROLL THAT ATE MY LEGS LIVES.
BECAUSE IT'S HAD A TASTE OF ME, IT CAN SENSE WHEN I'M NEARBY.
I HAVEN'T BEEN ABLE TO LEAVE MY BOAT WITHOUT THAT SPOT-EYED STINKER TRYING TO STUFF THE REST OF ME DOWN ITS GULLET.
WHEN THE SHERIFF BROUGHT ME TO THE STATION EARLIER FOR QUESTIONING, IT STARTED SNIFFING ME OUT, AND IT ALMOST CAUGHT ME WHEN I PULLED BACK TO SHORE FOR YOU KNUCKLEHEADS.
THE ONE THAT ATE YOUR LEGS... YOU SAY IT HAS A SPOT AROUND ITS EYE?
YEP. NASTY SLUGGER, THAT ONE.
WE KNOW. IT TRIED TO EAT US OUTSIDE THE PIZZERIA!
WELL, IT WON'T BE EATING ANYONE AFTER TODAY. NOT IF THIS BOMB WORKS THE WAY I HOPE IT WILL.
NOW I JUST NEED TO KEEP ON THE MOVE WHILE I FIGURE OUT WHERE THE TROLLS' LAIR IS. IF WE'RE LUCKY, I CAN FIND IT BEFORE THE TROLLS FIND ME.
MISTER BROGGLIN?

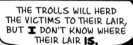

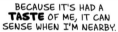

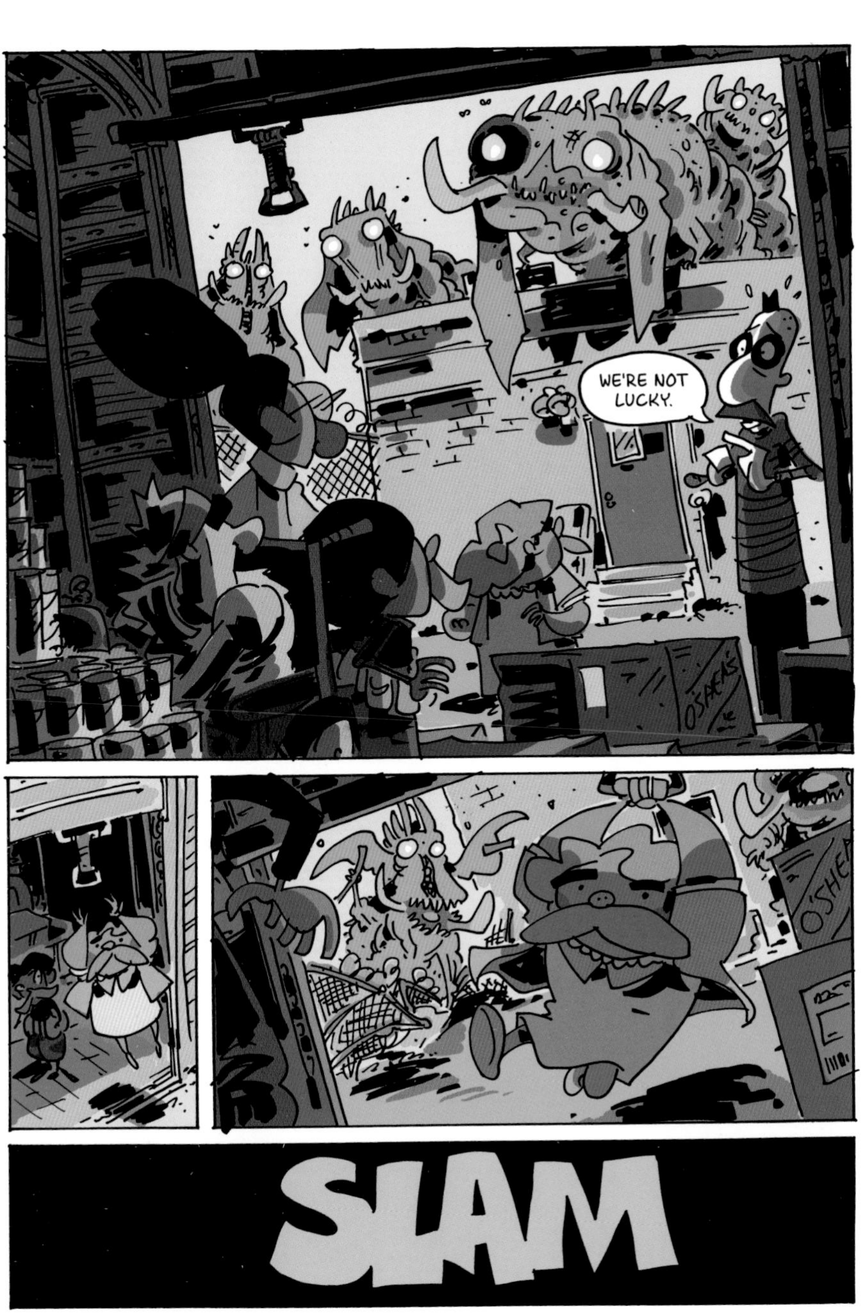
WE'RE NOT LUCKY.
SLAM

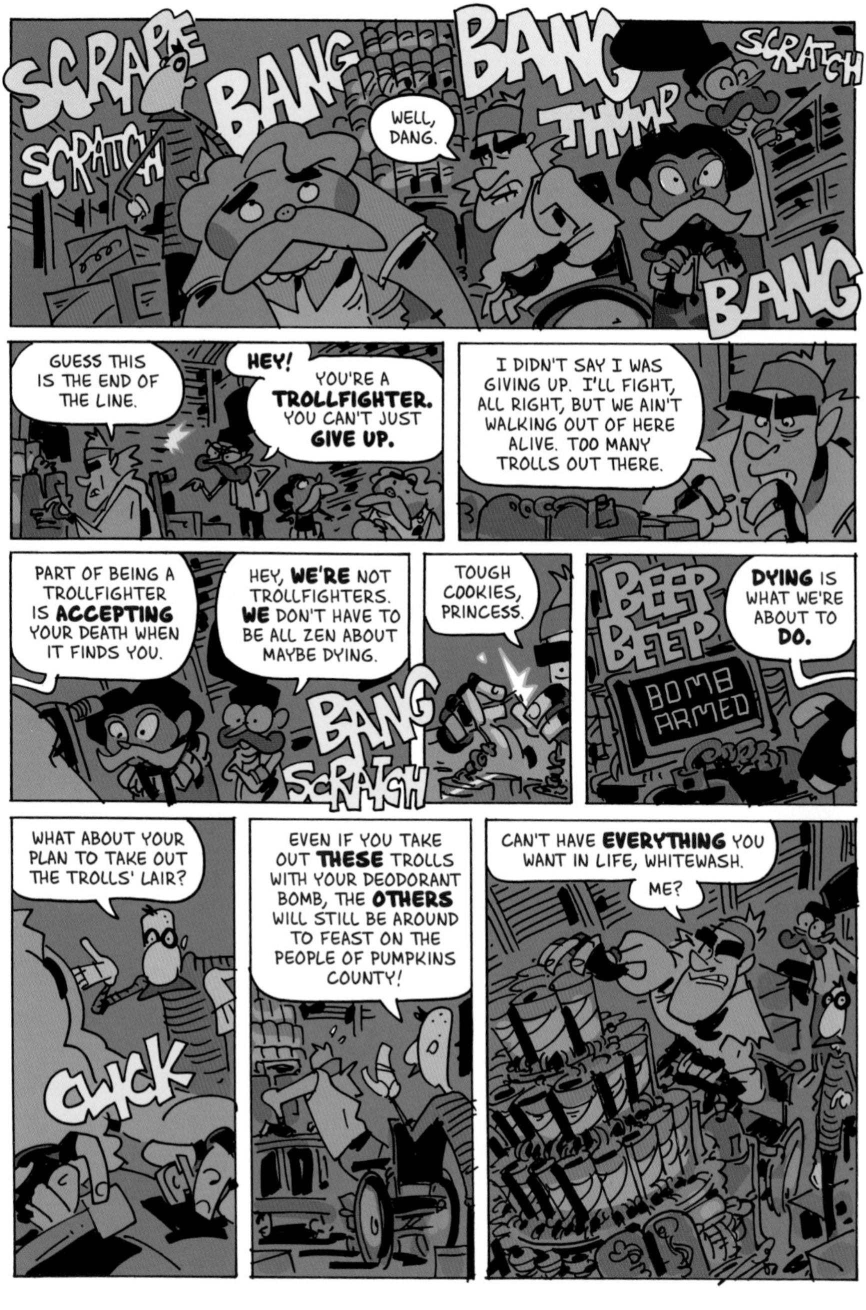
SCRAPE
SCRATCH
BANG
BANG
WELL, DANG.
THUMP
SCRATCH
BANG
GUESS THIS IS THE END OF THE LINE.
HEY!
YOU'RE A **TROLLFIGHTER.** YOU CAN'T JUST **GIVE UP.**
I DIDN'T SAY I WAS GIVING UP. I'LL FIGHT, ALL RIGHT, BUT WE AIN'T WALKING OUT OF HERE ALIVE. TOO MANY TROLLS OUT THERE.
PART OF BEING A TROLLFIGHTER IS **ACCEPTING** YOUR DEATH WHEN IT FINDS YOU.
HEY, **WE'RE** NOT TROLLFIGHTERS. **WE** DON'T HAVE TO BE ALL ZEN ABOUT MAYBE DYING.
BANG
SCRATCH
TOUGH COOKIES, PRINCESS.
BEEP BEEP
BOMB ARMED
DYING IS WHAT WE'RE ABOUT TO **DO.**
WHAT ABOUT YOUR PLAN TO TAKE OUT THE TROLLS' LAIR?
CLICK
EVEN IF YOU TAKE OUT **THESE** TROLLS WITH YOUR DEODORANT BOMB, THE **OTHERS** WILL STILL BE AROUND TO FEAST ON THE PEOPLE OF PUMPKINS COUNTY!
CAN'T HAVE **EVERYTHING** YOU WANT IN LIFE, WHITEWASH.
ME?

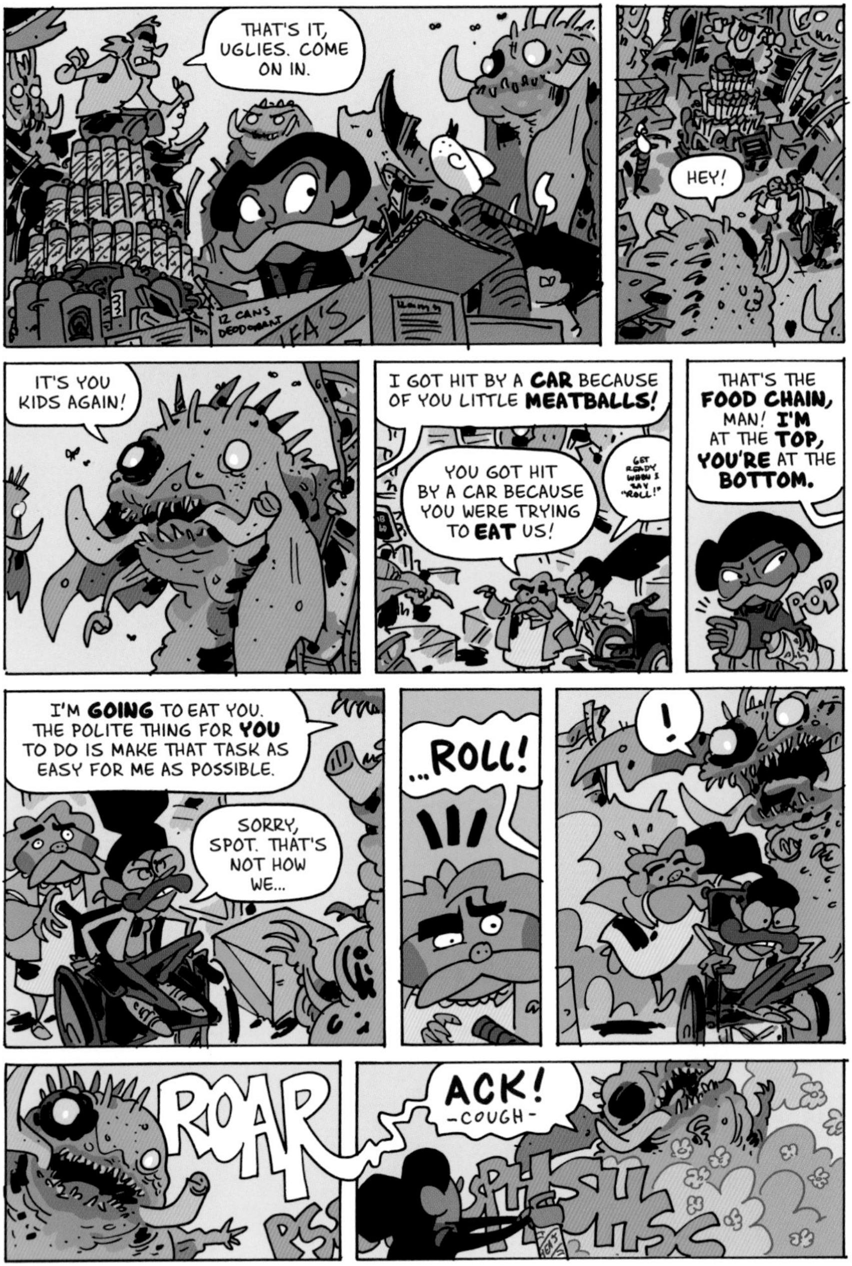

THAT'S IT, UGLIES. COME ON IN.
12 CANS DEODORANT
HEY!
IT'S YOU KIDS AGAIN!
I GOT HIT BY A **CAR** BECAUSE OF YOU LITTLE **MEATBALLS!**
YOU GOT HIT BY A CAR BECAUSE YOU WERE TRYING TO **EAT** US!
GET READY WHEN I SAY "ROLL!"
THAT'S THE **FOOD CHAIN,** MAN! **I'M** AT THE **TOP, YOU'RE** AT THE **BOTTOM.**
POP
I'M **GOING** TO EAT YOU. THE POLITE THING FOR **YOU** TO DO IS MAKE THAT TASK AS EASY FOR ME AS POSSIBLE.
SORRY, SPOT. THAT'S NOT HOW WE...
...ROLL!
!
ROAR
ACK! -COUGH-
PSSH
PHSHSHSC

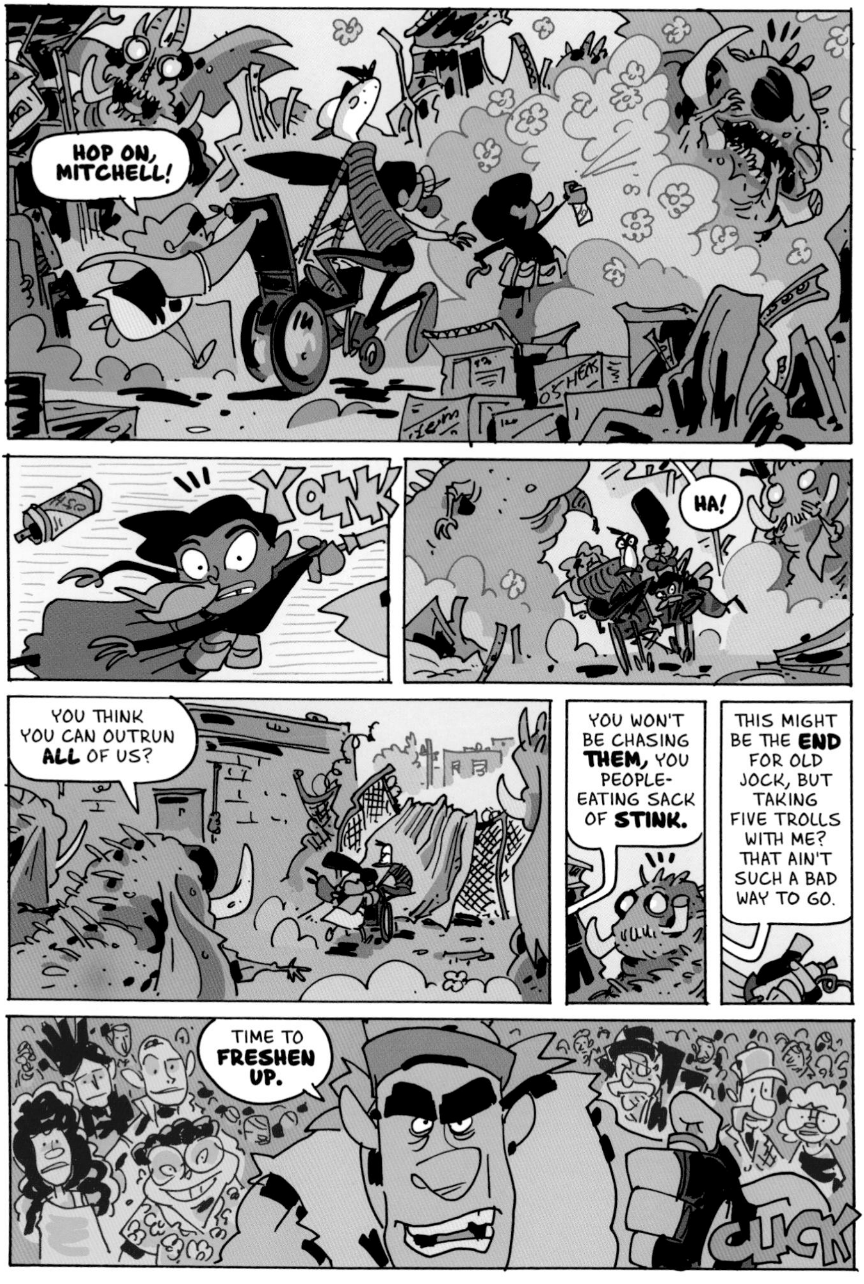
HOP ON, MITCHELL!
YONK
HA!
YOU THINK YOU CAN OUTRUN ALL OF US?
YOU WON'T BE CHASING THEM, YOU PEOPLE-EATING SACK OF STINK.
THIS MIGHT BE THE END FOR OLD JOCK, BUT TAKING FIVE TROLLS WITH ME? THAT AIN'T SUCH A BAD WAY TO GO.
TIME TO FRESHEN UP.
CLICK

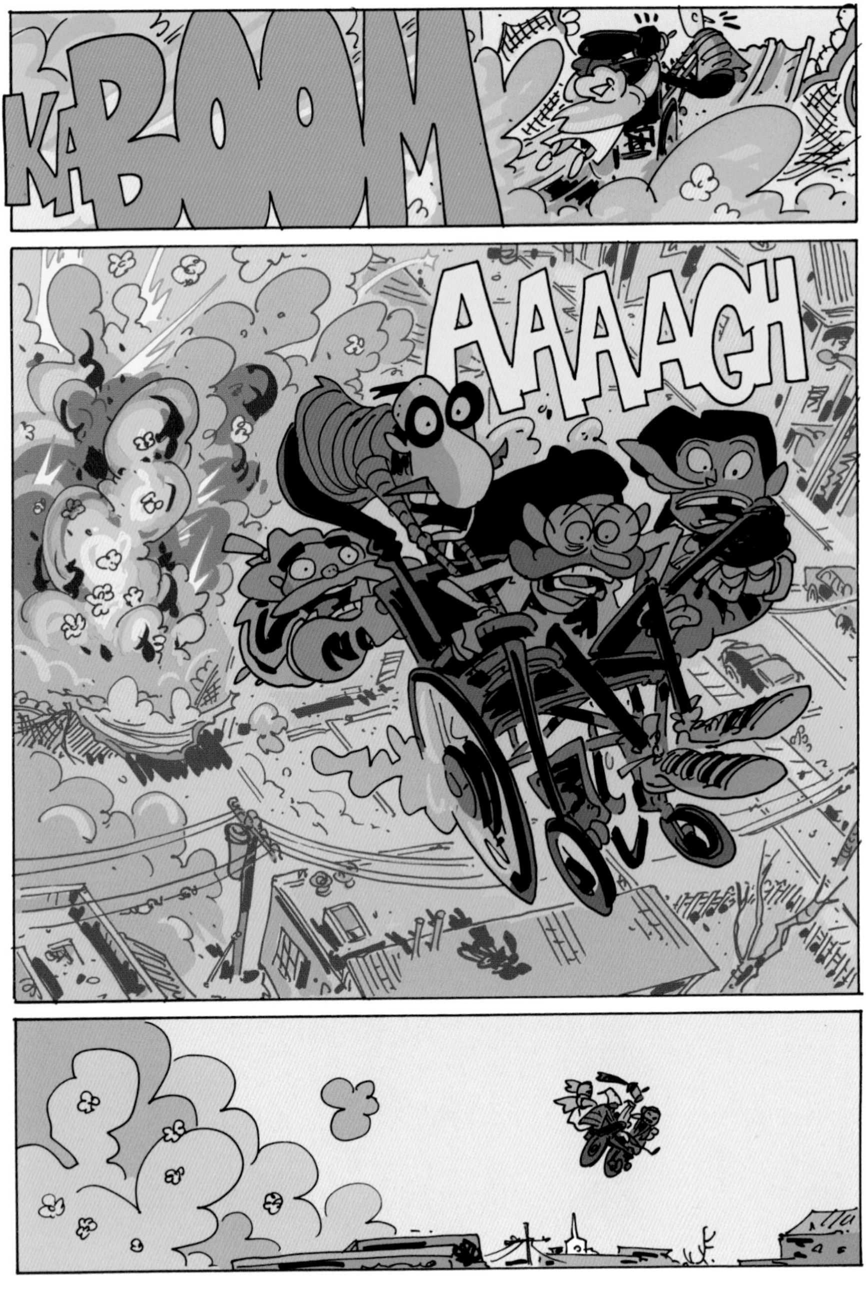
KABOOM
AAAAGH

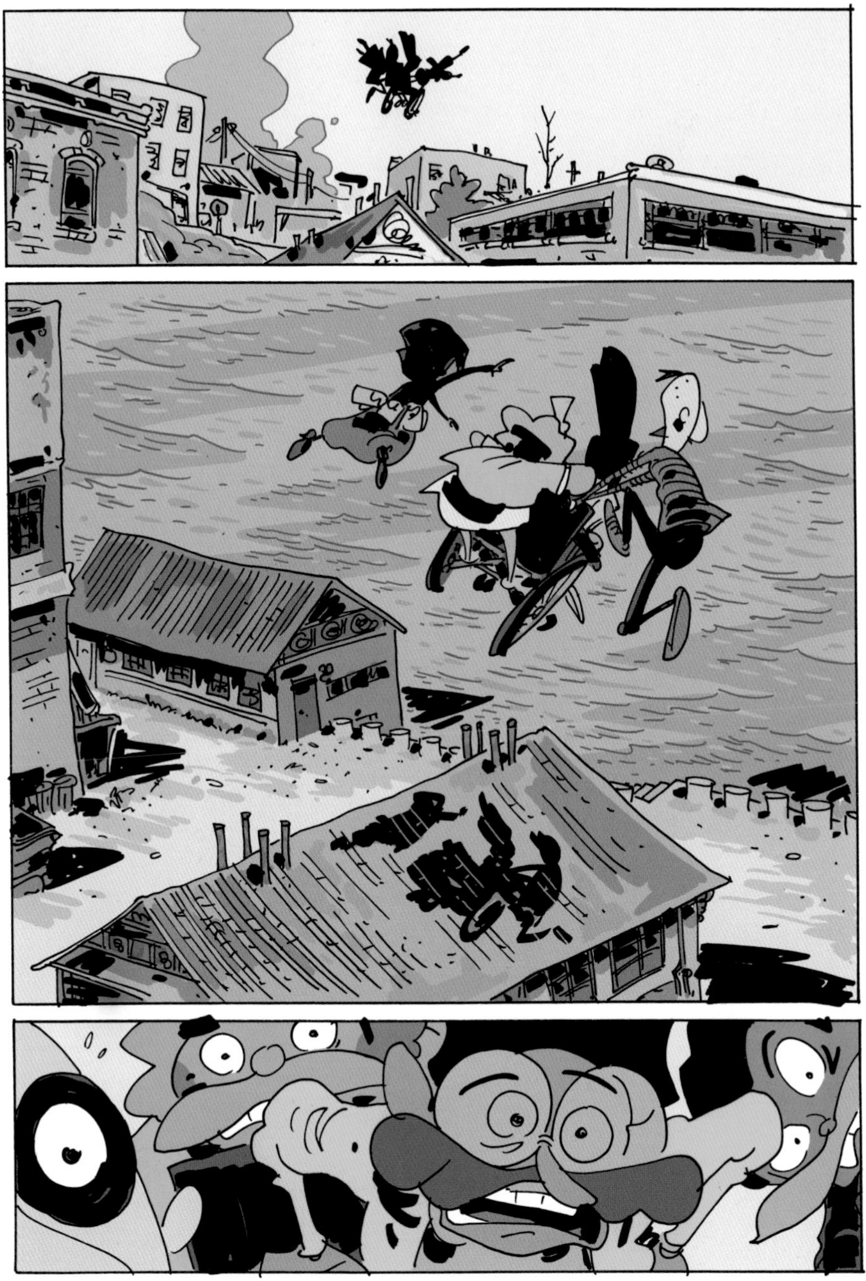

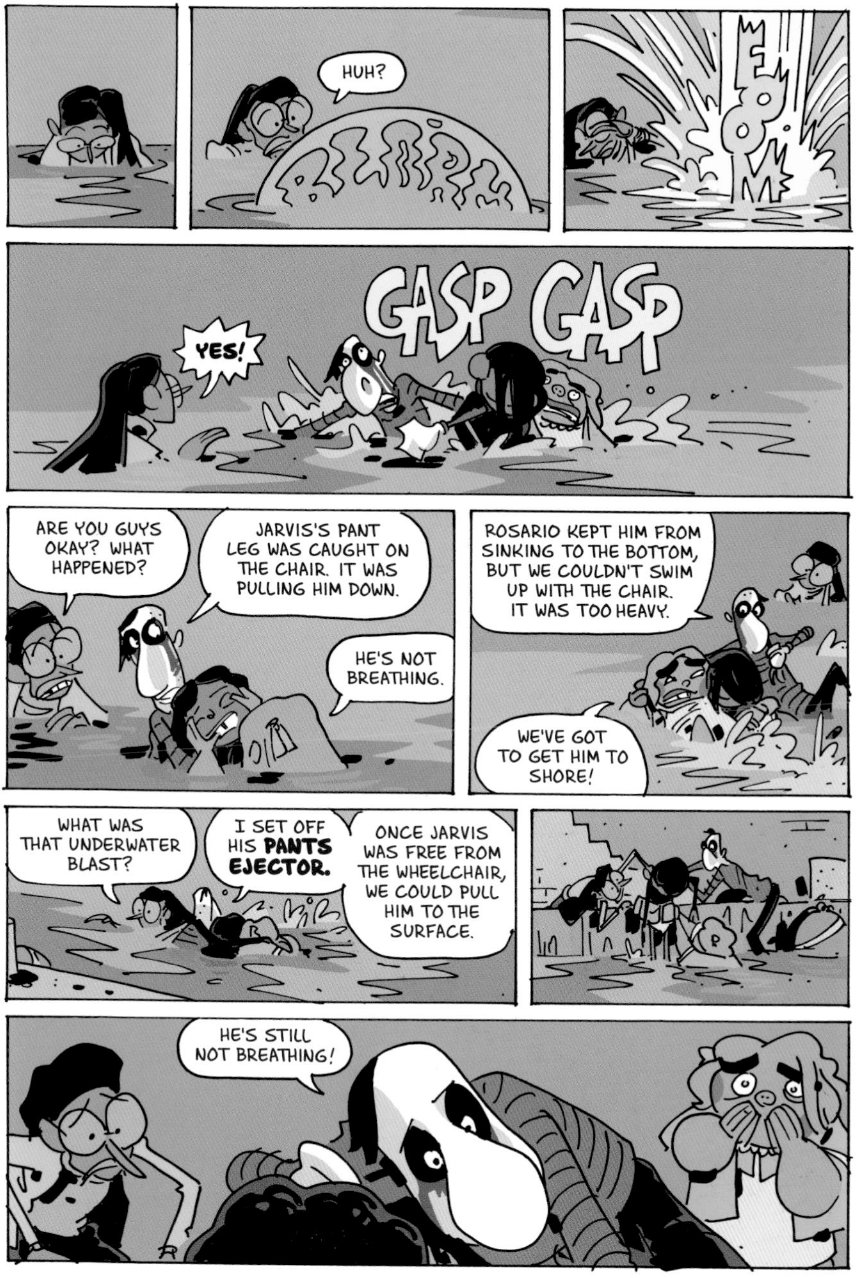
HUH?
GASP GASP
YES!
ARE YOU GUYS OKAY? WHAT HAPPENED?
JARVIS'S PANT LEG WAS CAUGHT ON THE CHAIR. IT WAS PULLING HIM DOWN.
HE'S NOT BREATHING.
ROSARIO KEPT HIM FROM SINKING TO THE BOTTOM, BUT WE COULDN'T SWIM UP WITH THE CHAIR. IT WAS TOO HEAVY.
WE'VE GOT TO GET HIM TO SHORE!
WHAT WAS THAT UNDERWATER BLAST?
I SET OFF HIS **PANTS EJECTOR.**
ONCE JARVIS WAS FREE FROM THE WHEELCHAIR, WE COULD PULL HIM TO THE SURFACE.
HE'S STILL NOT BREATHING!

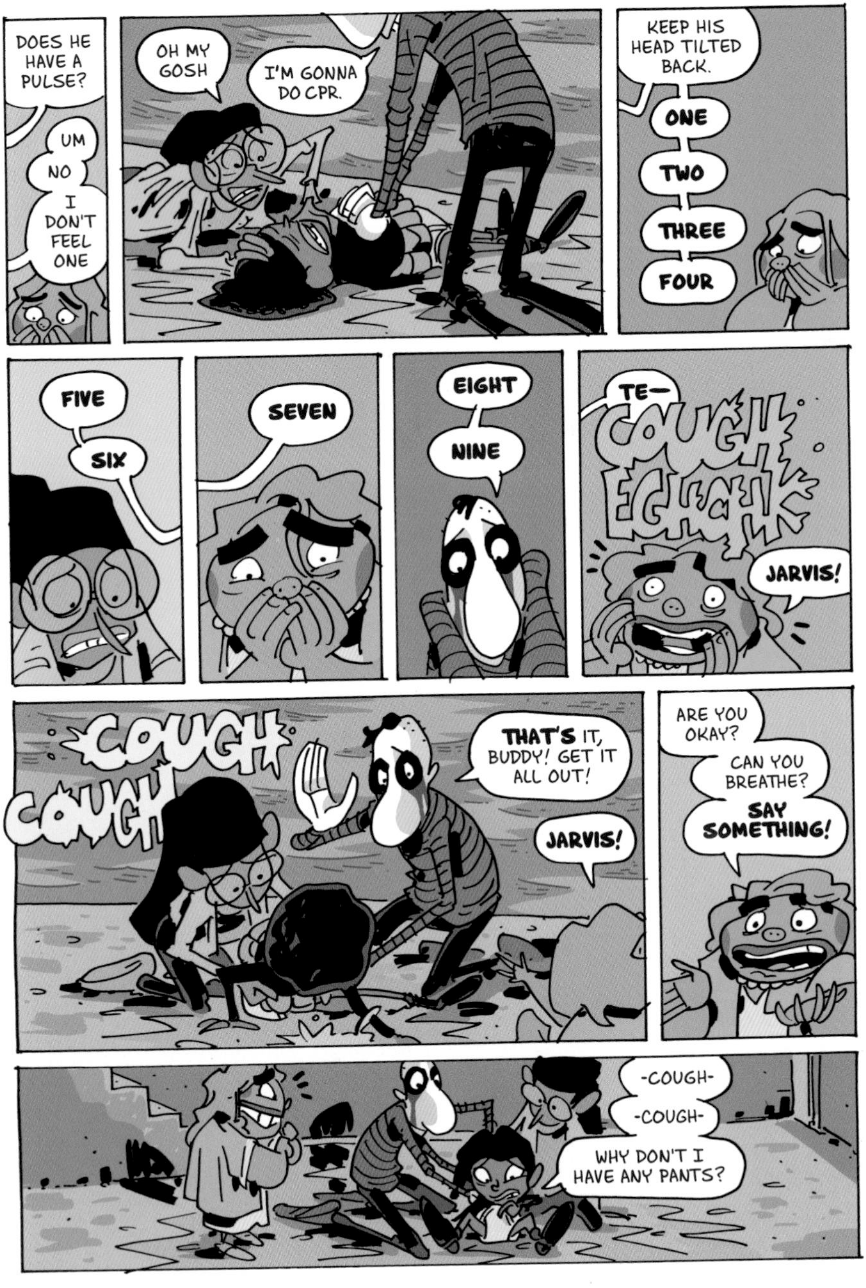
DOES HE HAVE A PULSE?
UM
NO
I DON'T FEEL ONE
OH MY GOSH
I'M GONNA DO CPR.
KEEP HIS HEAD TILTED BACK.
ONE
TWO
THREE
FOUR
FIVE
SIX
SEVEN
EIGHT
NINE
TE—
COUGH
EGHGHK
JARVIS!
COUGH
COUGH
THAT'S IT, BUDDY! GET IT ALL OUT!
JARVIS!
ARE YOU OKAY?
CAN YOU BREATHE?
SAY SOMETHING!
-COUGH-
-COUGH-
WHY DON'T I HAVE ANY PANTS?

STILL NO SIGNAL.

CAROL, I **DON'T** NEED AN AMBULANCE. MY CHEST IS A LITTLE SORE, BUT OTHERWISE I'M **FINE.**

BUT THERE'S A PHONE TOWER RIGHT DOWN THE STREET.

I **SHOULD** BE GETTING **GREAT** SERVICE HERE.

PEOPLE HAVE BEEN HAVING PHONE TROUBLE ALL DAY.

I'M NOT ABLE TO GET ONLINE, EITHER.

NO MESSAGING, NO E-MAIL, NOTHING.

THE ONLY THING THAT SEEMS TO BE WORKING IS TATTLER.

OH MY GOSH! HAVE YOU KIDS BEEN **SWIMMING?**

FANCY SPRING SP

NOT ON **PURPOSE!**

YOU NEED TO GET TO THE HOSPITAL RIGHT AWAY!

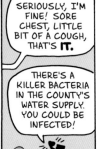

SERIOUSLY, I'M FINE! SORE CHEST, LITTLE BIT OF A COUGH, THAT'S **IT.**

THERE'S A KILLER BACTERIA IN THE COUNTY'S WATER SUPPLY. YOU COULD BE INFECTED!

GREAT. AS IF WE DIDN'T HAVE **ENOUGH** TO STRESS ABOUT ALREADY!

HOLD IT RIGHT THERE, YOU!

WHO, US?

YES, YOU! WHAT PROOF DO YOU HAVE THAT YOU'RE NOT FROM **GREENLAND?**

UM...**NONE,** I GUESS.

IT'S NOT THE SORT OF THING I'VE EVER HAD TO **PROVE** BEFORE.

THAT'S EXACTLY THE SORT OF THING A **GREENLANDER** WOULD SAY!

BEAT 'EM DOWN, LADIES! IT'S OUR PATRIOTIC DUTY!

WHOA, THERE!

WHY DO YOU WANT TO FIGHT PEOPLE FROM GREENLAND?

BECAUSE THE GREENLANDERS HAVE **INVADED!**

THEY'VE ATTACKED THE CAPITOL AND ARE SENDING AN ARMY SWEEPING ACROSS THE COUNTRY.

THREE MONTHS!

ONLY **THREE MONTHS** UNTIL THE **ASTEROID** HITS!

ASTEROID?

WORTHLESS! IT'S ALL WORTHLESS! YEARS OF SAVING, FOR NOTHING!

WHAT IS GOING **ON?!**

PHONES ARE DOWN, THE INTERNET IS DOWN, THE INVADERS HAVE SHUT OFF ALL MEANS OF COMMUNICATION.

EXCEPT FOR TATTLER. **IT'S** WORKING.

YES, THANK HEAVENS FOR TATTLER! IT'S THE ONLY WAY THAT THE RESISTANCE CAN KEEP US INFORMED ABOUT THE INVASION!

WE'RE ALL SUPPOSED TO RENDEZVOUS AT THE CITY DUMP. STRENGTH IN NUMBERS, KIDS!

SEEMS LIKE A LOT HAS HAPPENED SINCE WE FLEW OUT OF THE SHERIFF'S STATION.

YEAH. IT **"SEEMS"** LIKE A LOT HAS HAPPENED.

SCREEEEE!

AW, JEEZ! I THOUGHT YOU GUYS WERE AT THE **DUMP!**

HEY, BIG BROTHER!

WAIT, YOU MEAN THERE REALLY **ARE** INVADERS FROM GREENLAND?

WHAT?

NEVER MIND. FORGET WHATEVER WEIRD STUFF YOU'RE DOING.

MOM SENT ME A MESSAGE OVER TATTLER SAYING THAT YOU HAD AN ACCIDENT AT THE DUMP. I WAS HEADING THERE NOW!

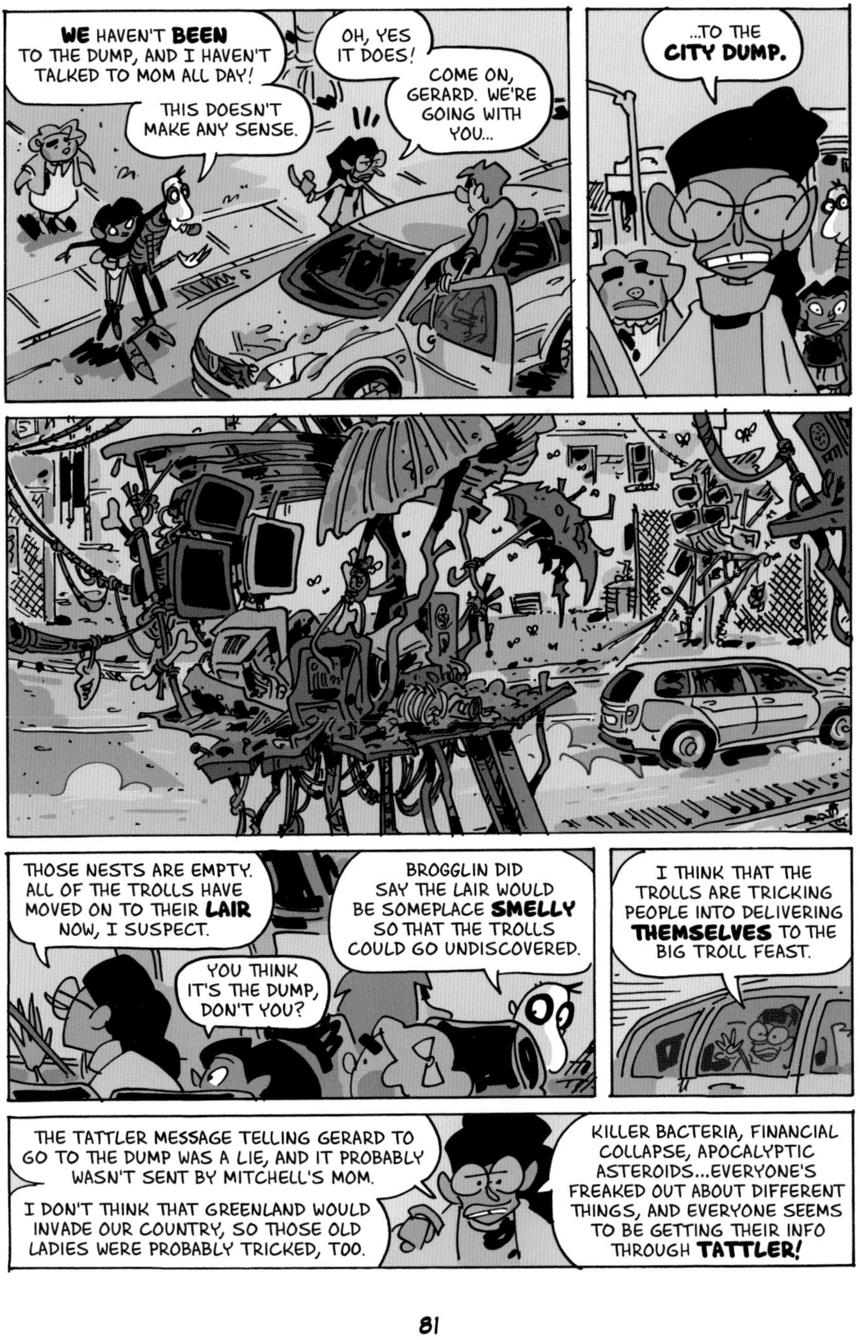
WE HAVEN'T BEEN TO THE DUMP, AND I HAVEN'T TALKED TO MOM ALL DAY!
THIS DOESN'T MAKE ANY SENSE.
OH, YES IT DOES!
COME ON, GERARD. WE'RE GOING WITH YOU...
...TO THE CITY DUMP.
THOSE NESTS ARE EMPTY. ALL OF THE TROLLS HAVE MOVED ON TO THEIR LAIR NOW, I SUSPECT.
YOU THINK IT'S THE DUMP, DON'T YOU?
BROGGLIN DID SAY THE LAIR WOULD BE SOMEPLACE SMELLY SO THAT THE TROLLS COULD GO UNDISCOVERED.
I THINK THAT THE TROLLS ARE TRICKING PEOPLE INTO DELIVERING THEMSELVES TO THE BIG TROLL FEAST.
THE TATTLER MESSAGE TELLING GERARD TO GO TO THE DUMP WAS A LIE, AND IT PROBABLY WASN'T SENT BY MITCHELL'S MOM.
I DON'T THINK THAT GREENLAND WOULD INVADE OUR COUNTRY, SO THOSE OLD LADIES WERE PROBABLY TRICKED, TOO.
KILLER BACTERIA, FINANCIAL COLLAPSE, APOCALYPTIC ASTEROIDS...EVERYONE'S FREAKED OUT ABOUT DIFFERENT THINGS, AND EVERYONE SEEMS TO BE GETTING THEIR INFO THROUGH TATTLER!

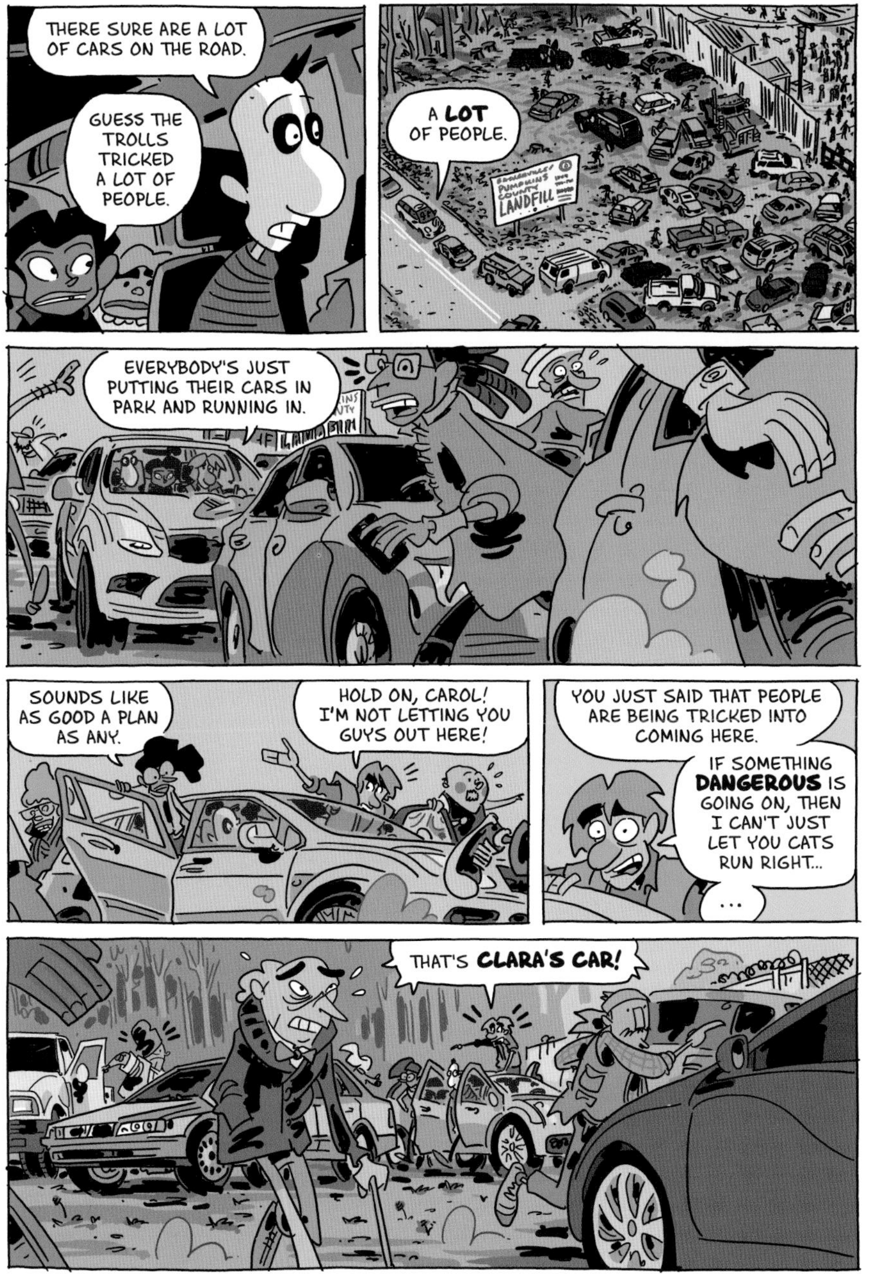
THERE SURE ARE A LOT OF CARS ON THE ROAD.
GUESS THE TROLLS TRICKED A LOT OF PEOPLE.
A **LOT** OF PEOPLE.
PUMPKINS COUNTY LANDFILL
EVERYBODY'S JUST PUTTING THEIR CARS IN PARK AND RUNNING IN.
SOUNDS LIKE AS GOOD A PLAN AS ANY.
HOLD ON, CAROL! I'M NOT LETTING YOU GUYS OUT HERE!
YOU JUST SAID THAT PEOPLE ARE BEING TRICKED INTO COMING HERE.
IF SOMETHING **DANGEROUS** IS GOING ON, THEN I CAN'T JUST LET YOU CATS RUN RIGHT...
...
THAT'S **CLARA'S CAR!**

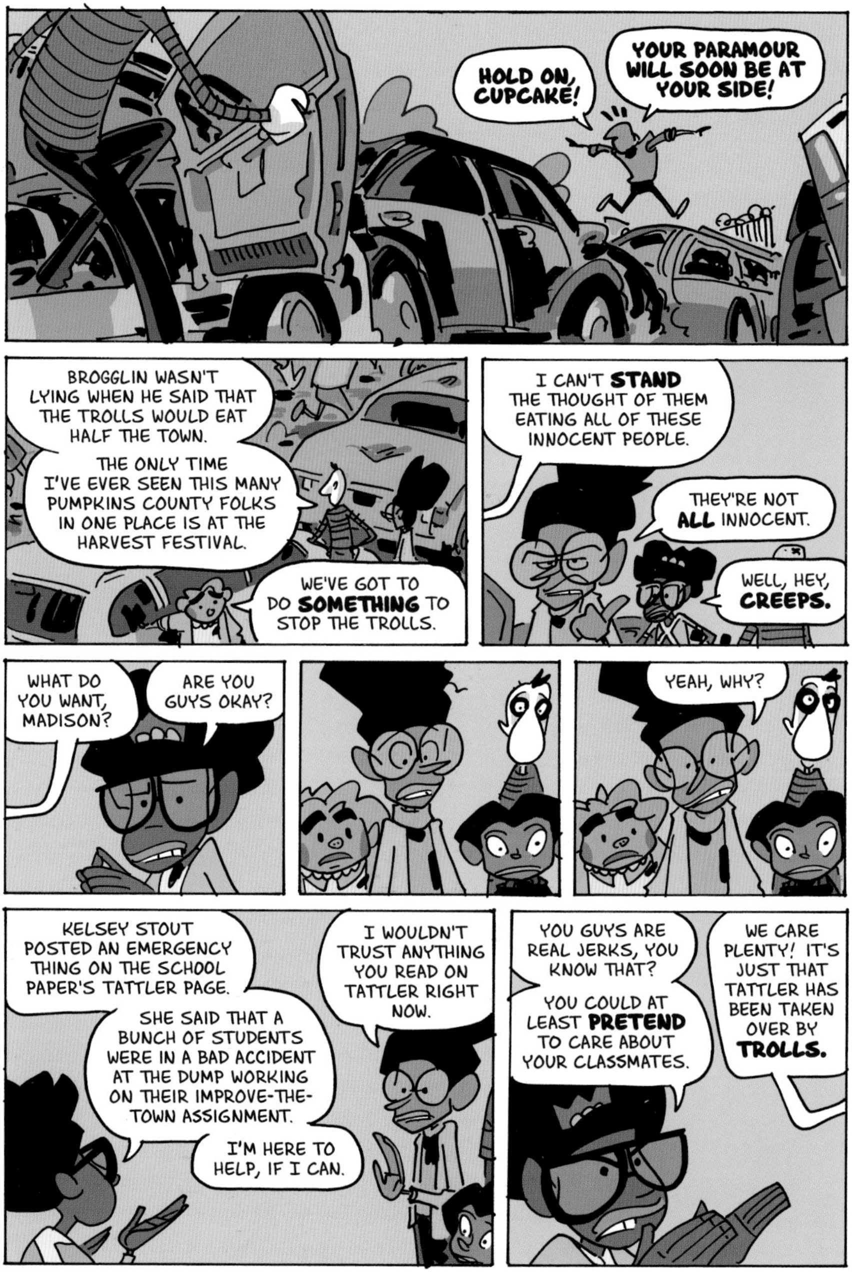

HOLD ON, CUPCAKE!
YOUR PARAMOUR WILL SOON BE AT YOUR SIDE!
BROGGLIN WASN'T LYING WHEN HE SAID THAT THE TROLLS WOULD EAT HALF THE TOWN.
THE ONLY TIME I'VE EVER SEEN THIS MANY PUMPKINS COUNTY FOLKS IN ONE PLACE IS AT THE HARVEST FESTIVAL.
WE'VE GOT TO DO SOMETHING TO STOP THE TROLLS.
I CAN'T STAND THE THOUGHT OF THEM EATING ALL OF THESE INNOCENT PEOPLE.
THEY'RE NOT ALL INNOCENT.
WELL, HEY, CREEPS.
WHAT DO YOU WANT, MADISON?
ARE YOU GUYS OKAY?
YEAH, WHY?
KELSEY STOUT POSTED AN EMERGENCY THING ON THE SCHOOL PAPER'S TATTLER PAGE.
SHE SAID THAT A BUNCH OF STUDENTS WERE IN A BAD ACCIDENT AT THE DUMP WORKING ON THEIR IMPROVE-THE-TOWN ASSIGNMENT.
I'M HERE TO HELP, IF I CAN.
I WOULDN'T TRUST ANYTHING YOU READ ON TATTLER RIGHT NOW.
YOU GUYS ARE REAL JERKS, YOU KNOW THAT?
YOU COULD AT LEAST PRETEND TO CARE ABOUT YOUR CLASSMATES.
WE CARE PLENTY! IT'S JUST THAT TATTLER HAS BEEN TAKEN OVER BY TROLLS.

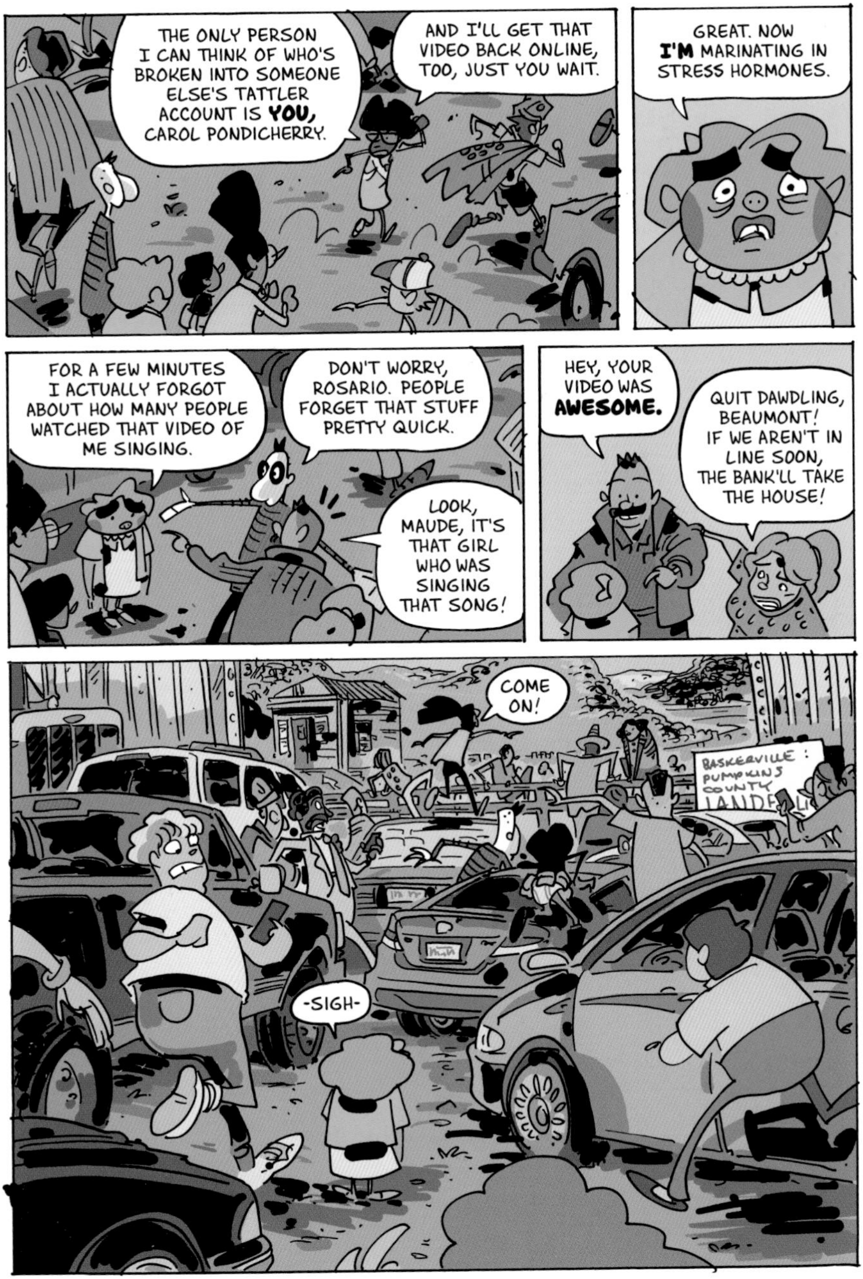
THE ONLY PERSON I CAN THINK OF WHO'S BROKEN INTO SOMEONE ELSE'S TATTLER ACCOUNT IS **YOU,** CAROL PONDICHERRY.
AND I'LL GET THAT VIDEO BACK ONLINE, TOO, JUST YOU WAIT.
GREAT. NOW **I'M** MARINATING IN STRESS HORMONES.
FOR A FEW MINUTES I ACTUALLY FORGOT ABOUT HOW MANY PEOPLE WATCHED THAT VIDEO OF ME SINGING.
DON'T WORRY, ROSARIO. PEOPLE FORGET THAT STUFF PRETTY QUICK.
LOOK, MAUDE, IT'S THAT GIRL WHO WAS SINGING THAT SONG!
HEY, YOUR VIDEO WAS **AWESOME.**
QUIT DAWDLING, BEAUMONT! IF WE AREN'T IN LINE SOON, THE BANK'LL TAKE THE HOUSE!
COME ON!
BASKERVILLE : PUMPKINS COUNTY
-SIGH-

86

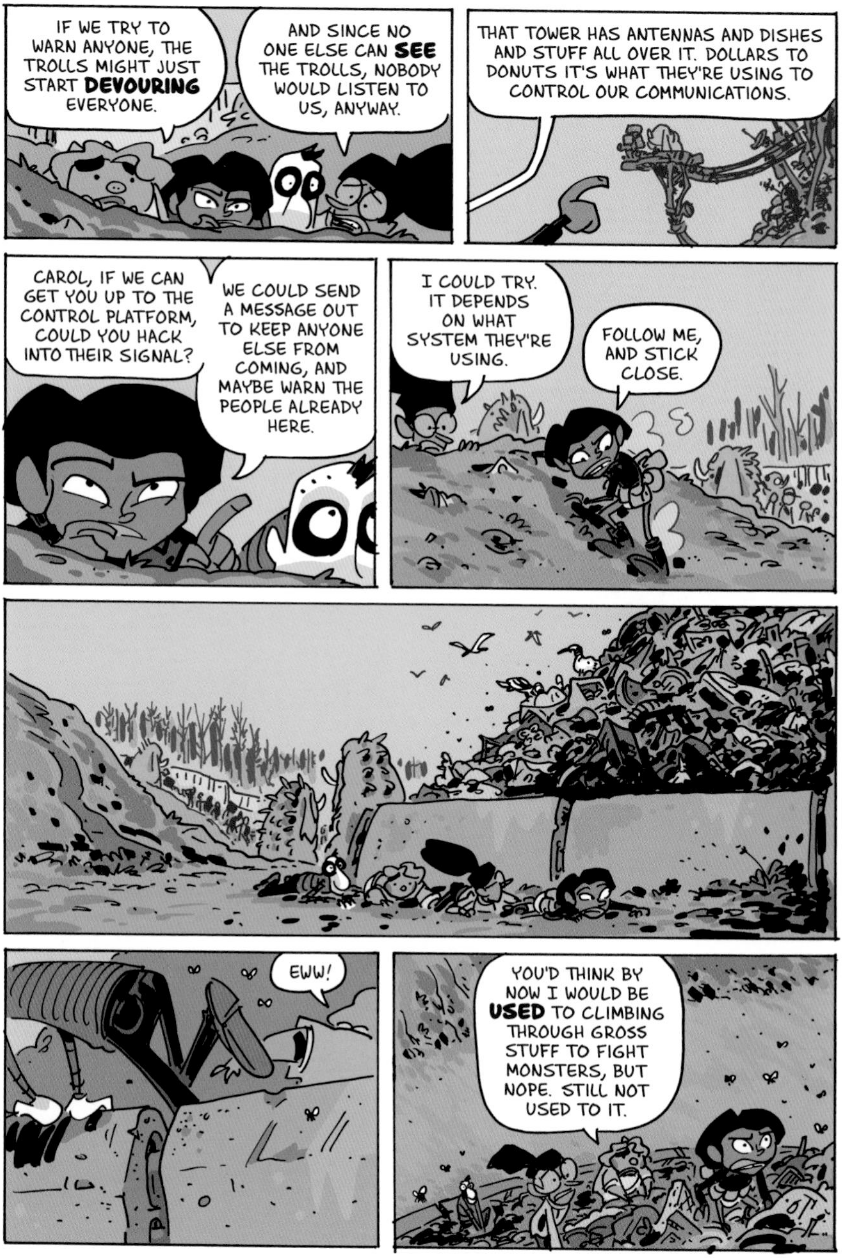

IF WE TRY TO WARN ANYONE, THE TROLLS MIGHT JUST START **DEVOURING** EVERYONE.
AND SINCE NO ONE ELSE CAN **SEE** THE TROLLS, NOBODY WOULD LISTEN TO US, ANYWAY.
THAT TOWER HAS ANTENNAS AND DISHES AND STUFF ALL OVER IT. DOLLARS TO DONUTS IT'S WHAT THEY'RE USING TO CONTROL OUR COMMUNICATIONS.
CAROL, IF WE CAN GET YOU UP TO THE CONTROL PLATFORM, COULD YOU HACK INTO THEIR SIGNAL?
WE COULD SEND A MESSAGE OUT TO KEEP ANYONE ELSE FROM COMING, AND MAYBE WARN THE PEOPLE ALREADY HERE.
I COULD TRY. IT DEPENDS ON WHAT SYSTEM THEY'RE USING.
FOLLOW ME, AND STICK CLOSE.
EWW!
YOU'D THINK BY NOW I WOULD BE **USED** TO CLIMBING THROUGH GROSS STUFF TO FIGHT MONSTERS, BUT NOPE. STILL NOT USED TO IT.

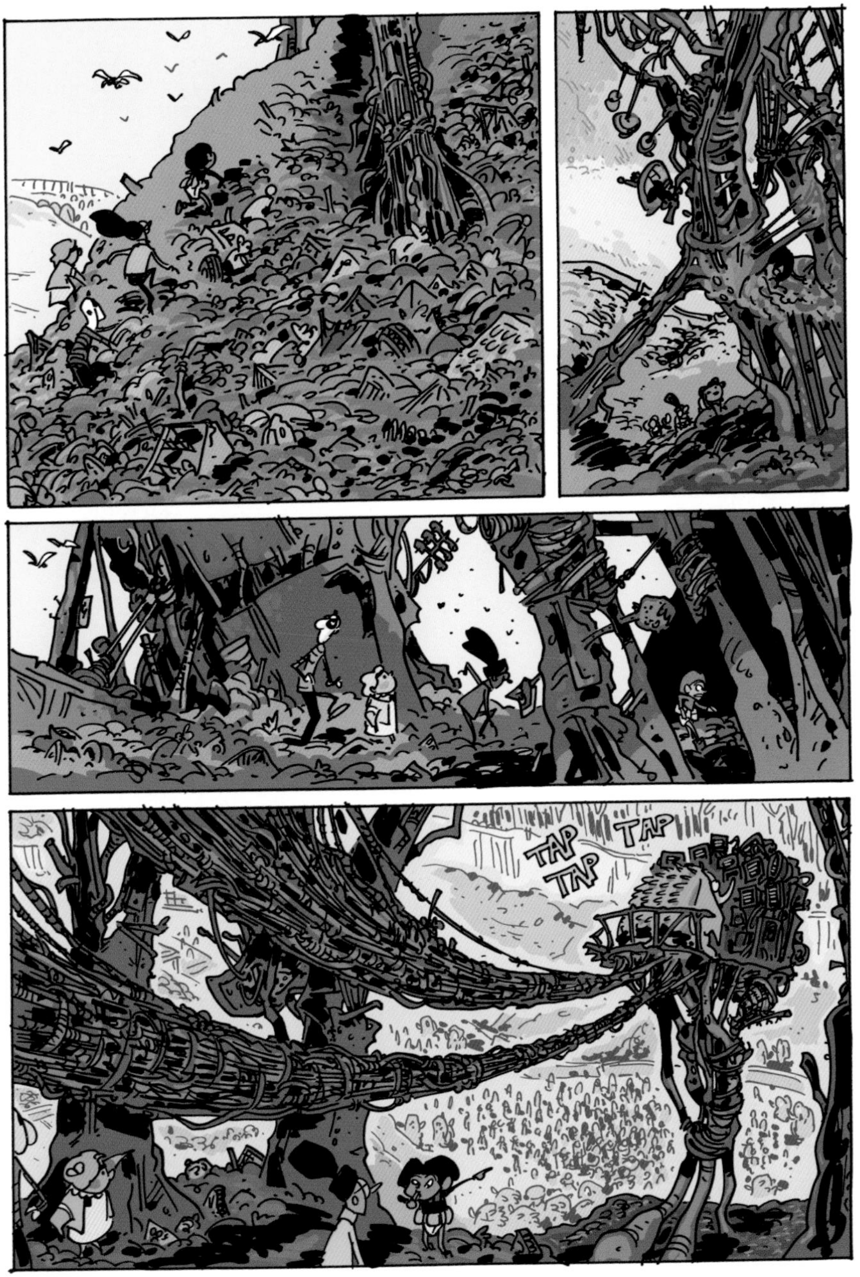
TAP
TAP
TAP

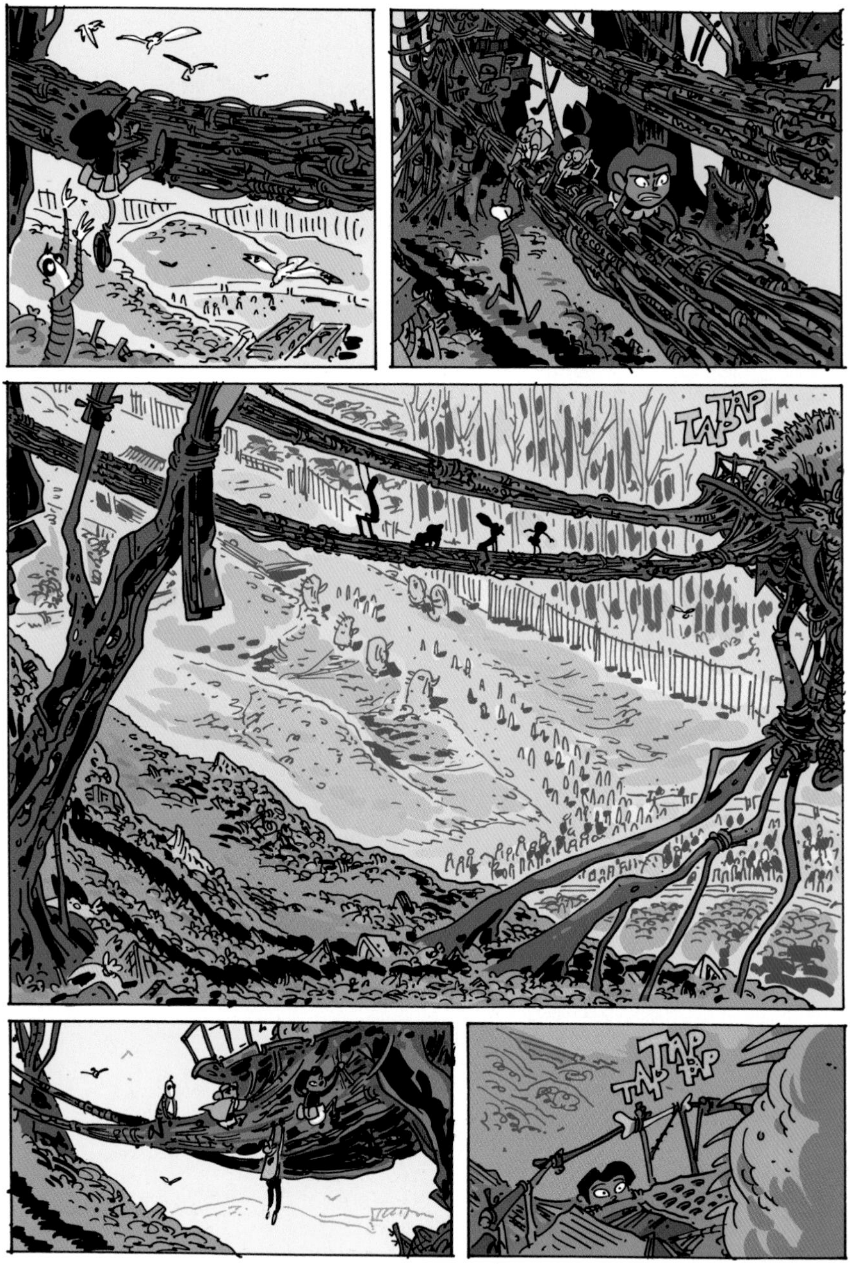
TAP TAP
TAP TAP TAP TAP

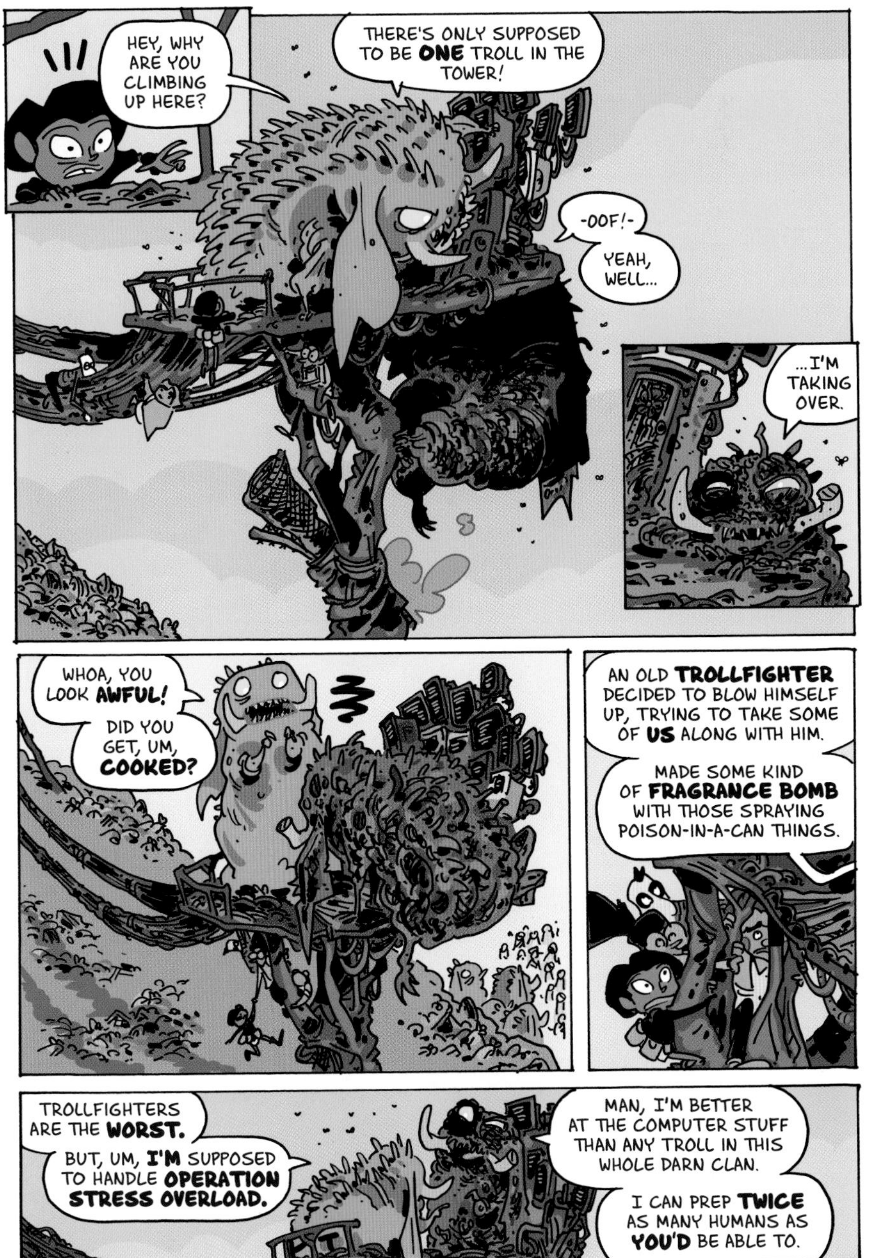
HEY, WHY ARE YOU CLIMBING UP HERE?
THERE'S ONLY SUPPOSED TO BE ONE TROLL IN THE TOWER!
-OOF!-
YEAH, WELL...
...I'M TAKING OVER.
WHOA, YOU LOOK AWFUL!
DID YOU GET, UM, COOKED?
AN OLD TROLLFIGHTER DECIDED TO BLOW HIMSELF UP, TRYING TO TAKE SOME OF US ALONG WITH HIM.
MADE SOME KIND OF FRAGRANCE BOMB WITH THOSE SPRAYING POISON-IN-A-CAN THINGS.
TROLLFIGHTERS ARE THE WORST.
BUT, UM, I'M SUPPOSED TO HANDLE OPERATION STRESS OVERLOAD.
MAN, I'M BETTER AT THE COMPUTER STUFF THAN ANY TROLL IN THIS WHOLE DARN CLAN.
I CAN PREP TWICE AS MANY HUMANS AS YOU'D BE ABLE TO.

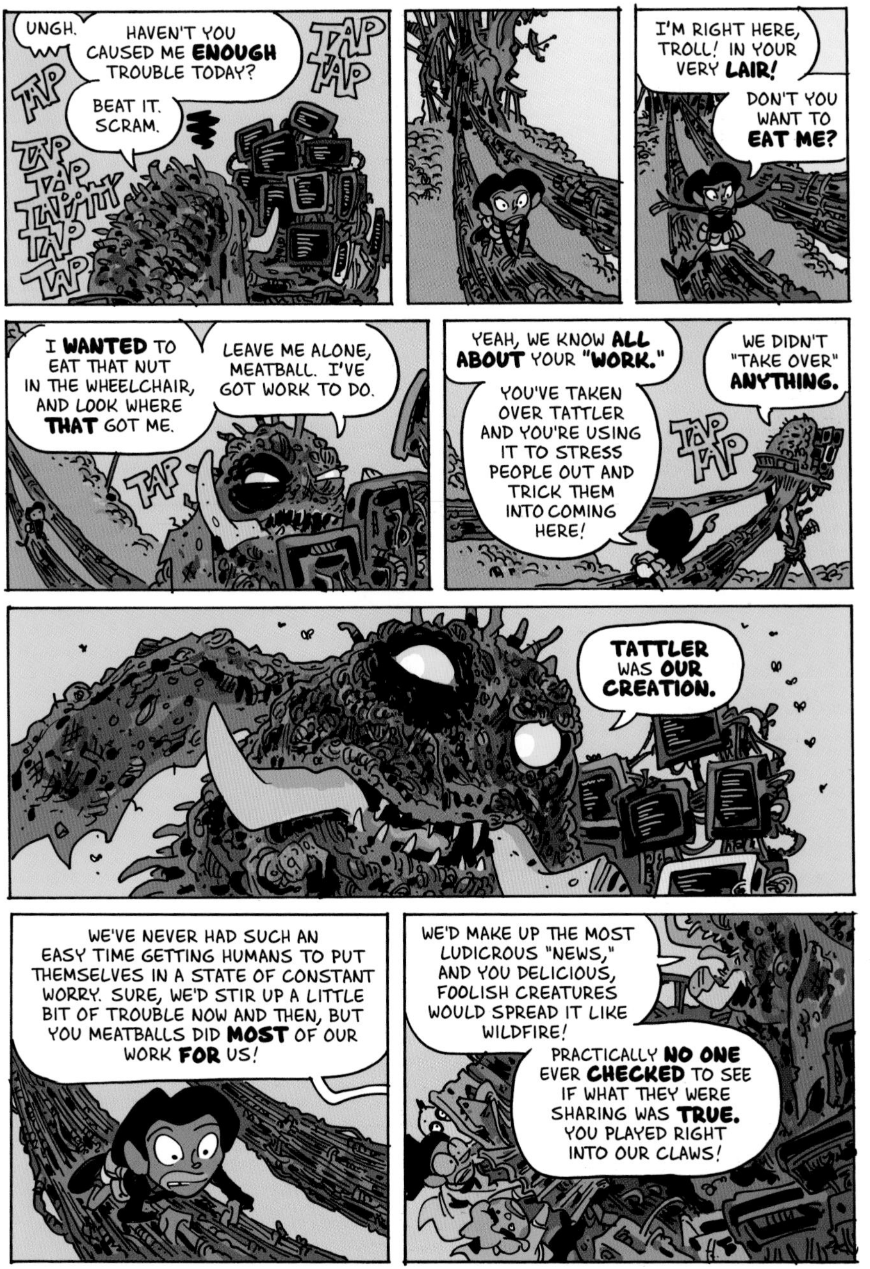
UNGH.
HAVEN'T YOU CAUSED ME **ENOUGH** TROUBLE TODAY?
BEAT IT. SCRAM.
TAP TAP TAP TAP TAP TAPPITY TAP TAP TAP
I'M RIGHT HERE, TROLL! IN YOUR VERY **LAIR!**
DON'T YOU WANT TO **EAT ME?**
I **WANTED** TO EAT THAT NUT IN THE WHEELCHAIR, AND LOOK WHERE **THAT** GOT ME.
LEAVE ME ALONE, MEATBALL. I'VE GOT WORK TO DO.
TAP
YEAH, WE KNOW **ALL ABOUT** YOUR **"WORK."**
YOU'VE TAKEN OVER TATTLER AND YOU'RE USING IT TO STRESS PEOPLE OUT AND TRICK THEM INTO COMING HERE!
WE DIDN'T "TAKE OVER" **ANYTHING.**
TAP TAP
TATTLER WAS **OUR CREATION.**
WE'VE NEVER HAD SUCH AN EASY TIME GETTING HUMANS TO PUT THEMSELVES IN A STATE OF CONSTANT WORRY. SURE, WE'D STIR UP A LITTLE BIT OF TROUBLE NOW AND THEN, BUT YOU MEATBALLS DID **MOST** OF OUR WORK **FOR** US!
WE'D MAKE UP THE MOST LUDICROUS "NEWS," AND YOU DELICIOUS, FOOLISH CREATURES WOULD SPREAD IT LIKE WILDFIRE!
PRACTICALLY **NO ONE** EVER **CHECKED** TO SEE IF WHAT THEY WERE SHARING WAS **TRUE.** YOU PLAYED RIGHT INTO OUR CLAWS!

BETWEEN THESE IMAGINARY CALAMITIES AND YOUR KIND'S PREDELICTION FOR BEING CRUEL TO ONE ANOTHER, WE COULD SIT BACK AND JUST WAIT FOR YOU TO **SIMMER.**

ANOTHER COUPLE OF WEEKS AND YOU'D HAVE BEEN **RIPE** FOR THE **FEAST.**

WE'VE **NEVER** HAD SO MUCH **LEISURE TIME!**

I EVEN HAD A **VACATION NEST** BY THE **WATERFRONT.**

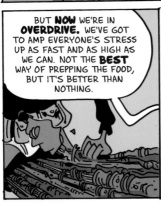

BUT **NOW** WE'RE IN **OVERDRIVE.** WE'VE GOT TO AMP EVERYONE'S STRESS UP AS FAST AND AS HIGH AS WE CAN. NOT THE **BEST** WAY OF PREPPING THE FOOD, BUT IT'S BETTER THAN NOTHING.

LIKE MICROWAVING SOMETHING THAT SHOULD BE SLOW-ROASTED—

HEY! WHAT ARE YOU DOING?!

I'M CUTTING THESE CABLES. FIGURE THEY'RE WHAT'S CARRYING YOUR COMMANDS TO THE ANTENNAS AND STUFF.

WELL, **STOP IT!**

NO WAY, BARBECUE.

YOU WANT ME TO STOP, YOU'RE GONNA HAVE TO **MAKE ME.**

YOU WANT ME TO EAT YOU?

FINE.

I'LL EAT YOU.

CONSIDER YOURSELF A **POWER SNACK.** A LITTLE BOOST OF ENERGY TO HELP ME FOCUS ON THE TASK AT HAND.

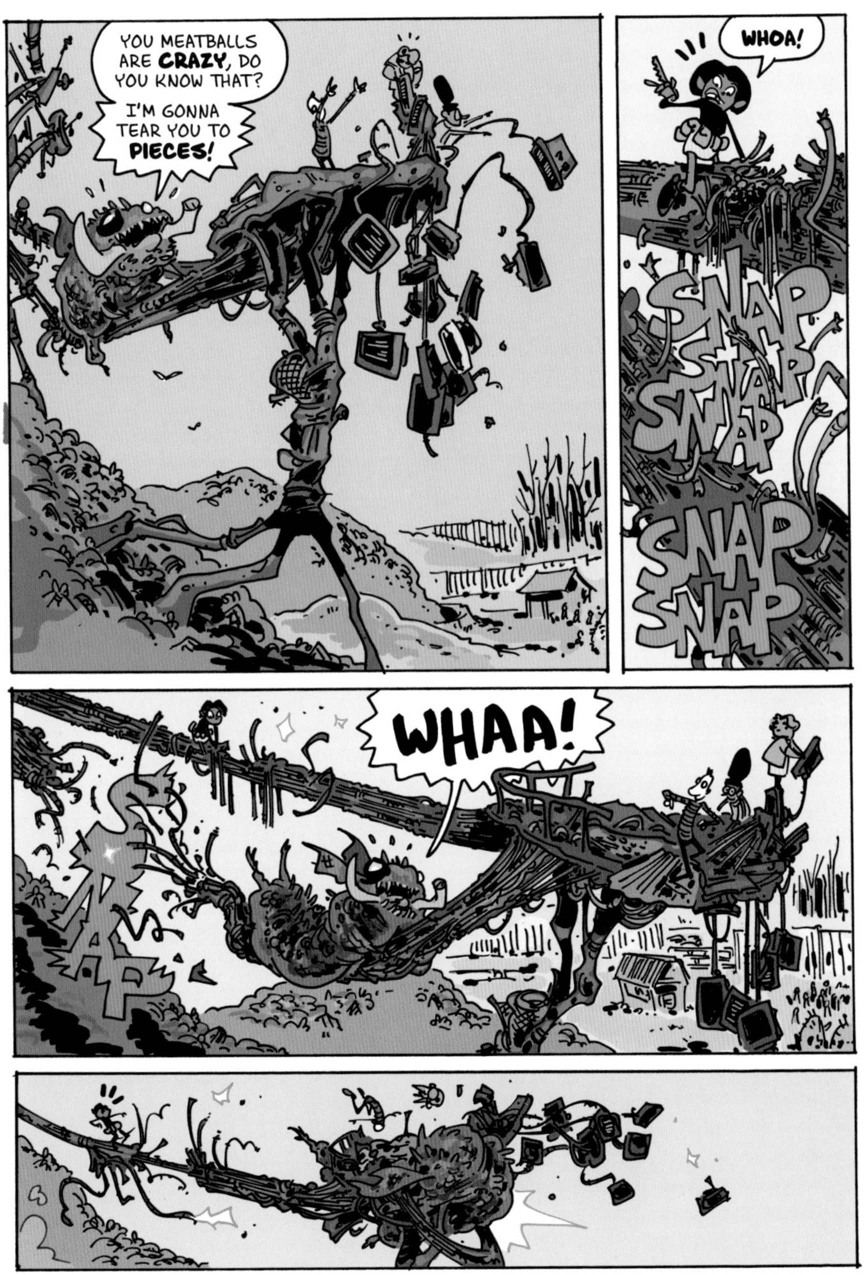

YOU MEATBALLS ARE **CRAZY**, DO YOU KNOW THAT?
I'M GONNA TEAR YOU TO **PIECES!**
WHOA!
SNAP SNAP SNAP
SNAP SNAP
WHAA!

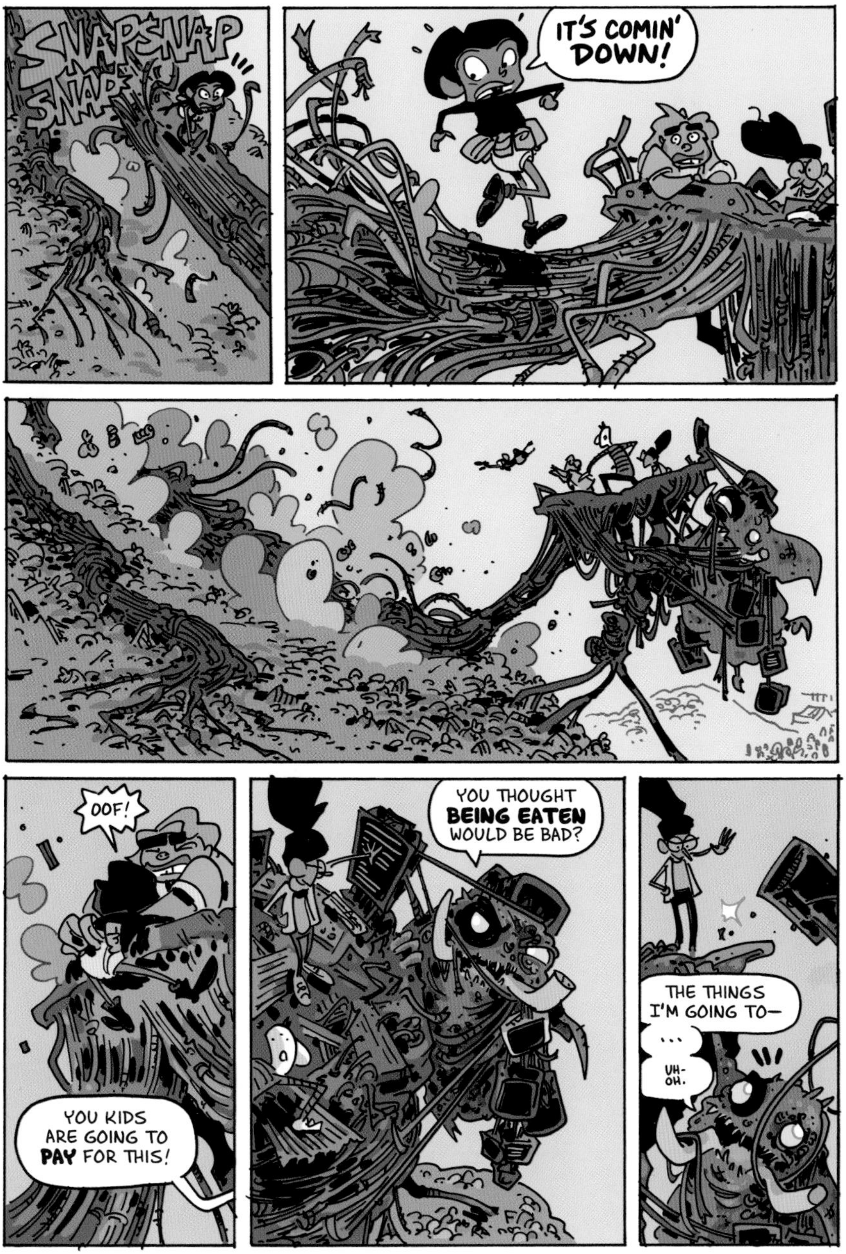
SNAPSNAP SNAP
IT'S COMIN' DOWN!
OOF!
YOU KIDS ARE GOING TO **PAY** FOR THIS!
YOU THOUGHT **BEING EATEN** WOULD BE BAD?
THE THINGS I'M GOING TO—
...
UH-OH.

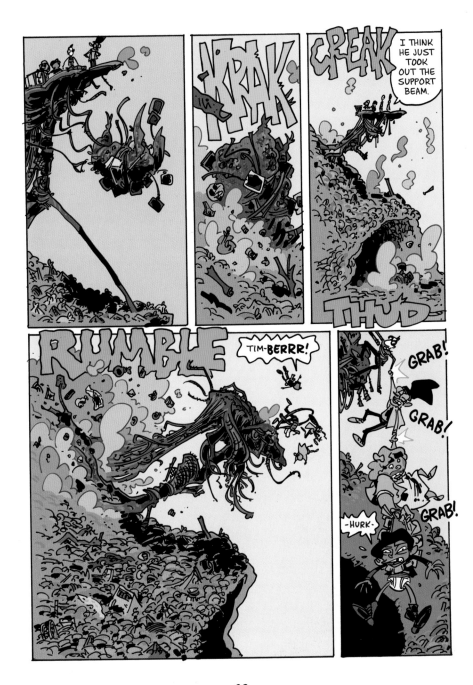

99

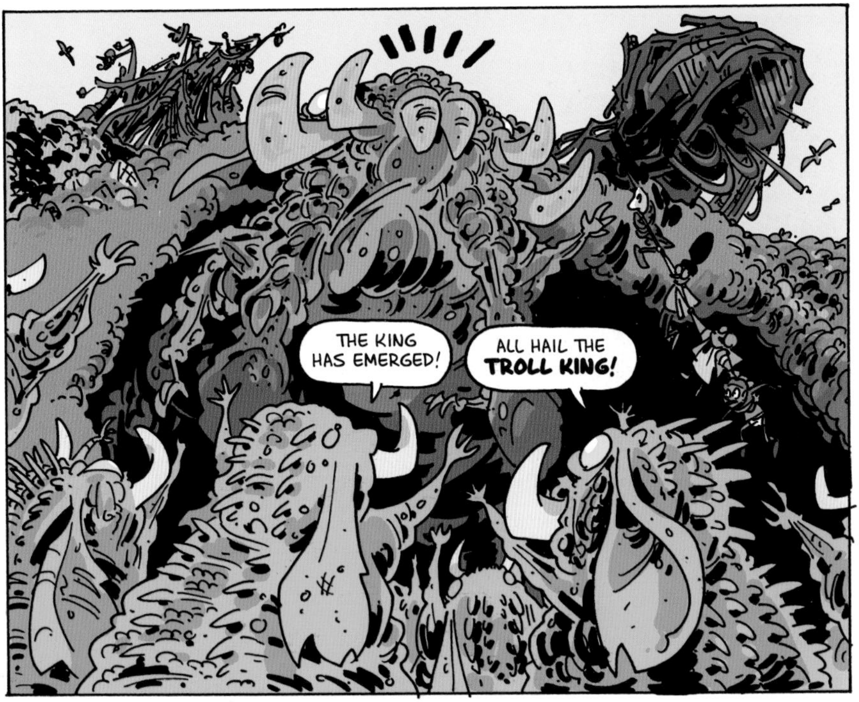
THE KING HAS EMERGED!
ALL HAIL THE **TROLL KING!**

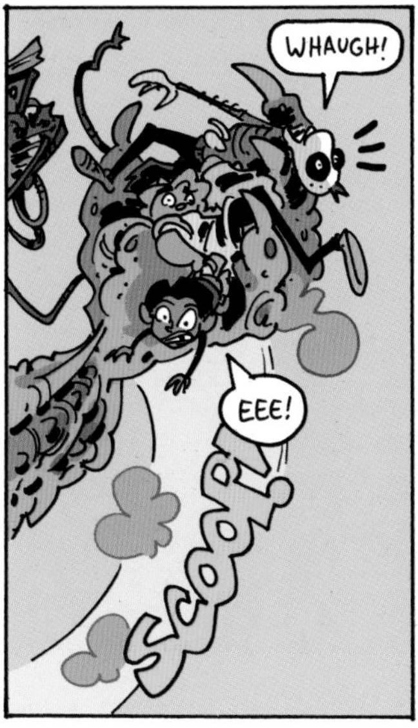
WHAUGH!
EEE!
SCOOP!

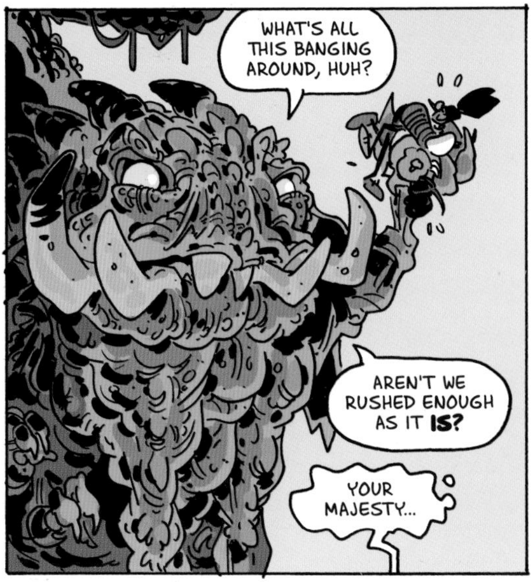
WHAT'S ALL THIS BANGING AROUND, HUH?
AREN'T WE RUSHED ENOUGH AS IT **IS?**
YOUR MAJESTY...

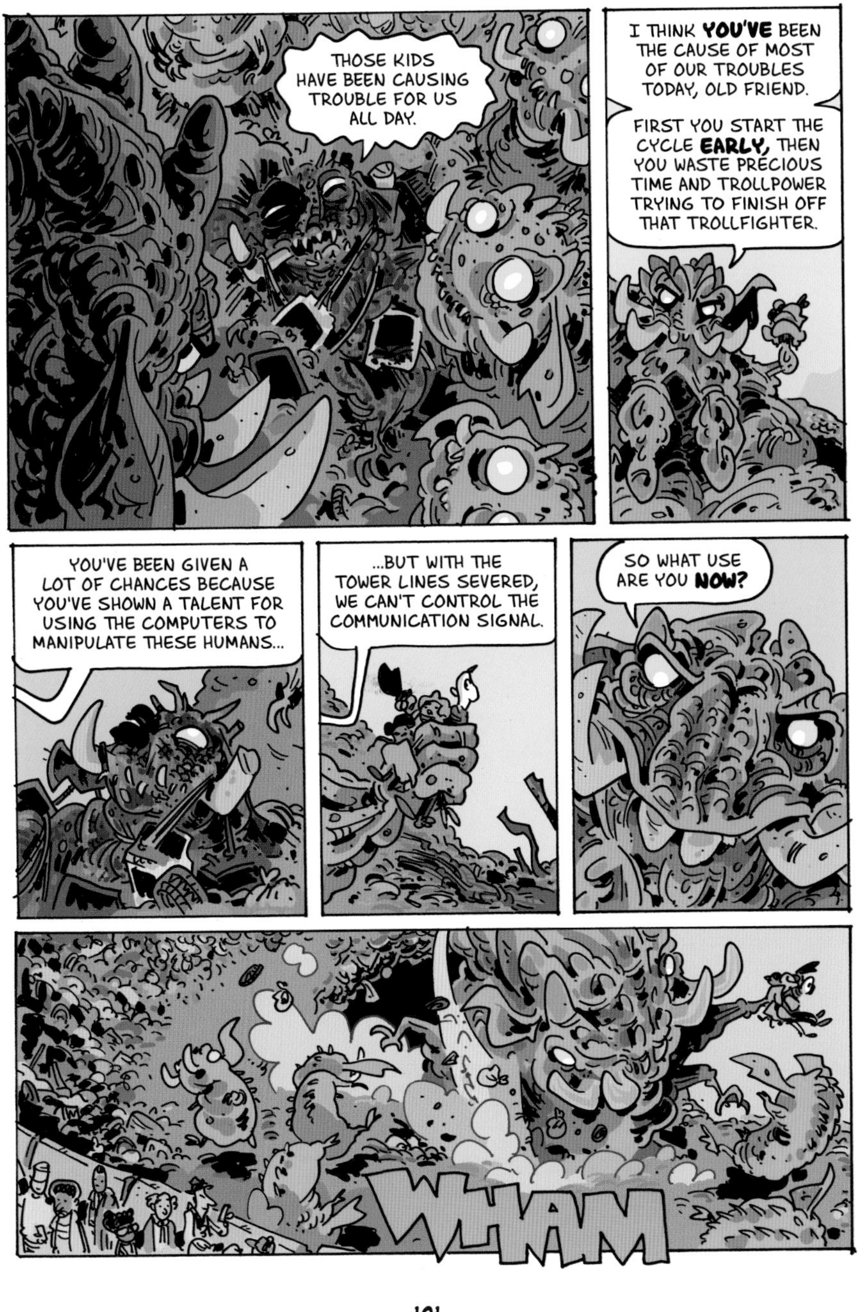
THOSE KIDS HAVE BEEN CAUSING TROUBLE FOR US ALL DAY.
I THINK **YOU'VE** BEEN THE CAUSE OF MOST OF OUR TROUBLES TODAY, OLD FRIEND.
FIRST YOU START THE CYCLE **EARLY,** THEN YOU WASTE PRECIOUS TIME AND TROLLPOWER TRYING TO FINISH OFF THAT TROLLFIGHTER.
YOU'VE BEEN GIVEN A LOT OF CHANCES BECAUSE YOU'VE SHOWN A TALENT FOR USING THE COMPUTERS TO MANIPULATE THESE HUMANS...
...BUT WITH THE TOWER LINES SEVERED, WE CAN'T CONTROL THE COMMUNICATION SIGNAL.
SO WHAT USE ARE YOU **NOW?**
WHAM

WE DON'T WANT THEM TO **PANIC** AND TRY TO **ESCAPE** BEFORE THEY'RE **PENNED IN...**

...BUT WE NEEDN'T WORRY ABOUT **THAT** WITH **YOU,** DO WE?

YOU WE CAN EAT **RIGHT NOW.**

ERRK!

OH, THAT IS **SO GROSS.**

WHY ARE YOU CREEPS ROLLING AROUND IN THE **GARBAGE?**

WE'RE FIGHTING A GIANT TROLL IN AN EFFORT TO SAVE AS MANY PEOPLE AS WE CAN FROM BEING EATEN.

RUN, MADISON! SAVE YOURSELF!

GIVE IT A **REST,** CREEPS!

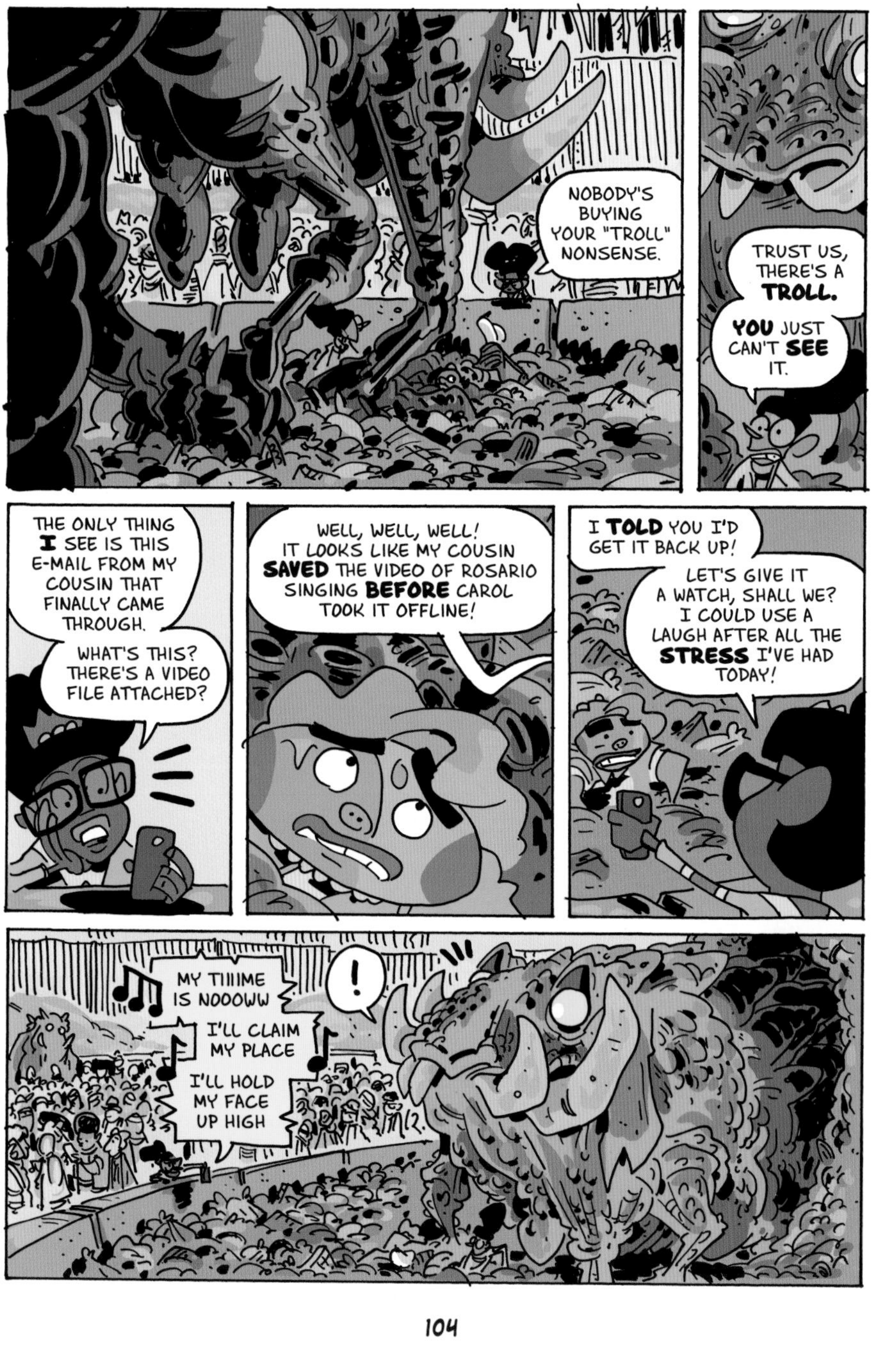
NOBODY'S BUYING YOUR "TROLL" NONSENSE.
TRUST US, THERE'S A **TROLL.**
YOU JUST CAN'T **SEE** IT.
THE ONLY THING **I** SEE IS THIS E-MAIL FROM MY COUSIN THAT FINALLY CAME THROUGH.
WHAT'S THIS? THERE'S A VIDEO FILE ATTACHED?
WELL, WELL, WELL! IT LOOKS LIKE MY COUSIN **SAVED** THE VIDEO OF ROSARIO SINGING **BEFORE** CAROL TOOK IT OFFLINE!
I **TOLD** YOU I'D GET IT BACK UP!
LET'S GIVE IT A WATCH, SHALL WE? I COULD USE A LAUGH AFTER ALL THE **STRESS** I'VE HAD TODAY!
MY TIIIIME IS NOOOWW
I'LL CLAIM MY PLACE
I'LL HOLD MY FACE UP HIGH
!

NOTHING'S GONNA STOP ME FROM BEING A PRINCESS ♪

ROAR

NOTHING'S GONNA STOP ME FROM BEING A PRINCESS ♪

SOME MAY POINT AND SOME MAY SCOFF ♪

TURN THAT **HORRIBLE** NOISE **OFF!**

BUT I WILL ONLY SHAKE IT OFF ♪

NOTHING'S GON—

CRASH

DID YOU GUYS SERIOUSLY JUST BREAK MY PHONE?! YOU ARE GONNA BE IN **SO MUCH TROUBLE!**

EVEN A HIDEOUS MONSTER CAN'T STAND MY SINGING!

AWW, WHAT DOES **HE** KNOW?

SURE, MAYBE YOU'RE A LITTLE **WARBLY,** BUT—

SHH!

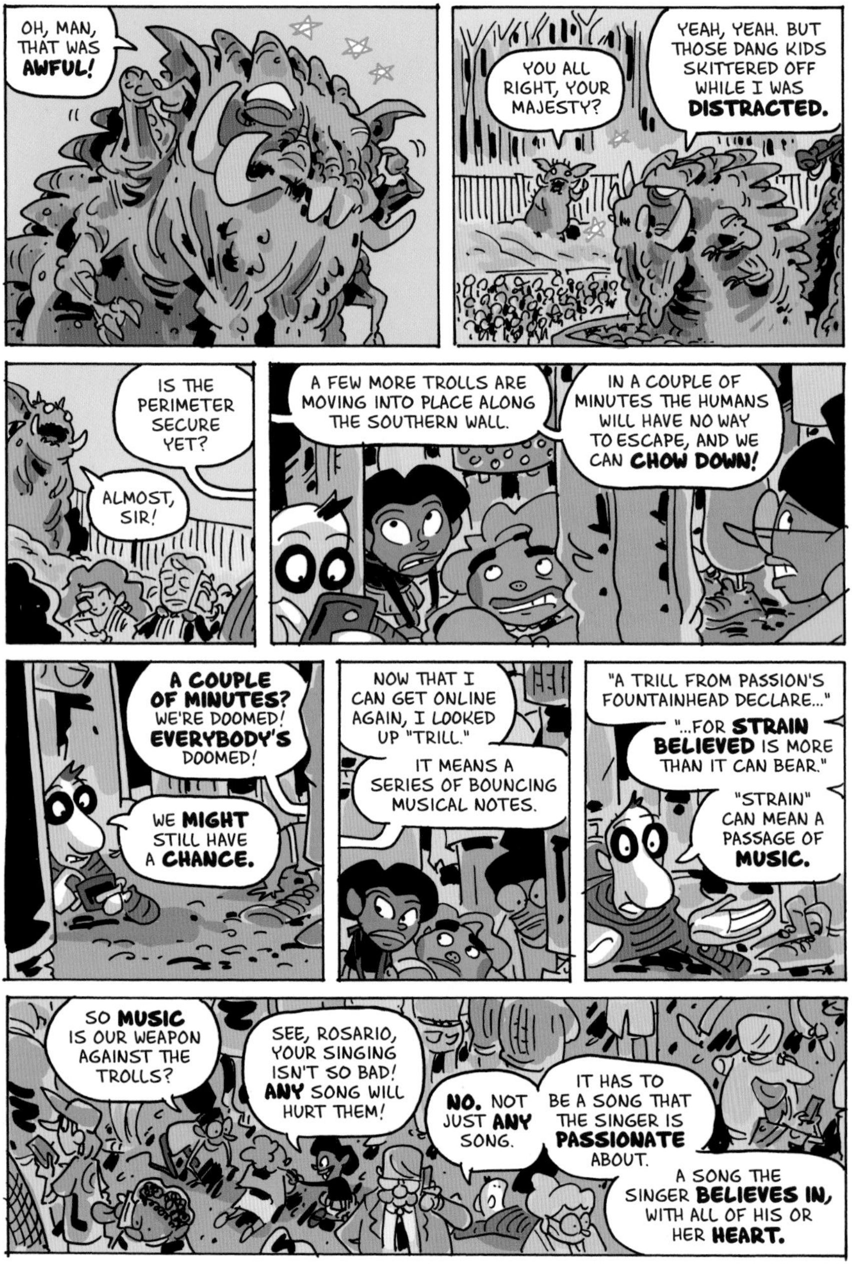
OH, MAN, THAT WAS **AWFUL!**
YOU ALL RIGHT, YOUR MAJESTY?
YEAH, YEAH. BUT THOSE DANG KIDS SKITTERED OFF WHILE I WAS **DISTRACTED.**
IS THE PERIMETER SECURE YET?
ALMOST, SIR!
A FEW MORE TROLLS ARE MOVING INTO PLACE ALONG THE SOUTHERN WALL.
IN A COUPLE OF MINUTES THE HUMANS WILL HAVE NO WAY TO ESCAPE, AND WE CAN **CHOW DOWN!**
A COUPLE OF MINUTES? WE'RE DOOMED! **EVERYBODY'S** DOOMED!
WE **MIGHT** STILL HAVE A **CHANCE.**
NOW THAT I CAN GET ONLINE AGAIN, I LOOKED UP "TRILL."
IT MEANS A SERIES OF BOUNCING MUSICAL NOTES.
"A TRILL FROM PASSION'S FOUNTAINHEAD DECLARE..."
"...FOR **STRAIN BELIEVED** IS MORE THAN IT CAN BEAR."
"STRAIN" CAN MEAN A PASSAGE OF **MUSIC.**
SO **MUSIC** IS OUR WEAPON AGAINST THE TROLLS?
SEE, ROSARIO, YOUR SINGING ISN'T SO BAD! **ANY** SONG WILL HURT THEM!
NO. NOT JUST **ANY** SONG.
IT HAS TO BE A SONG THAT THE SINGER IS **PASSIONATE** ABOUT.
A SONG THE SINGER **BELIEVES IN,** WITH ALL OF HIS OR HER **HEART.**

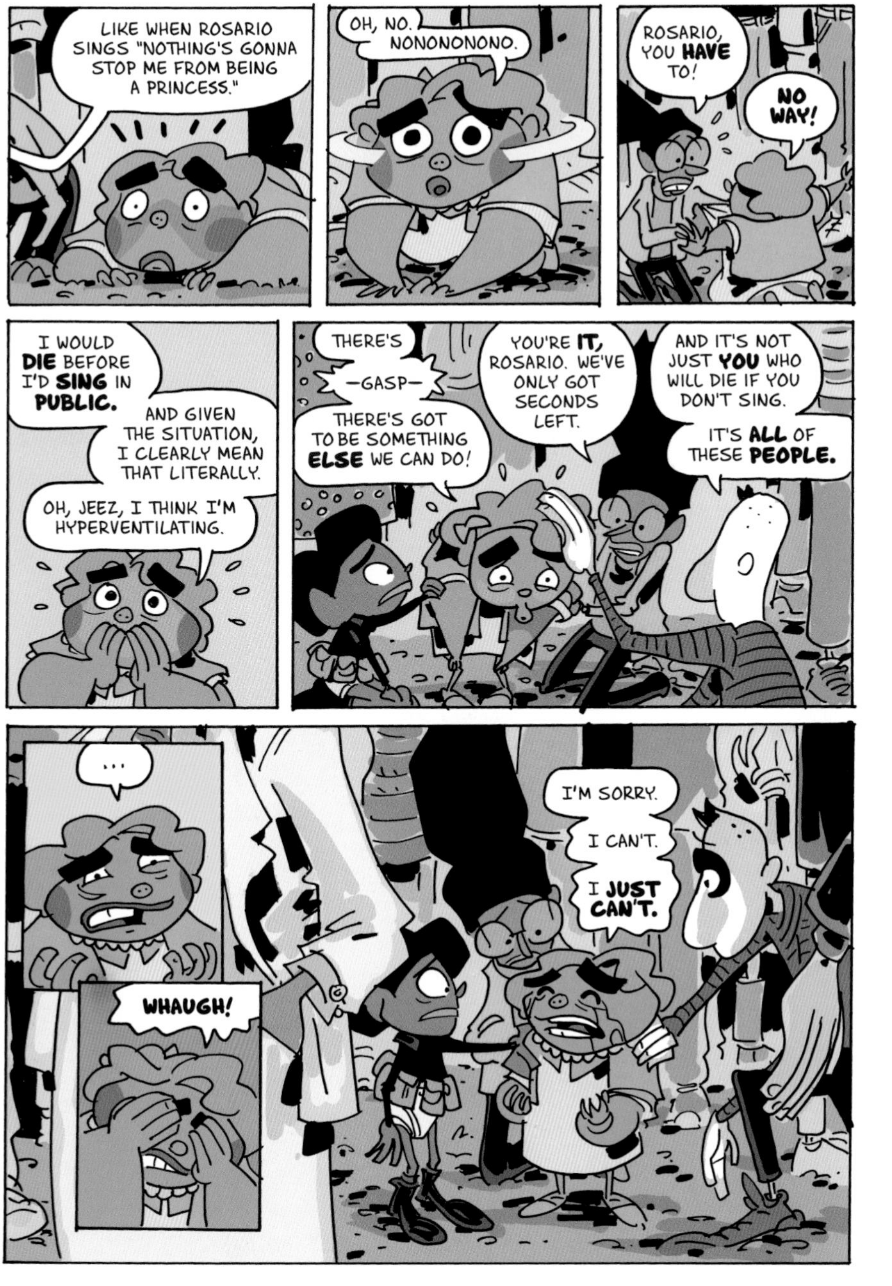

LIKE WHEN ROSARIO SINGS "NOTHING'S GONNA STOP ME FROM BEING A PRINCESS."
OH, NO. NONONONONO.
ROSARIO, YOU HAVE TO!
NO WAY!
I WOULD DIE BEFORE I'D SING IN PUBLIC.
AND GIVEN THE SITUATION, I CLEARLY MEAN THAT LITERALLY.
OH, JEEZ, I THINK I'M HYPERVENTILATING.
THERE'S
—GASP—
THERE'S GOT TO BE SOMETHING ELSE WE CAN DO!
YOU'RE IT, ROSARIO. WE'VE ONLY GOT SECONDS LEFT.
AND IT'S NOT JUST YOU WHO WILL DIE IF YOU DON'T SING.
IT'S ALL OF THESE PEOPLE.
...
WHAUGH!
I'M SORRY.
I CAN'T.
I JUST CAN'T.

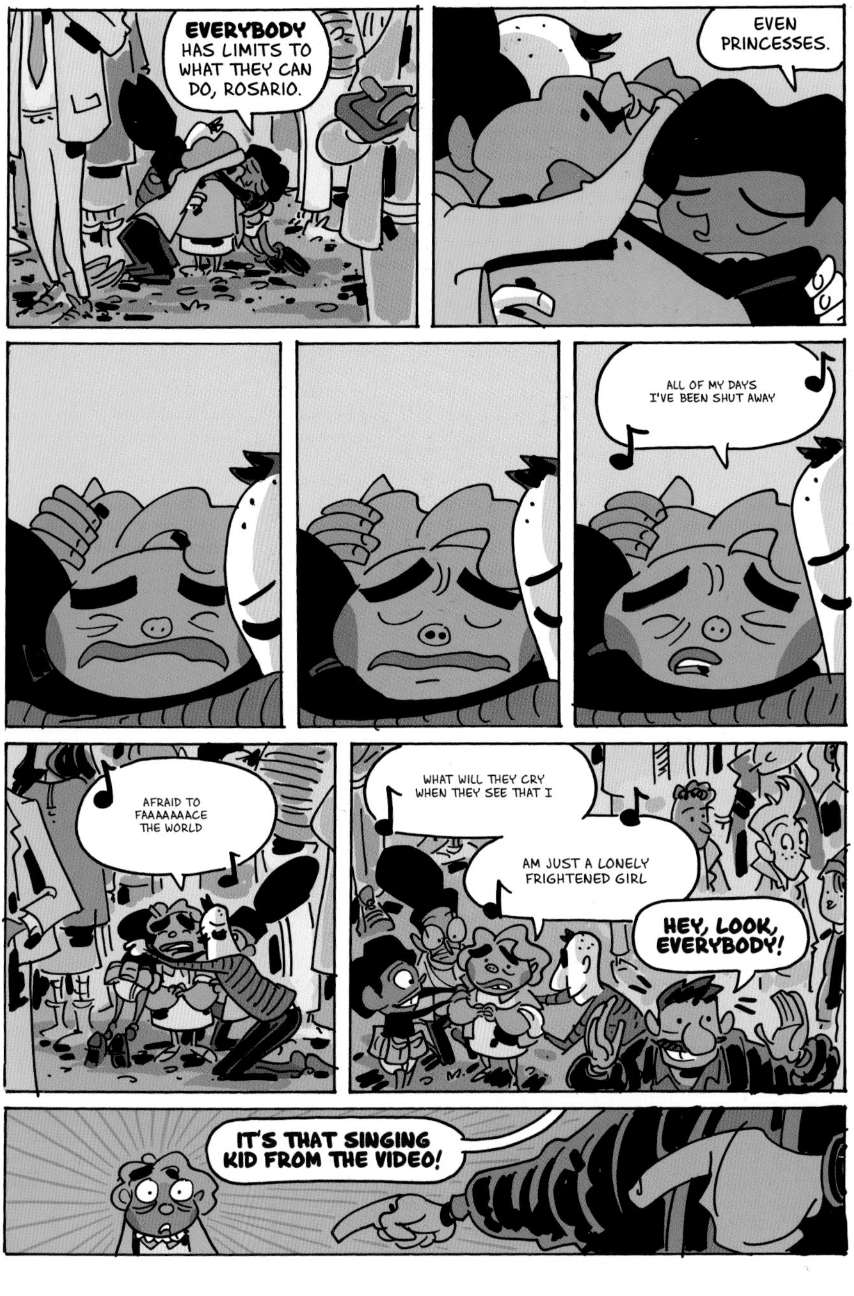
EVERYBODY HAS LIMITS TO WHAT THEY CAN DO, ROSARIO.
EVEN PRINCESSES.
ALL OF MY DAYS I'VE BEEN SHUT AWAY
AFRAID TO FAAAAAAACE THE WORLD
WHAT WILL THEY CRY WHEN THEY SEE THAT I
AM JUST A LONELY FRIGHTENED GIRL
HEY, LOOK, EVERYBODY!
IT'S THAT SINGING KID FROM THE VIDEO!

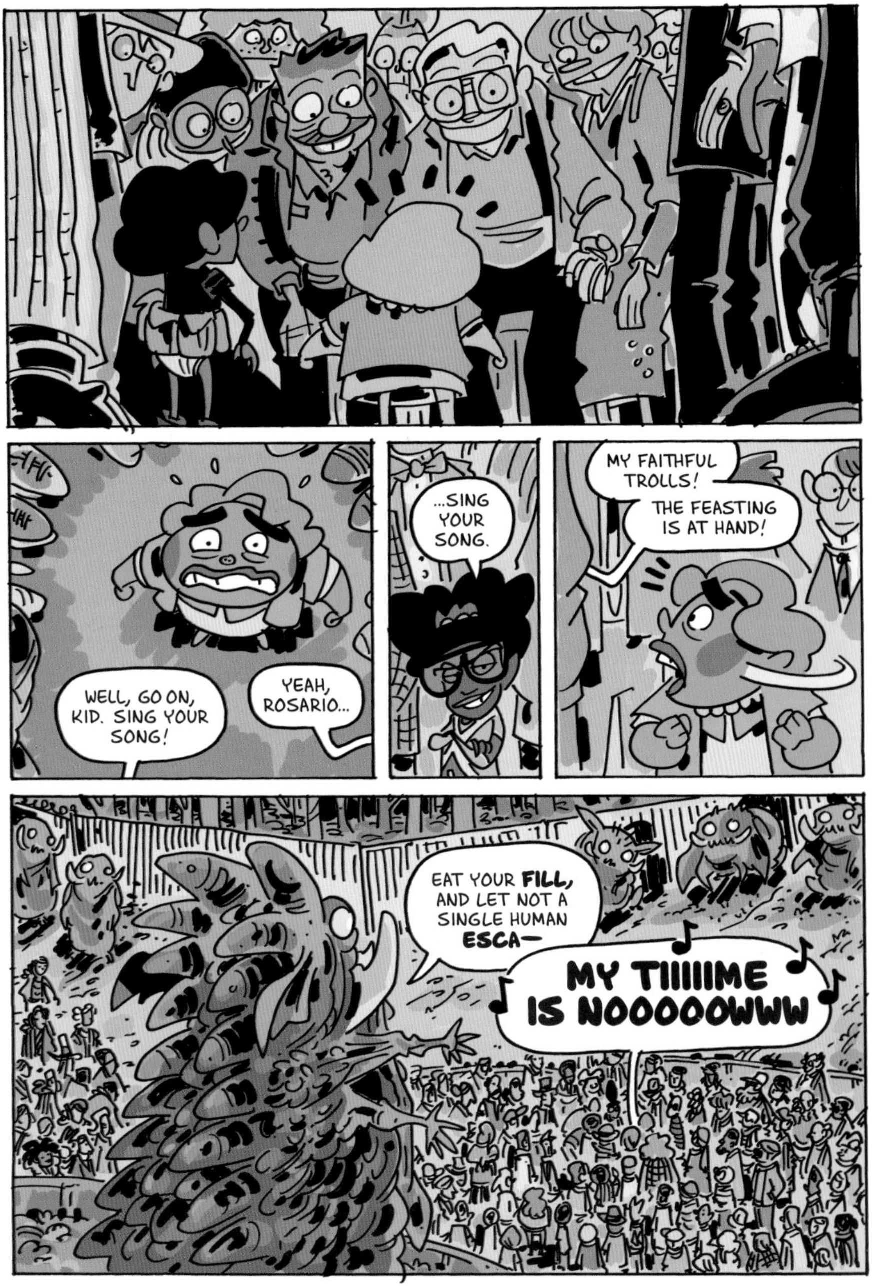

WELL, GO ON, KID. SING YOUR SONG!
YEAH, ROSARIO...
...SING YOUR SONG.
MY FAITHFUL TROLLS!
THE FEASTING IS AT HAND!
EAT YOUR **FILL,** AND LET NOT A SINGLE HUMAN **ESCA—**
MY TIIIIIME IS NOOOOOWWW

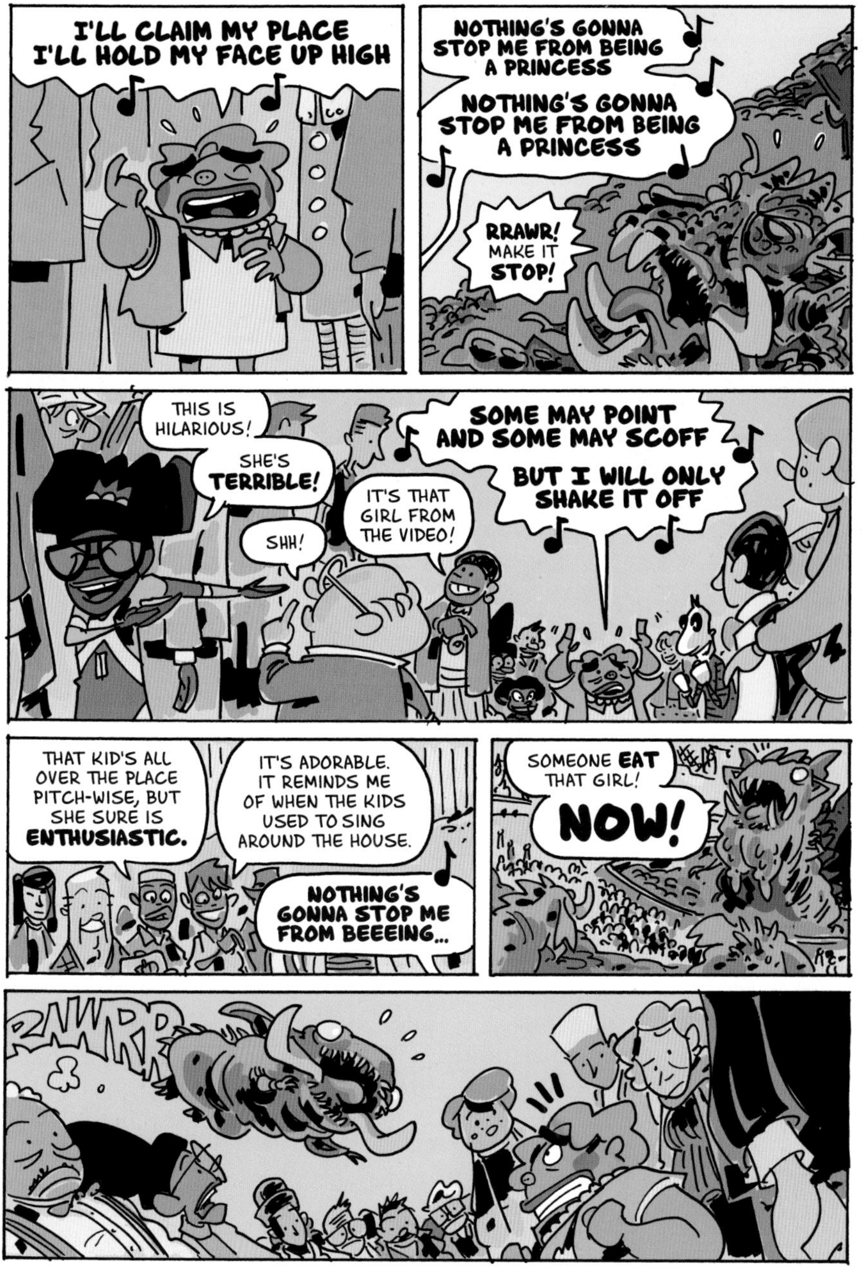
I'LL CLAIM MY PLACE I'LL HOLD MY FACE UP HIGH
NOTHING'S GONNA STOP ME FROM BEING A PRINCESS
NOTHING'S GONNA STOP ME FROM BEING A PRINCESS
RRAWR! MAKE IT STOP!
THIS IS HILARIOUS!
SHE'S TERRIBLE!
SHH!
IT'S THAT GIRL FROM THE VIDEO!
SOME MAY POINT AND SOME MAY SCOFF
BUT I WILL ONLY SHAKE IT OFF
THAT KID'S ALL OVER THE PLACE PITCH-WISE, BUT SHE SURE IS ENTHUSIASTIC.
IT'S ADORABLE. IT REMINDS ME OF WHEN THE KIDS USED TO SING AROUND THE HOUSE.
NOTHING'S GONNA STOP ME FROM BEEEING...
SOMEONE EAT THAT GIRL!
NOW!
RAWRR

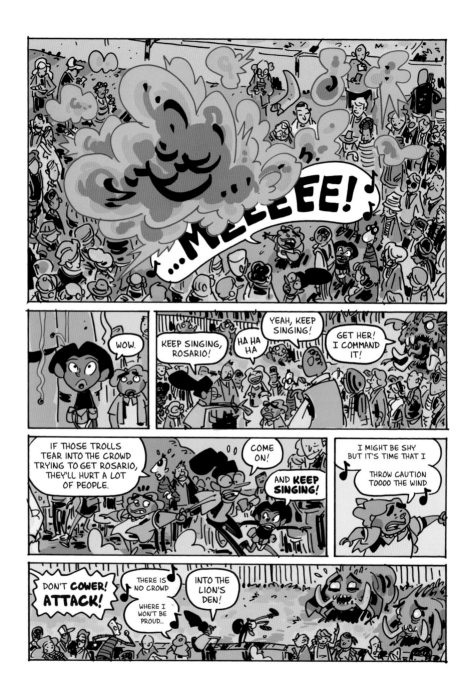

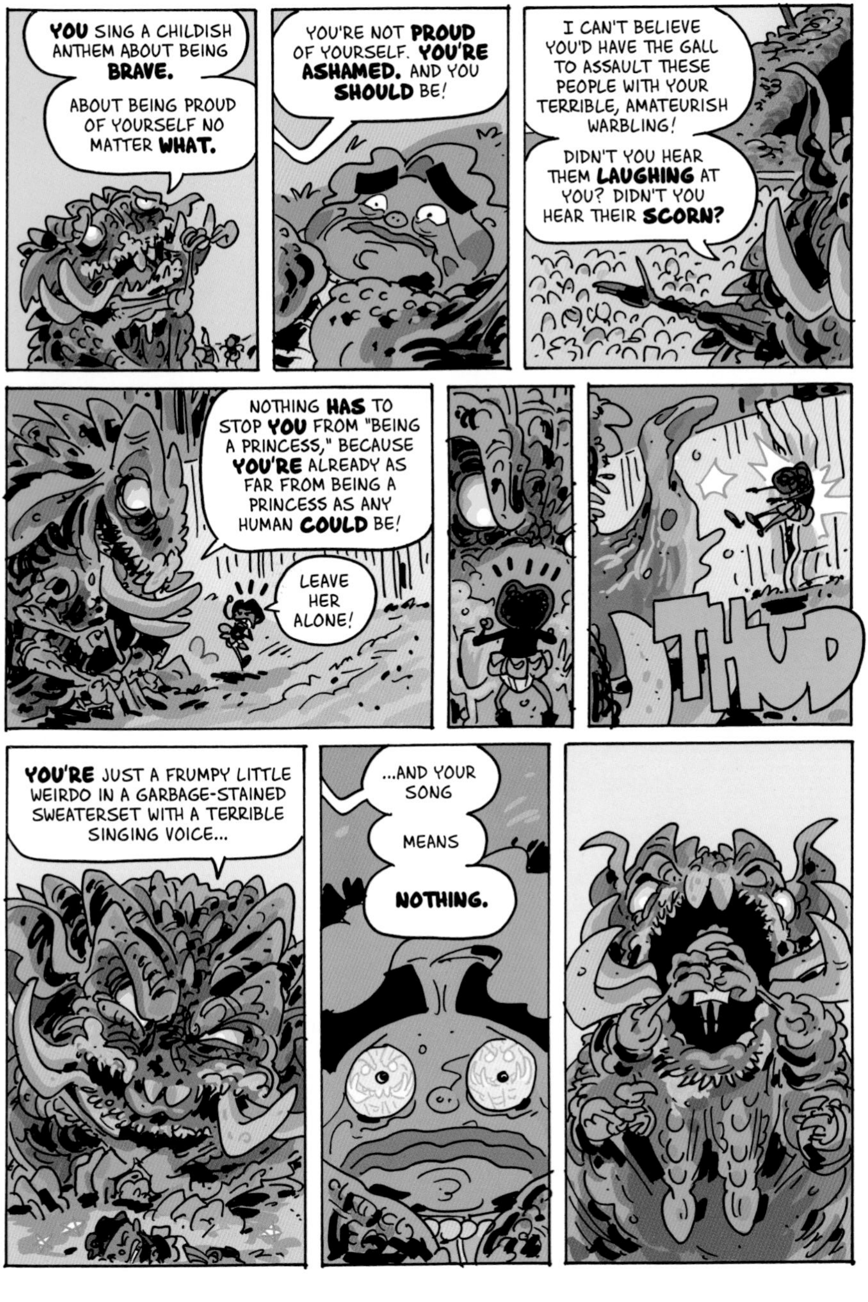
YOU SING A CHILDISH ANTHEM ABOUT BEING BRAVE.
ABOUT BEING PROUD OF YOURSELF NO MATTER WHAT.
YOU'RE NOT PROUD OF YOURSELF. YOU'RE ASHAMED. AND YOU SHOULD BE!
I CAN'T BELIEVE YOU'D HAVE THE GALL TO ASSAULT THESE PEOPLE WITH YOUR TERRIBLE, AMATEURISH WARBLING!
DIDN'T YOU HEAR THEM LAUGHING AT YOU? DIDN'T YOU HEAR THEIR SCORN?
NOTHING HAS TO STOP YOU FROM "BEING A PRINCESS," BECAUSE YOU'RE ALREADY AS FAR FROM BEING A PRINCESS AS ANY HUMAN COULD BE!
LEAVE HER ALONE!
THUD
YOU'RE JUST A FRUMPY LITTLE WEIRDO IN A GARBAGE-STAINED SWEATERSET WITH A TERRIBLE SINGING VOICE...
...AND YOUR SONG
MEANS
NOTHING.

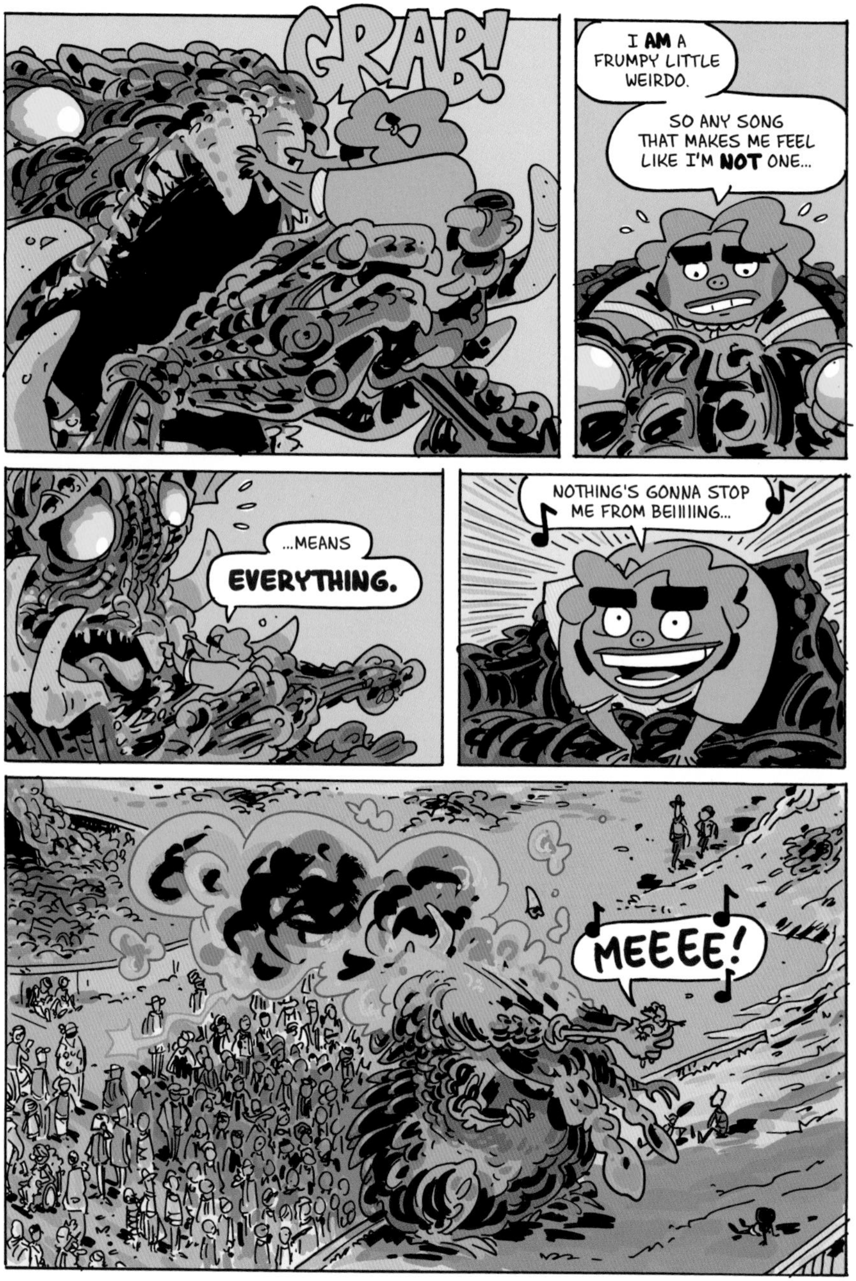
GRAB!
I AM A FRUMPY LITTLE WEIRDO.
SO ANY SONG THAT MAKES ME FEEL LIKE I'M NOT ONE...
...MEANS EVERYTHING.
NOTHING'S GONNA STOP ME FROM BEIIIIING...
MEEEE!

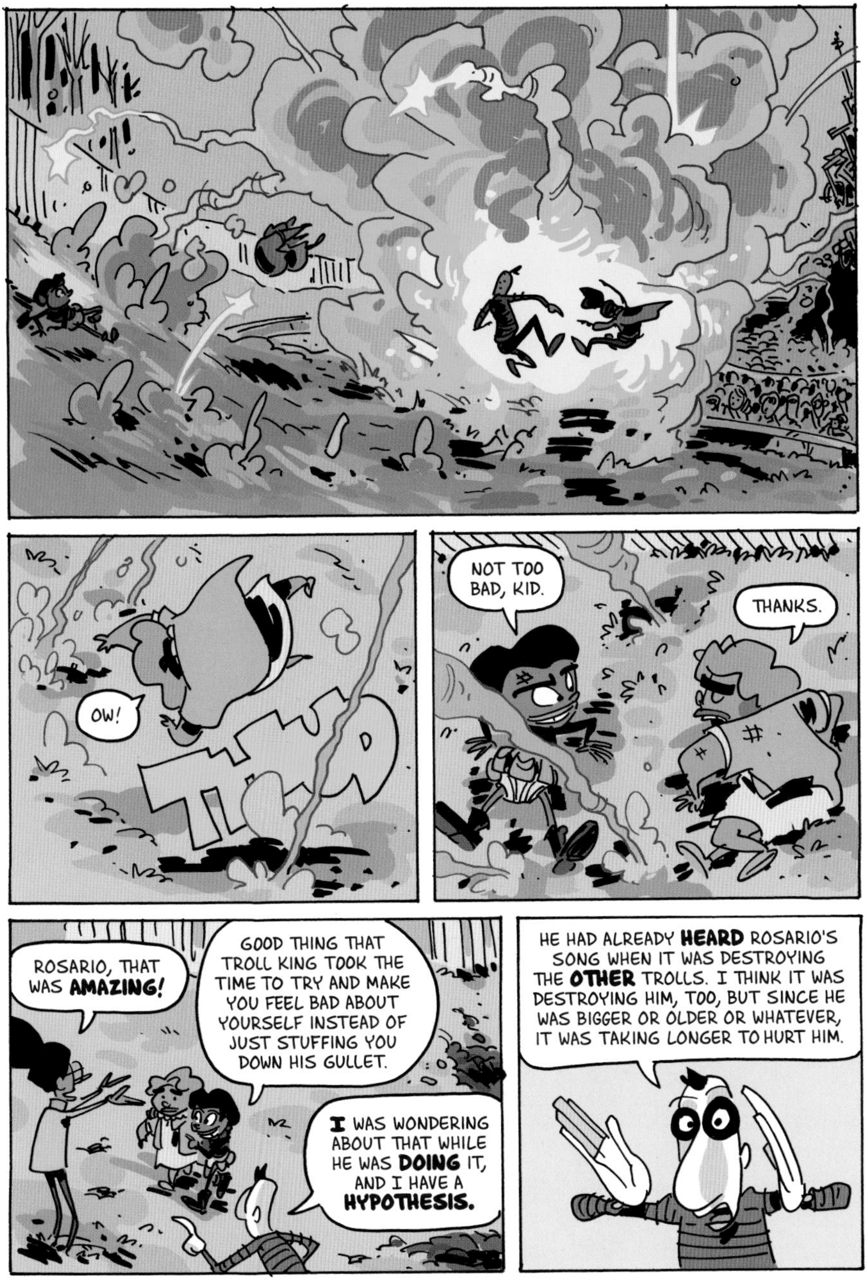
OW!
NOT TOO BAD, KID.
THANKS.
ROSARIO, THAT WAS **AMAZING!**
GOOD THING THAT TROLL KING TOOK THE TIME TO TRY AND MAKE YOU FEEL BAD ABOUT YOURSELF INSTEAD OF JUST STUFFING YOU DOWN HIS GULLET.
I WAS WONDERING ABOUT THAT WHILE HE WAS **DOING** IT, AND I HAVE A **HYPOTHESIS.**
HE HAD ALREADY **HEARD** ROSARIO'S SONG WHEN IT WAS DESTROYING THE **OTHER** TROLLS. I THINK IT WAS DESTROYING HIM, TOO, BUT SINCE HE WAS BIGGER OR OLDER OR WHATEVER, IT WAS TAKING LONGER TO HURT HIM.

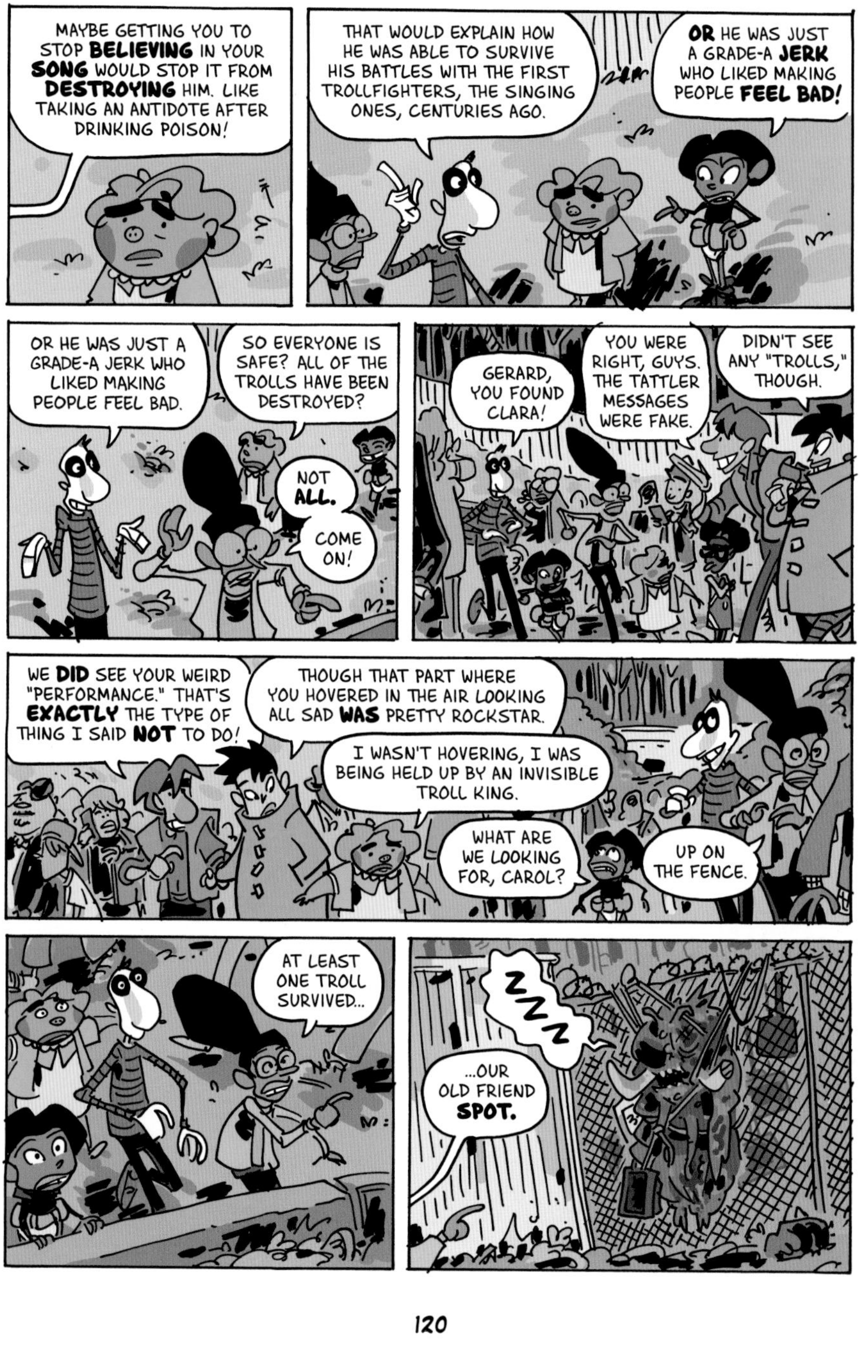
MAYBE GETTING YOU TO STOP **BELIEVING** IN YOUR **SONG** WOULD STOP IT FROM **DESTROYING** HIM. LIKE TAKING AN ANTIDOTE AFTER DRINKING POISON!
THAT WOULD EXPLAIN HOW HE WAS ABLE TO SURVIVE HIS BATTLES WITH THE FIRST TROLLFIGHTERS, THE SINGING ONES, CENTURIES AGO.
OR HE WAS JUST A GRADE-A **JERK** WHO LIKED MAKING PEOPLE **FEEL BAD!**
OR HE WAS JUST A GRADE-A JERK WHO LIKED MAKING PEOPLE FEEL BAD.
SO EVERYONE IS SAFE? ALL OF THE TROLLS HAVE BEEN DESTROYED?
NOT **ALL.**
COME ON!
GERARD, YOU FOUND CLARA!
YOU WERE RIGHT, GUYS. THE TATTLER MESSAGES WERE FAKE.
DIDN'T SEE ANY "TROLLS," THOUGH.
WE **DID** SEE YOUR WEIRD "PERFORMANCE." THAT'S **EXACTLY** THE TYPE OF THING I SAID **NOT** TO DO!
THOUGH THAT PART WHERE YOU HOVERED IN THE AIR LOOKING ALL SAD **WAS** PRETTY ROCKSTAR.
I WASN'T HOVERING, I WAS BEING HELD UP BY AN INVISIBLE TROLL KING.
WHAT ARE WE LOOKING FOR, CAROL?
UP ON THE FENCE.
AT LEAST ONE TROLL SURVIVED...
ZZZ
...OUR OLD FRIEND **SPOT.**

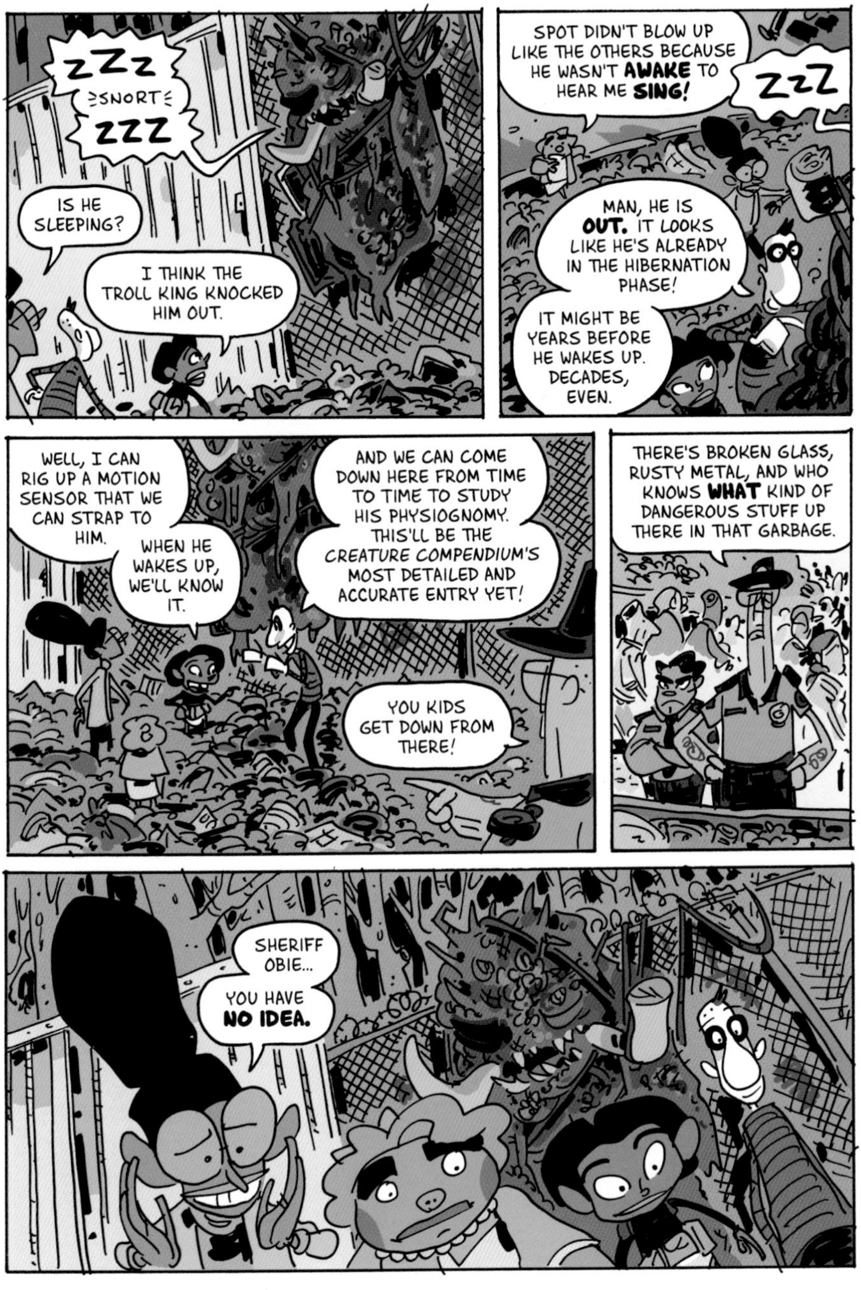
zZz
SNORT
ZZZ
IS HE SLEEPING?
I THINK THE TROLL KING KNOCKED HIM OUT.
SPOT DIDN'T BLOW UP LIKE THE OTHERS BECAUSE HE WASN'T **AWAKE** TO HEAR ME **SING!**
ZzZ
MAN, HE IS **OUT.** IT LOOKS LIKE HE'S ALREADY IN THE HIBERNATION PHASE!
IT MIGHT BE YEARS BEFORE HE WAKES UP. DECADES, EVEN.
WELL, I CAN RIG UP A MOTION SENSOR THAT WE CAN STRAP TO HIM.
WHEN HE WAKES UP, WE'LL KNOW IT.
AND WE CAN COME DOWN HERE FROM TIME TO TIME TO STUDY HIS PHYSIOGNOMY. THIS'LL BE THE CREATURE COMPENDIUM'S MOST DETAILED AND ACCURATE ENTRY YET!
YOU KIDS GET DOWN FROM THERE!
THERE'S BROKEN GLASS, RUSTY METAL, AND WHO KNOWS **WHAT** KIND OF DANGEROUS STUFF UP THERE IN THAT GARBAGE.
SHERIFF OBIE...
YOU HAVE **NO IDEA.**

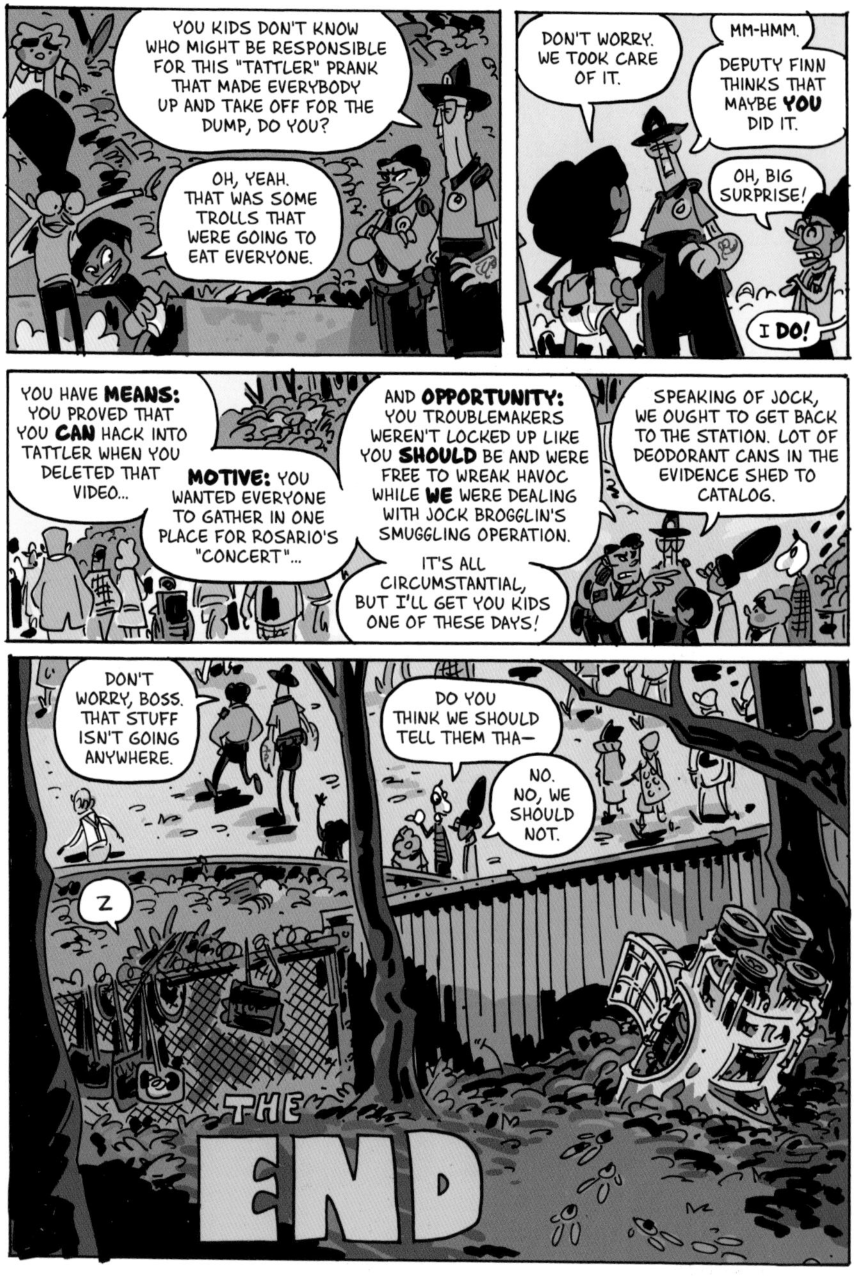
YOU KIDS DON'T KNOW WHO MIGHT BE RESPONSIBLE FOR THIS "TATTLER" PRANK THAT MADE EVERYBODY UP AND TAKE OFF FOR THE DUMP, DO YOU?
OH, YEAH. THAT WAS SOME TROLLS THAT WERE GOING TO EAT EVERYONE.
DON'T WORRY. WE TOOK CARE OF IT.
MM-HMM.
DEPUTY FINN THINKS THAT MAYBE **YOU** DID IT.
OH, BIG SURPRISE!
I **DO**!
YOU HAVE **MEANS:** YOU PROVED THAT YOU **CAN** HACK INTO TATTLER WHEN YOU DELETED THAT VIDEO...
MOTIVE: YOU WANTED EVERYONE TO GATHER IN ONE PLACE FOR ROSARIO'S "CONCERT"...
AND **OPPORTUNITY:** YOU TROUBLEMAKERS WEREN'T LOCKED UP LIKE YOU **SHOULD** BE AND WERE FREE TO WREAK HAVOC WHILE **WE** WERE DEALING WITH JOCK BROGGLIN'S SMUGGLING OPERATION.
IT'S ALL CIRCUMSTANTIAL, BUT I'LL GET YOU KIDS ONE OF THESE DAYS!
SPEAKING OF JOCK, WE OUGHT TO GET BACK TO THE STATION. LOT OF DEODORANT CANS IN THE EVIDENCE SHED TO CATALOG.
DON'T WORRY, BOSS. THAT STUFF ISN'T GOING ANYWHERE.
DO YOU THINK WE SHOULD TELL THEM THA—
NO. NO, WE SHOULD NOT.
Z
THE END